# CRY WOLF

## CJ Wheeler

Jacket Art & Design © 2025 by Jared Greenleaf with assistance by Roman Nikolić

Printed in the United States of America

*For my wife, Kami. My coach, my cheerleader, my greatest champion—for without you, this book would not exist. For promises kept and broken, for the laughter and the tears, for never giving up on me even when I had given up on myself. For your unwavering love and belief in me.*
*This book is, and always will be, for you.*

# CHAPTER ONE

**M**ichael opened his eyes and watched the shadow people as they danced across the grey room. It was an unusual sight that would have frightened most people, but not him. He had witnessed their graceful nocturnal movements since childhood. Michael had been scared then, but over the years the shadow people had become mundane if not comforting to him. Often, he would fall asleep as they spun in graceful pirouettes around him.

As he had done countless times before, Michael looked at his wife and watched her sleep. Perpetually cold, Steph had the blanket cocooned around her so that only a hint of her face was visible. Michael had mentioned the shadow people to her once. Steph had cupped his face with her tiny hands, smiled sweetly at him, and shook her head. One of her great strengths, or at rare times, a weakness, was that she was a strictly a see it to believe it type of person.

Even as a child Steph hadn't believed in ghosts or anything supernatural. Her parents had never been able to convince her that there was an Easter Bunny, a Tooth Fairy, or even Santa Claus. One Christmas Eve, she had even laid in wait behind the tree and then jumped out and scared her parents when they came to set presents out.

Oddly, for someone that was firmly rooted in reality, her faith was even stronger. Steph went to church every week and participated in as many church related activities as her busy schedule would allow. She read her bible every day and said her prayers every morning and night. She was a righteous person and Michael loved her for it. Inexplicably, she loved him as well, even though he was far from being righteous.

After a few months of dating, he had asked Steph about the duality of her nature as he drove her home from the movies. Instead of answering, she had grown strangely quiet and turned away to look out of the passenger side window. Michael had apologized, thinking that his question had upset her.

Steph looked at him, smiling that sweet, endearing smile of hers, and said, "No, you didn't offend me, my love. My religion and my faith are very personal to me, very private. I love you like the dawn, and I think you're the one for me, but I am not ready to share that story with you. Not yet." Then she leaned over, gave him a quick peck on the cheek then burrowed under his arm. That was Steph; beautiful, poetic, and perfect.

Michael had felt bewildered then as Steph had often made him feel. After a few minutes of silence, he asked, "Do... do you really think I'm the one?" Steph erupted into a silvery peal of laughter, then wrapped her arms around his chest and pulled herself tightly to him. "Maybe." She'd replied, her voice coy and her eyes sparkling with mischief. "Maybe one day you will find out if you're lucky." And he had felt lucky that night, driving home with a beautiful young woman snuggling under his arm. He was the luckiest man in the world.

Michael smiled at the memory and ran his fingers through

Steph's hair so that it framed her sleeping face. Her lips drew up into a pout for a moment and then she breathed "brat" before relaxing back into sleep. Michael grinned. Steph hated when he did that, even when she was sleeping. And so he did it every night because it was the only time he could get away with it.

The shadow people caught his attention again. They seemed restless, their dance wild and erratic. Michael really didn't see them directly as he could only see them out of the corner of his eyes. He'd notice a quick movement and look over at it and there would be nothing. Then at the edge of his vision, he would catch movement again. Tonight they seemed different, almost tangible, visible for a split second before they faded like a ghost afterimage.

Michael looked over at Steph again and considered waking her to see if she could see them. No, no point in waking her. He knew she wouldn't see the shadow people, and she'd only tease him the next day and mock grumble about him waking her up because he was scared of the dark. He settled back and closed his eyes. In the morning the shadow people would be gone. He relaxed and let sleep overtake him.

Startled, Michael sat up against the tree branch, his heart thundering in his chest. The dream still echoed within his mind, bringing about feelings of happiness and safety. Dangerous emotions that he didn't deserve to feel. He shook his head to clear it and looked around. It was nearly dusk and he had slept too long. They would be out soon, hunting.

He had dreamed of her again and it left him feeling raw and hollowed out. He seemed to only dream in memories now, of a former life that would inexorably turn into an absolute nightmare. That night was the last time he had felt happy, and safe before his life shattered and the world had become a dark, twisted reflection of itself. The old world seemed so far away that sometimes he wondered if it had all been a dream.

But Michael knew the truth, the constant pain of it. Nearly every waking moment he thought about his life before, and his dreams were there to haunt him while he slept. This had to be a form of purgatory because the only place he could be now was hell. He was burning for the sins of his past and for the sins of all mankind.

They were in hell, the few that were left. Most had died within hours of the event. Died a horrible death and they were the lucky ones. There were things that were much worse than death. Nightmares come to life. The boogieman was real after all and he was hungry.

Michael looked down at the leaf cluttered ground forty feet below him. It was late September and while plenty of leaves covered the forest floor, there were still enough on the tree to keep him hidden. The treetop was safer than being on the ground and even if something tracked him to the tree they would have a hard time surprising him while he slept during the day. The tree wouldn't be safe at night, however. It would be a trap.

He braced his feet to pull himself up and then froze, listening. The sound came again from below, footsteps shuffling through dead leaves. They came up to his tree and stopped. Had they found him? He itched to reach for his rifle, lying in the crook of the branch next to him but remained still.

A desperate whimpering came from below. Michael slowly shifted his weight so that he could look down between his legs. A young blonde woman in a light pink jacket that practically screamed *kill me now*, was leaning against his tree. Breathing rapidly, her head shot back and forth, looking frantically in every direction.

*Is she tracking me?* Michael knew how to hide his trail, but he also knew that there were some people, some *things* that might be able to find it. Worse, some of them could track by smell. He stayed still and waited, on the edge of bursting into action.

There was a startled intake of breath from the girl and she clamped her hands over her mouth in horror, her eyes fixated on something in the brush. Letting out a low moan, she took three slow steps backward and then spun around and took off. Maybe she was human after all. *Or a very clever wolf*, he thought with a shudder.

He closed his eyes to heighten his hearing and listened to see if anything was following the girl. His breathing rasped too loudly so he took a large gulp of air and held it, listening intently to the ambient forest sounds. It was quiet aside from an occasional rustle as a gentle wind caressed the dead leaves. There didn't appear to be anything following the girl but Michael couldn't be certain. He forced himself to release the pent-up air slowly and then took a slow deep breath to ease the burning in his chest.

Survivors were rare, especially now, nearly six months after the event. Rare enough that it piqued his interest and he wanted to take a closer look at the girl. He'd then be able to decide whether to kill her or not. *Wolves amongst the sheep*. He shook his head angrily. That voice was unwanted as well. This nightmare was bad enough before *she* had defined it for him.

After looking around one more time, Michael threw the

pack on his back and slung the rifle over his shoulder. He quickly navigated down the tree and was on the ground in seconds. He paused and listened, taking in the surroundings. No immediate threat that he could detect. He found the girl's tracks right away though he didn't need them. She made an incredible racket as she broke through the brush. *How had she survived this long?*

He went from tree to tree like a ghost walking past gravestones. As he approached the girl, Michael could hear her talking and estimated that she was now only about twenty yards ahead of him. When he drew to within a few yards of her, he silently unlimbered his rifle and continued to follow the sounds.

"Zack," the girl whispered through chattering teeth, "You had to go and get yourself killed, didn't you? You said we needed to risk it, that we were almost out of food. So we risked it and you became food!" She gave a hysterical giggle and covered her mouth with both hands, looking around her with wide, fearful eyes as her body shook violently. After her fit had passed, she started whispering again, "You promised, Zack, you promised. You promised that you would take care of me. You knew I was too weak to do it myself. You promised one bullet was all it would take. Your final gift. Now you're dead you selfish BASTARD!" The last came out as an explosive shriek that echoed through the forest.

Michael shook his head sadly. The girl was clearly out of her mind and at the rate she was going would attract some unwanted attention soon. He had heard enough to know that she wasn't one of them. On a sudden impulse, he raised his rifle and aimed it at the girl's heart. For a long agonizing moment he considered putting her out of her misery but then lowered the gun. He had killed enough innocents. Powerful emotions rose in him but he choked them back down.

He stopped following the girl and watched until she disappeared behind some trees and then set off on a perpendicular route. He wished the girl a quick death and hoped that when she met her end, it would be painless. Only the damned deserved to live.

Michael slung the rifle back on his shoulder and turned his thoughts back to his own survival. His supplies were still plentiful, but he was always of a mind to be proactive about securing new ones. Last night had been colder than expected, with the promise of an early winter. He needed to find warmer clothing soon especially since a fire would draw the monsters quick as a moth to flame. They hated the light but hated him more. Tomorrow he would have to risk going into the town he had carefully passed a few miles back. He was sure he would find some winter gear there and maybe, if he was lucky, some ammo as well. If he was unlucky, something would find him.

A scream echoed flatly through the trees, thin with distance. Michael froze as another one followed. It was the girl. He turned towards the sound and listened. The scream came again, filled with fear and hysteria. Wracked with indecision, he took a step away and stopped, hating himself. "Help me!" The girl screamed and Michael's former self came welling up inside, filling him with emotions he'd long thought dead.

Cursing under his breath, Michael pulled the rifle from his shoulder and took off at a dead run. He was furious with himself, with the girl, with the world. He wanted only to be left alone. Alone in his self-hatred. Alone in his private hell until the real hell came for him. There was no redemption for him, nor did he want it. He did not deserve absolution.

Michael arrived at the place where he had left the girl and quickly found her trail. Another scream came, much closer this time, tinged with pain. He ran towards the sound as if there was a monster at his back. Maybe there was.

He cleared the top of a hill and instantly took in the sight below him. A large man in hunting fatigues had the girl by the throat and was walking towards a deep drop-off several yards away. The girl struggled against his grip, her feet dangling a foot off of the ground. Reaching down, she grabbed for something at the man's side and pulled a pistol out of his waistband. The man casually swatted the gun away and the girl screamed again. He just grinned at her and kept walking.

Michael quickly dropped to one knee and raised his rifle in a smooth, practiced motion. He sighted the man through the scope, looking for a shot but his breathing was ragged, throwing off his aim. He needed to take the shot now, as the hunter and the girl were nearing the edge of the precipice. It was a gamble as he risked hitting the girl but that would be a moot point in a second. He aimed center mass and fired. The shot went wide hitting a nearby tree with a sharp crack. The hunter's head whipped around to look at him, his face going red with rage. He snarled and drew his arm back to throw the girl.

Michael forced himself to hold his breath. It was an effort as his chest was still heaving from running. His training kicked in and he aimed for the man's chest again and fired. A red spot bloomed on the man's ribs and he flinched from the impact. The hunter glared at Michael and hissed as his arm shot forward and the girl screamed. It was not a man but a wolf!

Michael let his instinct override his training and fired again. The wolf's wrist shattered and the girl dropped, just short of going over the edge. The creature howled in fury and charged uphill toward Michael with inhuman speed. He only had time for one more shot before the monster would be on him. Hitting its chest again would be worthless. The first shot had struck the thing's heart and hadn't even slowed it down.

Hoping for a headshot, Michael aimed high and fired as the thing reached him. The side of the thing's throat exploded in a bloody, ragged hole, but the wound didn't slow it down. Wheezing, it bowled into him at full speed, sending both of them tumbling down the hill. Michael grunted with pain; it felt like a linebacker had just slammed into him.

He rolled to a stop and the wolf was instantly on him, pinning him to the ground. The creature swung wildly, hitting his face and chest and shrieking in fury. Michael tried to block the hits but his arms were swept aside like twigs. Blood showered down on him from the thing's ruined throat but it showed no signs of weakening.

The wolf clamped its good hand around Michael's throat and squeezed. Frantic, Michael tried to pry the hand away to no avail as the creature was unbelievably strong. It dropped its face close to his and roared its hatred of him, spraying Michael's face with bright, arterial blood. It began to pummel him with its ruined hand, each blow bringing him closer to blackness.

Michael gasped as his lungs burned for air. He knew there was no way he could physically defeat the wolf. He'd be dead long before the creature bled out. He needed to switch tactics. He fumbled with numb fingers at his right side until his hand found his hunting knife. He quickly drew it and slammed the large knife into the creature's ear with as much violence as he could muster.

The wolf's head rocked to the side from the strike. Its screeching cut off abruptly and it looked at him, eyes wide with shock. Michael twisted out from under the creature until their positions were reversed. Despite its mortal wounds, the wolf's hand was still tight around his neck. Screaming with effort, Michael pushed down on the creature's chest. The hand finally tore away suddenly, nails leaving deep burning furrows on his throat.

Michael grabbed the knife and gave it a quick, brutal twist. The wolf made an odd groan as its body went rigid then settled back against the ground with a sigh. The thing's eyes never left him, burning with hatred as it died.

Michael fell to the ground, exhausted. A deceptively beautiful sunset greeted his eyes as his heart thundered in his ears. Slowly the sound quieted down and his breathing returned to normal. He forced himself to sit up and look for the girl. He wasn't surprised to see she was gone.

Shaking his head, he got to his feet and then looked at the wolf's body. It appeared to be dead but Michael needed to make sure. Slowly, despite the pain, he leaned over and grabbed it by the arms, and dragged it to the drop-off. He rolled the corpse over the edge with his foot and watched as it broke and splattered upon the rocks below. For a moment Michael considered following it in. He shook his head and took a firm step back. That wasn't his decision to make.

Michael painfully limped back up the hill to get his pack and rifle. There was a surprising amount of blood on the ground. He looked down and found his clothes saturated with it. At least most of it wasn't his. His throat was on fire and his head and chest were a mass of bruises, but overall he had been lucky. He needed to get away from the area as quickly as possible. The hunters would be out soon if they weren't already and they were attracted to places where violence had occurred.

Michael then walked over to where the wolf had dropped the girl. He found her trail in the dying light and followed it several yards over to the spot she had entered the brush. She was bleeding slightly, but her steps were strong. A thought occurred to him and he looked back along her trail and confirmed his suspicion. The pistol was missing.

Apparently, the girl in the pink jacket wasn't too badly injured and now she was armed. Good. He was better off without her and she was better off without him. Plus he wasn't exactly thrilled about following an armed, frightened person into the brush, crazy or not. Would she want his help or would she simply shoot him on sight if he approached her?

Michael started to walk away and then slowly turned back, ashamed. He could lie to himself all he wanted and it wouldn't assuage his conscience. In her current state, the girl would die soon, gun or no gun. They all were on a very short timeline so did it matter? If he helped her then he would only be prolonging the inevitable and he would have another innocent's death on his soul. *Though did it really matter after the first one?* Michael thought bitterly.

Still, he couldn't stop his eyes from following her trail in the faint light until it disappeared behind a tree. His gut began to burn with a familiar feeling, urging him to go after her. He stood there for a full minute trying to resist it. Finally, he cursed and followed the girl's trail into the dark woods.

# CHAPTER TWO

Rachel hadn't felt so devastated and helpless since the night Zack died. Throat still burning from the horrible man's grip, she ran as fast as she could. A numbness filled her, pervading her limbs with weakness. She *was* weak, she knew, fragile, and worthless. Zack had been her strength, her protector, and now he was dead. Her mother had been right after all. Like every other worthless man in her life he had failed her. *I will take care of you if it comes to it. I will take care of you if there is no way out. They won't get you, I promise.* Zack was gone, his promise broken, and now she had to take care of herself. She cussed him out as she ran, knowing that she wouldn't survive long without him.

Exhaustion made her legs feel like heavy, wet sacks of flesh. She stumbled over a fallen tree and caught a branch to steady herself, listening for a moment. Nothing. Rachel wasn't fooled. She knew it was there, behind her, coming for her. It had killed the idiot that had come to her rescue, and now it was after her again. Death was coming for her, its scythe hungry for the last of the harvest.

She began running again as fast as her exhausted body could take her, weeping at the futility of it. Tears made the trees blur as Rachel ran past them. She tripped again and slammed headfirst against a stump. Pain erupted in her head, drowning out the burning in her chest and legs. She lay gasping for a moment and then struggled to get up. She needed to keep moving. It was coming for her. She needed to… she tried to get to her feet, but her legs were like jelly, refusing to support her. She settled down against the stump, resigned. This was it then. This was the moment where her broken life had come to and where it would end. She pulled the pistol from her waistband, holding it loosely in one hand.

This spot seemed as good as any other to face her fate. At least it would be on her terms. She did not want to die. Choice was an illusion. She lifted the pistol to her lips and kissed it, tasting oil and metal. Maybe that would somehow remove some of the violence and ugliness of what she was about to do. Tears welled up in her eyes again and she furiously wiped them away. No matter how she tried to romanticize it, the cold gun would never play Romeo to her Juliet.

Placing the gun to her temple, she closed her eyes and prayed for the strength to pull the trigger. It would be quick and hopefully painless, a better death than the monsters of this world would have granted her. Taking a deep breath, she cursed Zack again and placed her finger on the trigger.

A twig snapped close by. *It found me!* Screaming wildly, Rachel fired a shot at the sound and a little puff of leaves and dirt kicked up about twenty yards away. "S-stay back! Stay back! Stay back! Or I will kill you." She promised through clenched teeth.

"Fair enough." The voice was quiet and deep but laced with exhaustion and pain. It didn't sound like that man, that *thing* that had tried to kill her. Confused, Rachel looked towards the voice, trying to determine where it was coming from. Trees were all around her and he could be hiding behind any of them. *Can't see the monster for the trees.*

"Come out to where I can see you."

"Sorry, can't do that." The deep voice rumbled.

"Why not?"

"Not sure what your intentions are."

Intentions? What were her intentions? A hysterical snort came from her throat, almost unnoticed. Did she want to die? No. Did she want to stay in this world with its waking nightmares? No. The only real choice she had left now was death by monster or bullet, and well, that wasn't much of a choice at all. It was more of a preference, really. *Go away, Mr. Monster. I will be killing myself shortly.* "Leave me alone."

"No, I just want to talk." The voice sounded closer.

Not likely, she thought and raised a hand to her aching head as a wave of dizziness hit her. Blackness crept in at the edge of her vision. She needed to do it soon or she wouldn't be able to. She was sick of this conversation. Suicide was very personal and intimate, a selfish moment that she'd rather not share. "I've had enough of this. Either come out or leave me alone." She would murder-suicide his ass.

"Not until you put the gun down. I'm not going to hurt you."

Rachel snorted in response. "Why should I believe you?"

"I killed that wolf back there."

Startled, she lowered her gun and asked, "W-what did you call it?"

"A wolf, that's what they are." The man repeated as he stepped out from the tree closest to her.

Rachel almost shot him on sight. He was a large man with long curly black hair. His scraggly bearded face had a fierceness to it, and his icy blue eyes had a haunted intensity that made them seem magnetic. They contrasted with the blood on his face so sharply that they appeared to glow in the dying light. If anyone looked like a wolf, he did. The stranger was by far the most intimidating person she had ever seen and it didn't help that his fatigues and face were covered with blood. He hovered at the edge of the tree, eyeing her gun.

"Why did you call him-it, that thing, a wolf?" she asked him. The man just looked down at the ground and said nothing.

"Tell me!" She said, aiming the gun at the stranger.

He looked back up at her, and the intense blue eyes seemed to see right through her. "Who is Zack?"

Stunned, all she could do was stare in shock. How did he know about Zack? Had he been *following* her? Anger sparked deep inside her and she snarled, "Dead, that's who he is, okay? That *wolf*, monster, whatever, it killed…" She jabbed the gun at the man. "Why are you following me? What do you want from me?"

"I want to help you."

"H-help me?" Rachel let out a derisive laugh. She motioned to his hunter fatigues with her gun. "What are you going to do? Teach me how to hunt, how to survive? You couldn't even sneak up on me without snapping that twig." She began to laugh again.

The man looked at her for a moment, his eyes unreadable, and then he slowly raised and opened his hands. The end of a broken twig lay resting on each palm. Her laughter choked off as she stared at the broken twig.

"Just figured you would shoot at the first thing that

moved." He said without humor.

Maybe there was more to him than being big and scary after all. Rachel nodded slowly and lowered her gun. "You're going to help me?" She meant it to be sarcastic, but instead it came out as a plaintive whine. Maybe she wasn't ready to die after all.

The stranger nodded and let the twigs fall. She watched them hit the ground and then asked, "Why?" She asked suspiciously. "You don't know me. Why do you care whether I live or die?"

His haunted eyes dropped to the ground, then he said in a wary voice, "I just have a... feeling. I get them sometimes. That you need help."

"A feeling? Really? Ya think?" Okay...

The big man sighed. "Yes."

"You're going to help a stranger 'cause of a feeling?" That set her off on another round of laughter. She couldn't help it. Men were so stupid. Humanity's light may be burning out quickly but there was no doubt in her mind the last spark would be a woman.

The stranger's eyes tightened, and he gave her a look that could kill cancer. It only made Rachel laugh harder. There was a hysterical edge to it and she felt like giving in and fading away into oblivion. She broke off mid-laugh as a thought hit her and she pointed the pistol at him again. "I will not sleep with you. Think otherwise and I will kill you. I'm a very good shot."

"Fair enough," he said, then looked down at her pistol. "Safety's on."

"What?" She said, turning the pistol to see.

The stranger's hand whipped out and snatched the pistol

from her hand.

"Hey! Give that back!" She lunged forward but he smoothly backstepped away.

"Not until you calm down." He told her as he examined the pistol.

"I am calm!" She shrieked at him.

The stranger snorted, slipping the pistol into the waistband at the small of his back.

Rachel forced herself to calm down. She was *calm* and could be *calm* when she wanted to. And as soon as she got the pistol back, she'd calmly kill him too.

"Can I *please* have my pistol back?" She said as evenly as she could.

"No."

"Fine!" She shrieked even louder. Her vision went black as a wave of vertigo hit her. Rachel fell back against the tree trunk and moaned as a hot angry pain bloomed inside her head. She heard a rustle as he got down on his knees next to her. "Get away from me!" She yelled at him or attempted to yell as the pain worsened. It trailed off in a plaintive wail instead.

"Don't be a child." The stranger growled. "Be still!"

Rachel flinched as his hands touched her face. "Just want to check your head." He said in a softer voice as he turned her face towards him. His large hands were surprisingly gentle. "Keep your voice down. Some of those things have excellent hearing, and we are in no shape to defend ourselves."

Rachel mulled that over in her head, trying to find a weak point to get at him. She was not a child after all; he had no call to be so condescending.

"Can you open your eyes?" He asked her.

"Why?"

"I want to see if you have a concussion or not."

She popped one eye open and then the other. The pain and the dizziness didn't come rushing back and she sighed in relief. Maybe her brains wouldn't melt out of her ears after all. The stranger leaned in close to her and she tensed and leaned back as he studied her eyes.

"Eyes look fine. Do you feel nauseous or confused? Headache or feel numbness anywhere?"

She shook her head and immediately regretted it. Dizziness made the world spin and she clenched her eyes shut until the sensation passed. "No," she said, opening her eyes again, "Just lightheaded and dizzy. Very. Dizzy."

He nodded and settled back. "I don't think you have a concussion."

"How would you know?" She snapped, voice dripping with sarcasm. "Are you some kind of doctor or something?" She doubted it; he would scare his patients away with a face like that.

"Something." The stranger said in a tone that firmly ended that topic. He shrugged his pack off his back and began rummaging through it. She studied his face again in the low light and could tell he knew she was studying it. That seemed to bother him. Good.

She missed Zack. Sure, she had easily manipulated him and used him for his money before the world had gone to H. E. double hockey sticks, but she had loved the idiot boy in a way. He had been sweet and nice to her and had not in any way intimidated her., unlike this big ox of a man. Thinking of him as just the man was beginning to irritate her. Time for introductions. "I'm Rachel."

"Michael." He replied as he pulled a water bottle from his pack and handed it to her. She took a big gulp and then coughed hard, spitting some of the water out. The liquid made her dry throat feel like she had just drunk razor blades.

"Slowly," Michael admonished and returned to rummaging through his pack. In a short time he produced a small first aid kit and a bottle of alcohol. As he turned back to her, he hissed and grabbed his side.

"You're not doing too hot either are you?" Rachel asked, making special note of the spot he touched in case she needed to exploit it later.

Michael shook his head. "First you, then we'll worry about me later. You have a nasty cut that requires stitches but I don't have any needle or thread. The best thing I can do is clean it and bandage it. You're going to have a scar."

"Wouldn't be the first one." Not even close. She had scars so deep that even her soul had them.

Michael poured some alcohol on a white bandage and then looked at her. "This will sting." He warned.

"Just do it," Rachel said, bracing herself. Michael placed the bandage against her temple and she groaned, clenching her teeth tightly together. It felt as if he'd just placed molten fire on her cut. A few seconds later, he removed the bloody bandage and the pain slowly burned away.

"Hard parts over," Michael said, pulling another bandage from his kit. He put some ointment on it and then placed it on her cut. He worked quietly and efficiently. It was obvious that he had done this before. She allowed herself to relax a little and tried to ignore the pounding in her head. She needed some distraction from it to distance herself from the pain. "Why did you call that thing a wolf?"

Michael paused in his ministrations and looked at her momentarily, his face unreadable. Then he began bandaging her cut again. She was about to ask again when he replied. "It is getting dark and talk of such things is best done during the day." He trailed off and sat back, the bandage finished. He looked at the darkening sky and sighed, "It's never a good time to talk about such things."

Rachel felt a chill going down her spine as she looked at the forest around them. Twilight permeated the woods, making the shadows dark and threatening. She drew her knees in and hugged them to her chest. "Can we have a fire?"

Michael shook his head. "Can't chance it. It would be like a beacon to anything out there." He said, putting the first aid kit and alcohol back in his pack.

Rachel sighed and stared forlornly at a spot on the ground, imagining a campfire burning there before forcing the thought out of her head. Dwelling on it made its absence worse.

Michael pulled out several cans of soup and set them on the ground. He then removed a light grey flannel blanket and handed it to her. "This will have to do for now."

Rachel only had eyes for the soup. It had been *days* since she had last eaten. Starving herself for beauty had not prepared her for starving to death. Absently wrapping the blanket around her, she pointed to a can and asked, "Can I please have some?" She realized that she had decided that she would play nice for now.

Michael's mouth twitched as he handed her a can. "Sorry, I'm used to traveling alone."

"Don't care. Um, sorry, I mean it's okay." Lifting the can to her lips, Rachel took a big swig of the thick liquid and grimaced at the greasy taste. Well, it wasn't her first time eating cold soup from a can. In fact, she had eaten far worse over the past few months. Rachel went through three cans before her hunger calmed down.

Michael finished his first can as she finished her last. "Better get some sleep," He told her, setting his empty can to the side. "We have a busy day tomorrow."

"Why?" Rachel asked, looking up in surprise. "What do you mean?"

Michael shrugged as he tended to his backpack. "We need supplies. There is a town to the south. Called Joshua Creek, I think. We'll head there at first light."

A chill came over Rachel. Death waited in the towns.

# CHAPTER THREE

The dawn's weak light peeked over the distant mountains in a cloudless sky. After a long night on watch, Michael stared at it blearily through red eyes. While he welcomed the sun, it would not protect them where they had to go today.

Rachel mumbled something in her sleep and Michael turned to look at her. The girl had cried out several times during the night, perhaps reliving the nightmare from the day before. Michael hadn't tried to console her. He had no comfort to give. Why wake her from a bad dream only to bring her into a worse one? No doubt she wouldn't have appreciated it if he tried.

He turned back to face the rising sun but his thoughts remained on Rachel. The girl was a problem. She seemed ill equipped to survive in this hostile world and her sanity was questionable at best. It was a miracle that she had survived this long. He also suspected that she was only playing nice until she could get away from him. Or kill him.

He again questioned his feeling that he needed to help her. These feelings had never really steered him wrong in the past and had in fact saved his life on several occasions. At other times, frustratingly, nothing came of them. Maybe he was lying to himself. Maybe he was lonely. Maybe he was just stupid and had not learned his lesson yet, whatever that may be. Too many maybes. Michael sighed, rubbing at the painful knot in his side, tight from the cold. There was no choice but to accept that, for the moment, the girl had to travel with him.

There was a faint crinkling of leaves as Rachel roused herself, brushing sleep from her eyes. Sitting up, she squinted at him briefly then stared at the ground, misery stark upon her face. *Bad night for both of us.* Michael thought. He pulled two cans of soup from his pack and handed one to Rachel. She took it without thanks, then looked up at morning's sky.

Hugging her knees to her chest, she said, "Daddy used to say that on mornings like this, with the sun rising late, that the earth was sleeping in, resting from all the work it had to do in the spring and summer." She smiled briefly, the expression contrasting strongly with her sad eyes. Michael said nothing, refusing to reminisce about a world long dead. After a moment, Rachel turned away from him, looking despondently at the forest as she ate.

After a few minutes, she turned back to him, a worried expression on her face. "Still planning on going to that town?"

Michael nodded, finishing the last of his soup.

"Can I have my gun back then?"

Michael snorted at the predictable question. "No."

Rachel's eyes flashed. "I want it back."

"No."

"Well, when are you going to give it back to me?" She demanded.

"Eat your soup," Michael told her.

She raised her arm as if to throw it at him.

"Do it, and it will be your last."

Rachel gave him a long look but finally took another sip.

During the night he had decided the best thing to do was to head into town alone. He trusted his gut but he did not trust the girl. He stood up and grimaced at the sharp pain in his side. The ribs did not seem to be broken but they were definitely bruised. Michael pushed the pain into the background, letting it join the symphony coming from his head and neck. Bracing himself, Michael bent down and picked up his gear. The pain screamed to the forefront and he nearly blacked out from it. He locked his knees and forced himself straight, waiting for the blackness to burn off. The pain resided back to a dull roar.

"Are you okay?" Rachel asked, her voice dripping with concern.

Michael opened his eyes to look at the girl. Rachel looked worried. However, he noted, that her feigned concern did not reach her eyes. They were cold and calculating, lingering on his injured side as if trying to memorize the location, just as she had done the night before. Rachel's eyes flicked up to his. There was an odd beat, then she blinked and her eyes matched her face, concerned and worried. The mask was complete. Michael felt a cold shiver go down his back. This was the person his gut wanted him to help?

"I'm fine." He told her. "I'm going to town alone. You will be safer here."

Rachel shook her head. "No, I'm coming with you."

"No, you're not."

Rachel threw her soup can at him, narrowly missing his head, and stood up shouting, "No! I'm coming with you. I-I refuse to be left alone. You leave me and you might come back as one of those... those things!"

Michael glared down at the girl. This was the last thing he needed right now. "I won't come back as a wolf. It's daylight remember. Now quit wasting food, sit down, and wait for me."

Rachel walked up to him until their faces were only inches apart. Her eyes were wide with fear and there were tears-fake or real, it was hard to tell-forming in them. "Please, I need to go with you. I don't want to be left alone."

Being this close to her, Michael couldn't help but see through the cracks of her pretty veneer. Was she actually wearing makeup? The world had gone to hell but she was still worried about looking good? "No, you will stay here and that is final!" He turned away and started walking down the trail.

An ear-shattering scream broke the morning's calm behind him. Michael spun around, pulling the rifle from his shoulder. He expected to find Rachel dead or dying in the clutches of some monster. Instead, he found her smirking at him, arms folded across her chest.

"What is wrong with you?" Michael demanded in a hoarse whisper, the hair on his neck standing straight up.

"Please let me come with you," Rachel answered in an odd, quiet voice.

"No, and keep your damn voice down," He hissed. "Monsters aren't the only thing we have to worry about."

Rachel lifted her head and blasted another scream, easily twice as loud as the first.

Michael took a step towards the girl and hissed, "Will you please shut up? You are going to get both of us killed!"

Rachel shrugged and said. "I'm dead either way. You have your so called feelings? Well, guess what? I have mine too. I will die today if you are not around to protect me. I...will...die. Do you want my death on your hands?"

Michael snorted in response. He doubted the shallow brat had ever had a real feeling about anything.

Rachel switched back to pleading. It was chilling how quickly she could change masks. "Please let me come with you. Please! I don't want to die." Large, fat tears began to roll down her cheeks. "Either give me the gun at least so I can protect myself or take me with you."

"Rachel, no..." Michael started to say. Rachel took a deep breath and flung her head back with her arms spread wide. Michael threw out a hand to stop her. "No-no-no, FINE!" He roared so loudly it echoed, then turned and stomped away.

"Keep *my* voice down?" Rachel muttered under her breath behind him. She ran until she caught up to him and matched his quick pace. Michael looked at Rachel's smug face and shook his head in disgust. She was far more trouble than she was worth.

They backtracked most of the morning to get to the town Michael had passed the day before. He kept them off the roads as there tended to be fewer zombies in the woods. He wasn't sure why, except maybe the things took the least resistance path. That or the zombies somehow knew that more people would be on the road.

Rachel had complained at first about traveling cross-country until Michael silenced her with a look. A short time later, he heard a disturbance behind him. Looking back, he saw Rachel fighting with a branch that had caught her jacket pocket. She was making ineffectual swings at it while producing high-pitched, childlike grunts. She finally broke free and the momentum sent her reeling backwards. She fell into a dry thicket that snapped and popped like fireworks in the still forest. She immediately threw a fit, kicking and punching at the twigs while making closed mouth squeals of frustration.

This girl is going to get me killed! Michael thought, horrified at what he was seeing. How had Rachel survived this long? Did she not understand the danger that they were in? Was she that stupid or... Michael's mouth dropped open as a thought occurred to him. Was Rachel doing it on purpose, just to spite him? *She wouldn't go that far, would she?"* He quickly scanned the forest around them, looking for signs of danger.

Suddenly, it was quiet. Michael turned to find Rachel sitting still, giving him a look as if daring him to say something. He opened his mouth to remind her to be quiet, thought better of it, and clamped it shut instead. The last thing he needed was for her to start screaming again.

Around noon, they arrived at the town of Joshua Creek. It was a small town, even for the area, with a population of no more than probably a few thousand before the event. Michael hid by the 'Welcome to Joshua Creek' sign, studying the main street leading into town. Idyllic and Americana, old yet well-kept buildings lined the street until it curved away from view, all overshadowed by an ancient wooden water tower. Several cars were haphazardly parked in the street, dirty windshields dully gleaming in the bright sunlight.

He looked at the welcome sign. Population: 3,326. Michael did not have to wonder about where the former residents were. Hundreds of zombies wandered through the streets, unholy caricatures of their former selves. They contrasted strongly with the perfect setting around them. Every town seemed to be this way, infested with zombies. Cities were far worse.

Michael checked the sun's position. It was noon and it was directly overhead. The sky was clear except for some ominous dark clouds gathering around the peaks to the west. Now would be the best time to go since the light was at its strongest, and the zombies and other things would be at their weakest. If they did not get out of town before dark, they would be dead.

"Are you sure this is a good idea?" Rachel asked, voice full of dread. She had her arms hugged tightly to her chest.

"You wanted to come," Michael replied.

"I did. I do."

He shrugged. "We need supplies." Deciding to give it one more try he added, "It will be safer if you stay here. I'll be back in an hour."

Rachel shivered as if breaking free from a trance. She appeared to waver for a moment, then took a deep breath and said firmly, "No."

"Thirty minutes then. Just give me thirty minutes and..."

Her eyes shot to his face and her head turned slowly to follow. "I—will—scream." She hissed.

"Do that and you will bring the whole town down on us."

Rachel gave a helpless giggle. "I don't care! I will not be left behind. You will keep me safe."

Michael flinched and felt the anger drain from him. The last time he heard those words, tragedy followed shortly after. Michael closed his eyes, fighting to control the sorrow and grief that tried to overwhelm him. Guilt came shortly after, burning away the other emotions until they were gone. It threatened to overwhelm him as well, but he embraced it instead of fighting it as it was his only reason for living.

Michael opened his eyes and found Rachel staring at him.

The girl flinched back from whatever she saw in them. Michael pulled Rachel's pistol from his waistband and flipped off the safety. She eyed the gun and licked her lips nervously.

"A few ground rules if you are coming with me." He told her in a tired, dead voice. "No screams, no temper tantrums, no sounds at all. If you do anything, and I mean anything, I will shoot you in the leg and leave you for whatever finds you. Understand?"

Rachel swallowed hard, then nodded. "I'll behave."

"Good, let's go then."

The zombies outside of town were easily avoided since they were spread out. Several of them groaned and growled as Michael and Rachel passed their line of sight and began to follow them. The noises attracted the attention of others in the area. A zombie ahead of them turned around and began to shuffle towards them.

Rachel froze, watching as the zombie closed in on her. Michael grabbed the girl's arm and led her past the thing. It lunged at them, movements slow and clumsy, and fell to the ground. They were easy to avoid in their dormant phase. They were altogether another monster at night.

Another zombie closed in on Michael and he pistol-whipped it across the face, spraying the ground with gore. It toppled over from the blow and then began crawling after them. Up ahead, two zombies turned at the sound and began stumbling towards them. Michael sighed and reached into his pack, producing a flare. Wincing in anticipation, he slammed it against his thigh and was relieved to see a small green flame ignite. Fire acted differently after the event. Sometimes it acted normal. Other times it would burn poorly. Occasionally it would burn quickly and if you were very unlucky, blow up in your face.

The flare spit fitfully, a dark heady smoke pouring from the lit end as if the fuel was poor. The flame was pitiful, but the effect on the zombies was noticeable. As a whole, the zombies drew back from the small flame, hissing and growling. Michael felt resistance on his arm and turned to find Rachel eyeing the flare. She seemed to be more afraid of the flames than the zombies. "Come on, let's go," Michael growled, giving her arm a sharp yank. They only had a few minutes before the flare would burn out. Ahead of them, the zombies parted, fearful of the flare, then joined the ranks of the growing horde following behind.

As they approached the first few buildings at the beginning of Main Street, Michael felt a familiar prickly sensation on his neck as the tiny hairs stood up on end. They were being watched. He had expected this. What waited in any town was the reason that almost any building was a death trap. Rachel shuddered and whispered, "I hate this feeling. Hate it!"

Michael looked to where he felt the eyes watching him. They came from the second floor window of a bank on the shaded side of the building. The shadows moved for a moment, growing darker, almost forming the shape of something. Hatred roiled from the window like heat from a bonfire. It was a poltergeist. Michael imagined its eyes burning with hunger and hatred. He glared back at it for a moment and kept walking, dragging Rachel after him. He wasn't interested in the bank.

Main Street grew more crowded with zombies. as they traveled along it, making it harder to avoid them. The ones they passed formed a desiccated train that followed them. Eventually, if they kept going, they would have to stop and then they would be surrounded. The flare pushed the zombies back, but they needed to get off the street before it burned out.

A sign on the other side of the street caught Michael's eye. Jake's Hardware. *Perfect.* It was a large brick building with plenty of windows facing the street. "Come on," He said, grabbing Rachel's arm. "Not so hard," she complained, but Michael ignored her. Reaching the hardware store, Michael quickly peered through the windows, mindful that they were running out of time. The interior was well lit by the sun.

"Is it safe?" Rachel asked as she hovered by him. Her eyes grew large as she noticed the horde of zombies following in their wake. "Please say it's safe."

"No zombies that I can see, no shadows, except at the back." Michael said as he unclipped his rifle and sat it against the red brick. "So as long as we stay towards the front, in the light, we should be safe." He tried the door and found it locked. "Here," he said, shoving the flare into Rachel's hand. The girl squealed and thrust the flare a full arm's length away from her. She stared at it as if it would explode at any moment. *Maybe it will and put us both out of our misery*, Michael thought with dark humor. "Don't drop it."

"Oh!" Rachel said, grabbing the flare with both hands and holding it as far away as possible.

Michael quickly pulled his pack off and dug through one of the side pockets, producing a tiny metal box.

"W-what's that?" Rachel asked as he opened it.

"Home-made lock picking kit," Michael replied, removing a paperclip and a hairpin from the box. He looked around them; the zombies were still closing, forming a half-moon just a few feet away. The flare was starting to sputter. He quickly knelt and studied the hardware's lock. It was an older model, five or six decades by the look of it, and should prove easy to pick. He inserted the hairpin into the keyhole and began to feel for tumblers.

"How did you learn how to do that?" Rachel asked.

"Something I learned in a former life," Michael muttered around the paperclip in his mouth. The old lock was stubborn and in serious need of being oiled.

"Were you a thief or something?"

"Something." He felt the first tumbler give.

"Why not just bash the door in?"

"Because then we can't lock it and the zombies will get in," Michael growled, irritated. He looked up at the horde and saw that they were completely surrounded. Not good. Soon the zombies in the back would start pushing the ones in the front forward, despite the flame. The flare began to spit impotently. He needed to work quicker. He needed to concentrate...

"Um." Rachel began again.

"Not now!"

"Michael."

He ignored her, feeling the second tumbler give. Halfway there.

"We have a problem you idiot!" Rachel repeated as her back bump pressed against him, jostling his arm. Michael looked up angrily and instantly realized what the girl had been trying to tell him. The flare had died and the zombies were closing in from all directions. They had only seconds left.

He quickly turned his attention back to the lock. It was taking too long. The rusted tumblers resisted his probing. He wanted to jam the hair pin in but finesse was needed. He probed a little harder and felt another tumbler give.

Rachel backed up against the glass window next to him. "Hurry!"

"Trying to," Michael said as he probed the last tumbler. There was no give to it at all.

"Watch out!" Rachel screamed.

Michael spun around and found a zombie lunging for him. He sidestepped it and then used its momentum to smash it against the bricks, spraying black ichor across the window. Rachel lunged and pulled the pistol from his waistband. She aimed it directly at Michael. He braced himself, expecting the shot. Instead, she turned and fired at a zombie, hitting it high in the shoulder.

"Aim for the head!" Michael said as he picked up his rifle and clubbed another zombie down.

"I was!" Rachel asked, brandishing the pistol.

"Hold your breath," Michael said as he cracked another zombie across the face with the rifle. "When you shoot."

"Okay?" Rachel said, though it oddly sounded more like a question. She took an exaggerated breath and squeezed off a shot, then another.

Michael went back to work on the tumbler. It still wouldn't give. He heard several clicks behind him. "I'm out!" Rachel said. Looking back, he saw that the zombies were almost on them, far too many to fight off. He grabbed the hairpin tightly and jammed it hard into the lock. It bowed and he was afraid the weak metal would bend, but then it sunk in as the last tumbler gave. "Finally!" Michael said, the word coming out like an expletive. He slipped the paper clip into the lock and twisted the knob. The door opened. He grabbed Rachel by the back of her pink jacket and she yelped as he thrust her through the opening.

Michael scooped up his pack and felt something claw at his shoulder. He swung the pack around, knocking several zombies to the ground. Dozens more swarmed towards him. He grabbed his rifle and slipped through the door as another zombie reached for him. Michael slammed the door shut and flipped the lock.

He stepped back as the zombies darkened the door and the windows, banging on the glass and moaning. Luckily, it was safety glass and only moved a little under each hit. Michael quickly picked a snow shovel from an after season sale display and slipped it through the door handle for reinforcement. That should hold the zombies until nightfall. Hopefully, if they were lucky, they would be gone by then. If not, they would be dead.

# CHAPTER FOUR

Zombies crowded the door, their rotten bodies pressing against the glass, leaving dark, greasy smears. Feeling a macabre curiosity, Michael crept forward until he was only inches from the window. It was his first real chance to see a "living" zombie up close without it trying to bite his face off. Sure, he had seen "dead" ones after he had killed them, but unsurprisingly they just looked like rotten corpses. Lacking fine motor control, the zombies were in a constant state of motion, always moving, overcorrecting, like a drunk or some addict doing the junkie shuffle. *The zombie shuffle.*

Some had noticeable bite marks on their faces and throats, while others bore no mark at all. One was so rotten and masticated that Michael couldn't tell whether it had been male or female. What was left of their clothes was torn and stained from their bodies decomposing and the blood of unfortunate victims. The sickly-sweet stench of death permeated through the doorframe, burning his nose and twisting his stomach.

The eyes were the most disturbing. They were frozen in a rictus glare, never blinking, eyelids drawn back into their sockets. Michael felt an unsettling wrench inside when he made eye contact as if their gaze was somehow tainting his soul. There was an insanity in them that was strangely compelling, almost hypnotizing. *Join us,* they said. Michael shuddered and turned away. Maybe the dead weren't so lucky after all.

He found Rachel huddled behind the checkout counter with the empty pistol clutched tightly in her hands. She seemed frozen in time. Her eyes were fixed on the zombies at the windows, lost in the horror she saw. A single fat tear rolled down her cheek. Michael hesitantly put his hand on her shoulder. "Don't look at them." Rachel turned to him slowly as if in a trance. She blinked at him for a moment until recognition finally set in. She gasped and took a ragged breath. "Don't look at them," Michael repeated. Rachel nodded and sunk down, her back against the counter.

Michael picked up a candy bar from the rack, tore it open, and gave it to Rachel. She held it in her shaking hand and looked down at the ground, swaying slightly—like the zombies out front. The image of Rachel as a zombie flashed in his mind momentarily. Michael grimaced and forced it away. "Eat," he said, and the girl did so, her movements mechanical. The girl was exhibiting signs of shock. He didn't blame her.

Michael stepped to the back of the counter and kept a wary eye on the store behind them as the girl ate. It looked like the typical small town hardware store and smelled faintly of sawdust and motor oil. Several rows of shelves ran perpendicular to the front of the store and a large aisle filled with sale displays from last spring ran between them. Sunlight streamed in from the front and the side windows. The back of the store lay in shadow. If there was trouble then it would come from there.

"D-do you think it's s-safe?" Rachel asked loudly over the

rhythmic thumping of the zombies hitting the glass.

Michael froze and listened to see if anything responded to Rachel's voice. The hardware remained quiet. "I think it is better to assume otherwise until we know for sure." Keeping an eye on the back of the store, Michael walked over to a small fridge and pulled out a bottle of cola. He twisted off the cap and it gave a satisfactory hiss of carbonation. Taking a big swig, he reveled in its taste and bite for a moment. His taste buds were definitely not used to processed sugar anymore.

He opened a second bottle and handed it to Rachel. She took a sip and closed her eyes. "Mmm, I've missed this. It's been . . . it's been far too long since I had one of these. Reminds me of my childhood for some reason." She took another sip and closed her eyes, making contented sounds. Lost for the moment in the past, the nightmares of the present forgotten. Michael was surprised at how quickly her demeanor had changed.

Rachel opened her eyes and noticed him watching her. "What?" she demanded, her posture instantly defensive.

"Nothing. The camping gear is at the back of the store. Stay—"

"I'm going with you." Rachel looked back at the zombies and shivered. "I-I don't want to be left alone with them. I don't feel right around them. It will be worse if I'm alone. I swear I can hear them saying join us or something like that." Michael looked at Rachel sharply. She was echoing what he was thinking a few minutes ago. Rachel giggled and continued, "In my mind, I mean. Or maybe I'm just going insane."

"Maybe," Michael said.

It was her turn to look at him sharply.

"They make me feel crazy too sometimes." Who wouldn't

question their sanity with those things around." She continued to eye him, so he added, "Let's go find you a winter jacket."

"If you say so. Wait, what's wrong with my jacket?"

"Well, for one, it won't keep you warm for much longer," Michael said as he walked to the first aisle.

"Oh."

"And then there is the color," Michael said as he looked down one aisle and another. No monsters and nothing that they could use. His eyes returned to the shadows at the back of the store as he crept up to the next row. He was starting to get an uneasy feeling in his gut. It wasn't like a geist, the energy was different. Not rage, more like waiting. It almost felt like a premonition.

*Ambush.*

"What's wrong with the color of my jacket?" Rachel exclaimed as she looked down at her bright pink windbreaker.

"Hush."

Rachel glared at him but closed her mouth. Michael raised a finger to his lips anyway and then pointed towards the back of the store. Rachel swallowed hard, anger fading into understanding, then fear.

The thumping of the zombies faded into the background as they made their way toward the back of the store. Michael stopped at each aisle and looked, listening for a moment to ensure it was safe to continue. It was nervous work, especially as they approached the shadows in the back.

They passed several rows filled with gardening tools, plumbing, and furnace filters—nothing they could use. The next one had camping equipment. Good. Michael had been worried that the hardware would be too small to carry it. He motioned to

Rachel to follow him and turned down the row. He picked up a small propane stove and showed it to Rachel.

Tears filled her eyes. "I haven't had a hot meal since forever." She wrapped her arms around herself and began to cry. "I'm s-sorry, but I can't seem to stop." She turned away from him, shaking as quiet sobs wracked her body.

*Ask a simple question.* Michael studied the camp stove in his hands, awkwardly turning it over in his hands as he waited for Rachel to calm down. After a few moments, she sniffed and said, "I-I'm sorry. I don't know what's wrong with me."

Michael felt he had a good idea of what that may be but decided it was best to change the subject. "Daylight won't last. We better get a move on, " He said, turning back to the camping gear.

During the long night on watch he had decided that they should head deeper into the mountains. If they were lucky, they would avoid most of the zombies and other monsters. They would also need some hefty supplies and gear to see them through the winter.

Michael looked over at Rachel and sighed. He would have to change tactics now that she was with him. The days of sleeping in a tree were over. He doubted the girl had ever even climbed one before. They would need a tent then. *Tents*, he corrected himself. There was no way he was going to share one with Rachel. Plus, it was getting too cold to sleep in a tree anyway.

He walked over to the next section and found several small hunting tents rated for winter. They came with a rain cover that was double sided, green camouflage on one side and white snow markings on the other. "Perfect." He said to himself and picked up another one for Rachel.

He then selected two new backpacks, and in short order, Michael had each of their packs filled up with anything he thought they could use. A propane heater to go with the stove, several small propane canisters, cooking equipment, and a multi-tool. Michael thought about moving the contents of his old pack into the new one but decided to wait until they were at a safer place to do it. Sunlight was burning. He tied the tent and a sleeping bag to the side of his pack and then helped Rachel with hers.

The camping section bled into emergency supplies. Michael located a half-full box of flares and stuffed them in his old pack for easy access. Instant light was priceless, and the flares would provide a quick fire if needed. More importantly, they would help them escape the store.

Michael hefted the pack. It was about fifty pounds, a good weight with some room left over for any food found up front. He heard a grunt behind him and turned to find Rachel trying to pick hers up. She lifted it a few inches and then dropped it to the ground. "It's too heavy," She kicked the pack and gave him a look like he should have known better. "I'm not carrying it."

Michael sighed again and then transferred most of Rachel's pack into his. It was his turn to grunt when he picked up his pack. It weighed about seventy-five pounds now and he guessed that the girl's pack only weighed about twenty. Rachel picked it up easily yet frowned. "It's still a little heavy."

"Great. Let's get you some warmer clothes then." Michael said, ignoring the complaint. Rachel gave him another look but said nothing as she followed him out to the center aisle. Past the last row, Michael could make out a clothing area marked

"Rugged Wear." Behind the clothes in the shadows was a set of vinyl doors with black windows.

Rachel looked at the doors and shook her head. "Nope to that. I'll be fine with what I have already."

"No, we have to do it now. We might not get a chance to do it later." Michael dropped his pack by the new ones and started walking towards the coats, rifle held ready in his hands and keeping a constant watch on the doors at the back of the store. Stopping at the edge of the sunlight, Michael looked back and found Rachel hanging back by the packs. She was hunched over, watching him apprehensively with her folded arms shoved deep into her stomach.

Michael turned back to the double doors. The coats were just within grabbing distance. Rachel needed a coat to survive the winter so he would have to chance it. He reached for the closest one, and as his fingers touched it, the sun grew dim as clouds covered it. He froze as the shadows grew around him.

"Hey!" Rachel hissed. "Look at the doors!"

Michael looked up quickly and terror shot through him at what he saw. An evil, inhuman face leered at him through one of the windows. It was a thing of madness, with malice glowing like coals in its red eyes. The too wide mouth was drawn back in a huge, hungry grin. With a howl, it blasted through the double doors and charged at Michael with its large talon like claws spread wide.

Figuring that a gunshot would have little effect, Michael grabbed the barrel of his rifle and sidestepped the creature, swinging as hard as he could at the thing's knee. The wood stock shattered, and the beast went sprawling towards Rachel.

"Run," Michael yelled, but Rachel was frozen in place,

staring at the creature in horror. The thing crawled for her, dragging one leg behind it. It made a keening, hungry noise with each movement that sounded vulgar to Michael's ears.

There was no chance he could get close enough to club the creature again before it got to Rachel. He raised his rifle to fire and saw that the barrel was bent. "Shoot!" He yelled at Rachel and then swore as he remembered that she did not have any bullets. As the thing reached Rachel, the girl's eyes rolled up inside her head and she fell to the tiles, still holding the pistol in her limp hand.

Michael's jaw dropped. "She fainted! I can't believe-"

The creature reared up over Rachel and sniffed deeply. It snorted explosively, and then its head spun around until it was looking directly at Michael with its insane eyes. It sniffed at him, and a perverse expression of joy and hunger came over its insane face. The creature's body spun around to match the direction of its head and started crawling rapidly towards Michael, keening with need.

Michael knew it was too quick for him, even with a broken leg. The rifle was broken and useless to him now. His mind racing, he looked over at the outside windows. If only the sunlight would come back. Then looking closer, he realized that where the window ended was not a black wall as he had previously thought but actually two black painted windows that extended for another ten feet. Bright shafts of light began to bleed along the painted glass as a cloud passed the sun.

Michael threw the rifle toward the darkened windows as the creature slammed into him, bearing him to the ground. Agony erupted in his already injured side but Michael had no time for the pain as the creature thrust its slobbering mouth towards his throat. Michael pushed against the wet jaws but the beast was far too strong for him.

Glass shattered in the distance and then sunlight blasted them both. The monster reared up, screaming in pain, then dove out of the sunlight. Pitch black smoke rolled off its body in thick waves. There was a horrible smell, like hair on fire, but much worse. Yipping in pain, the creature crashed through the coat racks and tore through the back double doors, knocking one of them loose.

For a few minutes, all Michael could do was lie on the ground and try to catch his breath. His side was a screaming mass of pain, and several ribs were cracked if not broken. He gasped, fighting for air as he kept a wary eye on the doors. Just because he was in sunlight now didn't mean he was safe. He risked looking over at Rachel and found her still unconscious on the floor, her arm twitching.

A low, angry growl brought his attention back to the doors. It cut off and then began again, promising death. A second growl joined it, deeper and angrier than the first. One of the doors slowly opened.

Michael forced himself to roll away, not wanting to see what horror would come to join the first creature. Agony ripped up the side of his chest, and he doubled over in a fetal position. He fought against his body's involuntary response to the pain, knowing he'd die soon if he didn't move. Wheezing, he forced himself to his knees and lowered his head to keep from blacking out. Too dizzy to get to his feet, he began crawling towards Rachel.

"Wake up!" He gasped as he inched towards her. Her finger twitched slightly and the pistol fell from her grip. "Rachel, wake up!" He tried to shout but only managed a loud whisper. There was a sharp breaking sound behind him and he forced himself to move faster. The creatures couldn't cross the light but they could still cause harm. As if reading his thoughts, a green John Deere lawn tractor went spinning by, missing his head by mere inches. It crashed into the shelves next to Rachel, sandwiching them to the ground. She shot up with a grunt, her eyes wide and searching, seeing everything but taking nothing in.

"Rachel!"

The girl's eyes found him and she flinched as reality hit her. "No, no, no, no, no!" She moaned as she shook her head. As she looked behind Michael, her eyes widened and started rolling up again. Michael grabbed the girl's arm, twisting hard enough to make her squeal in pain.

"Look at me! Look!" Michael demanded and twisted her arm until she did. "They can't cross the light. No, don't look back there. Keep your eyes on me. Get the pistol, grab the packs, and head to the doors. Get out of here!" Rachel remained frozen. "Now!" he snapped. The effort nearly made him black out again.

Rachel swiped up the pistol and scrambled to her feet. She picked up the packs with shaking hands and screamed as a diesel generator crashed down next to her. The girl ran full out for the counter, dragging the three packs behind her.

Michael sighed in relief. Now, he just had to get himself out alive. He began inching towards the front of the store, still not able to trust his legs.

The creatures screamed in fury as they realized they were losing their prey. Hardware items began to rain down all around Michael. A basketball beamed him in the leg with a solid thump, and a pair of garden shears slammed into the floor next to his hand, emitting a loud humming sound as they vibrated.

A river of gasoline came towards him from the wrecked generator, reeking and reflecting rainbows in the sunlight. Michael moved out of its way and came to rest near another box of road flares. He snorted at the serendipity of it and picked up a flare, slammed it onto the tile, and its end erupted into green incandescent flame.

Looking back, he caught sight of another lawn tractor arcing towards him. With a grunt, he rolled out of the way. It landed upside down with a crash, and Michael winced as several shards of broken tile hit his face.

*Enough of this!* Anger drowning out the agony in his side, Michael stood and threw the flare all in one motion. It hit the generator squarely, then bounced up in the air, landed near the edge of the rainbow pool of gasoline, and rolled slowly towards it in an arc.

Michael didn't wait to see if the gasoline ignited. He could only hope for luck as he limped toward the door. A saw blade whipped by his head and buried itself into a wooden pole. A snow blower bounced off the shelves beside him, and a paint can followed it. "Come on, light! Light!"

There was a loud whoomph behind him. Flames erupted and followed the puddle of gasoline into the back of the store, igniting everything within reach. The rain of items ceased, and the two creatures screamed almost harmoniously in fear and pain as the fire closed on them. Roaring and spitting defiantly, they quickly moved back through the double doors with the fire chasing their heels.

Michael wasn't out of danger yet. The store had enough kerosene and propane tanks to level it if they caught. He broke into a painful stumble towards the front door, hoping momentum would get him through.

Rachel was standing a few feet in front of the door. Behind her, he could make out silhouettes of dozens of zombies pounding on the glass. He'd forgotten about them! Tears streamed down Rachel's face and he could see her lips moving. "Run!" they urged.

Just as Michael reached the door, the world around him ignited in a deafening roar. A fiery hand lifted him off his feet, and he flew forward in what seemed like slow motion. He could see Rachel's eyes widening and her mouth opening to scream. Time sped up and he slammed into the girl, the impact carrying them crashing through the door.

# CHAPTER FIVE

**M**ichael looked up at the cloudless blue sky and felt himself begin to drift away in its vibrant beauty. A rotten face appeared above him, juxtaposing with the crystal blue heavens. It began to descend as if to give him a kiss, and then its mouth opened impossibly wide, displaying jagged broken teeth that promised death with their bite.

Michael opened his own mouth to scream as the horror filled his vision. A sudden jolt rolled through him and a massive plume of flame engulfed the zombie. Stunned, Michael could only marvel at the beauty of the liquid flame rolling up toward the sky. Then it was gone and the zombie with it.

The sky filled his eyes again. It was a blank canvas so beautiful, yet far removed from the ugliness of the world. Michael reached for it and found it unattainable. His hand caught his eye and he looked at it. It was covered with blood and his sleeve was on fire. Alarmed, he swiped at it with his other hand as a familiar pain shot through his side. It cleared his head, bringing him back to reality. *The zombies!* He thought, struggling to sit up.

He froze in awe at the carnage around him.

There was an empty area around the shattered front of

the store. Beyond that, zombies and pieces of them littered the street, ripped apart by the explosion and shrapnel. Several were on fire, spraying bright, iridescent sparks like the cheap fireworks from his childhood, mewling as they were consumed.

Hundreds shambled towards them from outside the explosion's radius, their faces twisted with hate and rot. The nearest ones hesitated near the sparking zombies. That would not last long. They needed to get moving! Rachel! Where was Rachel? Looking around, Michael couldn't discern Rachel's body from the others scattered around him. Had she been killed in the explosion? Then the familiar pink of her jacket caught his eye.

Rachel lay still by the broken remains of a plastic bench, her eyes staring up at the sky. Dead. Another person he had failed. Suddenly, Rachel convulsed, her whole body seizing. No, Michael realized with astonishment, she was laughing! It shook her petite frame and tears rolled down from her eyes. She broke off mid-laugh into a scream of release as she rocked back and forth, kicking at the ground with her heels. Rachel rolled to face him, her face serious now despite an occasional aftershock of giggling that shook her body. She said in a weary voice, "I'm so tired of being scared, so very tired." She closed her eyes, and lay still.

Michael stared at Rachel in disbelief. The girl's mind had finally snapped. He looked up at the approaching wall of zombies around them. The only way out was the alleyway next to the hardware, and in a few seconds, that would be closed off. Michael forced himself to his feet and nearly blacked out from the effort. He closed his eyes until the dizziness passed and then limped over to the girl.

"Rachel, get up." He told her in a voice that seemed coated

in ash. "The zombies are coming."

She didn't respond aside from her mouth grimacing for a moment. His old pack lay near her, thrown out by the explosion. Michael looked around for the two new packs and then realized they had been the source of the secondary explosion. Unable to bend over, he dropped to his knees next to the pack and quickly assessed it. Aside from some char and a few scrapes, it seemed whole.

"Rachel!" He yelled, picking up his pack. She popped one eye open and looked up at him.

"We need to go."

"Why?" She asked, closing her eyes and chewing at her bottom lip.

"What?"

"Why? Why should we go looking for death when it is already here?" Rachel sat up and looked at him with dead eyes. The fear, the anger, everything was gone, leaving only an empty shell. "WHY?" She shrieked and then fell to the ground, laughing hysterically.

Michael reached down to yank Rachel to her feet and suddenly a pistol was in his face. He froze and debated whether he was fast enough to swipe it from her hand. He doubted it.

"Don't!" Rachel said, shaking her head. Then her face softened and she pleaded, "Don't. Just let me be, please."

Michael looked at the alleyway and saw that several zombies had already passed it. There wasn't any more time to spare for Rachel, yet he couldn't abandon her either. Could he? He felt helpless but realized he couldn't do anything else for her.

He backed off, and Rachel gave him a thankful smile. Then, reversing the pistol, she tossed it to him. "Here, it's empty." Her smile turned wistful. "Thanks for putting up with me. Now go." She settled back on the ground as if preparing to take a nap. *Preparing to die.*

Hundreds of zombies closed in from all directions. Michael shoved the pistol into his belt and pulled two road flares from his pack. He slammed one on the ground. Red flame jetted from the other end. He laid the flare next to Rachel in a futile attempt to ease his conscience. "In case you change your mind." He said, but she didn't respond.

Shouldering the pack on his good side, Michael turned towards the approaching horde and ignited the other flare against his hip. The closest zombies hissed and backed away from it. Holding the flare aloft, he looked at Rachel one last time. She laid still, her face serene and her arms folded across her chest as if she were in a coffin.

Michael snarled as he waded into the zombies, brandishing the flare in a semi-circle before him. The zombies backed away as the flames came near and crowded in as soon as it passed. One bite and he was dead. It became harder to force them away as he got deeper into the mass.

One of the things lunged at him, and Michael slammed the flare into its gaping mouth. He pulled it out, and the zombie vomited green sparks. Its head caught fire and was quickly consumed by green flames. It bumped into another zombie, and it too went up in a shower of sparks as if covered in some type of accelerant. Howling, it stumbled into the zombie next to it and that one also went up. The other zombies backed away, leaving a narrow space wide enough for Michael to get through.

He made it to the alley opening and stopped. Looking back, he caught a brief glimpse of Rachel in her burned pink jacket before the zombies closed together in his wake. "Sorry, I failed you," Michael repeated and began walking as fast as he could down the alley, determined to put as much distance between him and what would soon happen. He hit the woods behind the hardware store and pushed himself to move faster, knowing the flare would only last so long.

After a few minutes, his injured side began to spasm, forcing him to stop. He collapsed to the ground and tried to breathe past the hitch in his side. He could only manage short, shallow breaths. Looking back towards the town, he could still make out the tops of some of the buildings, so he hadn't gone as far as he had hoped. His side tied up in knots, he could go no further.

Michael propped the flare against a fallen tree before him and focused on the flame. Minutes passed as he silently urged the flame to burn a little longer, knowing that it wouldn't. He watched it with dread as the flare began to spit and sputter. It spat one more time and went out, trailing smoke. Michael closed his eyes and waited.

Agony filled screams started coming from the town. Michael flinched with each one as if they were a physical blow. Anger and shame filled him, but he forced himself to listen to the screams, damning himself to hell with everyone. As the screams worsened, he started to cover his ears with his hands and then forced them down. No! He needed to hear this. Another person he had failed. Another person he had killed.

Suddenly, the screams broke off. Michael lifted his head and looked at the town. The forest was still and silent around him. He let out a large breath he hadn't realized he'd been holding. Rachel was finally dead. She was gone but the guilt would live on in him forever. Just like... He forced himself to his feet, anxious to get away.

Then Rachel screamed again, her voice filled with so much pain and agony that she sounded inhuman. Michael took an involuntary step back toward the town and stopped as the scream died. He waited in the aftermath that was so silent it made his ears pound. Sometime later, Michael turned away from the town and limped into the brush. He did not look back.

He traveled throughout the rest of the day and night as guilt drove him deep into the woods without rest. He had failed Rachel, just as he had failed Steph, and failed others. The old wounds in his heart threatened to burst open, and he shuddered away from them.

Why had he gotten the feeling to save the girl only to have it end this way? His gut had never been this wrong before. Had he done something wrong? There was no reason for it and no answers to be found. Rachel's last agonized scream echoed repeatedly in his mind, and he pushed himself harder, trying to escape it.

By morning, he was mentally and physically exhausted. His legs shook, threatening to give out with every step he took. The angry knot in his side wouldn't allow him to take a full breath, and he was having difficulty raising his arm over his shoulder. There would be no sleeping in a tree for him today. Still, he pushed on, tormented by the day before.

Sometime later, the woods broke open onto fallow farmland. An old haystack lay before him, slightly flattened by the elements. He considered hiding in the hay for a moment and then limped past it. Not only was it far too small for his large frame, but he would be completely blind and defenseless if he hid in it.

He stumbled forward, looking very much like a zombie himself. Painful thoughts of Rachel gave way to numbness as his brain shut down. Eventually, his only thought was to put one foot ahead of the other, which was getting harder to do with each step.

A loud crack of thunder shocked him out of his reverie sometime later. Michael quickly looked up and stared in awe at the menacing storm that had snuck up on him. Pitch-black clouds boiled above, bringing darkness in their wake. Frantic, he pulled a parka from his pack and scrambled to put it on. Thunder crashed again, the heavens opened up, and a torrent of rain fell from the sky.

*Idiot.* Michael thought, furious at himself for being caught unaware. Nearly blinded and half-deaf from the storm, he was vulnerable to anything on the prowl. Worse, it was dark enough that the zombies would be nearly at full strength. He was so drained that he doubted he could handle a dormant zombie, let alone a quickened one. He needed to find a place to hole up and soon.

Minutes went by as the downpour continued without lessening. Cold, wet, and miserable, Michael reloaded the pistol with the remaining six bullets and kept it cocked and ready in his hand. He stayed to the wood line as much as possible, moving carefully, sometimes freezing when he thought he heard or saw something.

Dusk fell, the deluge finally weakening into a drizzle as a cold wind began to pick up. Michael kept going, shivering until his teeth chattered, passing several dark houses in the distance. He stopped at each one, then reluctantly moved on. They all felt wrong. He thought he could even make out the dark forms of zombies by some of them. He would need to find one that felt right soon, or he'd freeze to death.

With the feeble light dying in the distance, Michael crested a hill and could make out the back of an old farmhouse across a large field with several barns and a silo. Next to the largest barn was a massive oak tree, a wooden platform cradled in its large outstretched branches like a platter held by a server. The remnants of a treehouse.

Michael studied the farm. He didn't see any zombies, and his gut remained quiet. Could he trust it again after Rachel? The farm was either salvation or a death trap. He would have to chance it either way. He doubted that he would be able to go much further. The temperature was dropping fast, and his legs were trembling violently. He began limping towards the house and prayed that his legs wouldn't give out on him.

He was halfway across the open field when three figures stepped out of the woods beside him.

# CHAPTER SIX

The zombies shrieked in rage and charged at Michael. Quickened by the night, their movements were fast and graceful like a predator. He barely had time to raise the pistol before the first one was on him. It may have been a woman once, though it was hard to tell. Michael shot the zombie in the head and it fell to the muddy ground, sliding to a stop before him.

The other two zombies leaped over the body and came full speed at Michael. Two more shots and they collapsed in a tangle and lay still. Michael slipped the pistol into his waistband and made for the farmhouse as fast as possible. He could only manage a stumbling jog and silently urged his exhausted legs to go faster. He didn't want to be caught in the open with only two shots left.

Behind Michael came a chorus of shrieks as zombies poured out of the forest directly at him. He pivoted and ran towards the closer oak tree, fear resurrecting his dead legs.

The zombies caught up to Michael as he reached the tree. He jumped for one of the low branches, and a zombie crashed into him from behind, slamming him to the ground. Michael's breath left his lungs in a loud whoosh, and his vision dimmed momentarily as he nearly passed out from the pain in his side. The zombie rolled off, spun around, and launched itself at Michael again in one graceful motion.

Its jaws immediately went for Michael's neck, and he grabbed the zombie by the throat in an attempt to stop it. The thing's mouth clamped down on his coat instead and began to shake its head, ravaging his arm through the thick fabric. Screaming in horror and pain, Michael yanked the pistol from his waistband, placed it against the zombie's head and pulled the trigger. A cone of gore blasted out the side of its head, and the zombie collapsed on top of him.

Michael freed his arm from the zombie's mouth and pushed the lifeless body to the side. Was he infected? There was no time to check as another zombie ran at him, screeching its hatred of the living. Michael sidestepped, but the zombie swiped the pistol away as it passed. It crashed into the tree with a stomach-turning crunch and fell prone against the trunk.

There wasn't any time to search for the pistol. Dozens of zombies were running towards him. Michael looked up and made out the remains of an old rotted rope used for getting to the wooden treehouse platform. He quickly dropped the pack and, using the prone zombie as a stepping-stone, launched himself up and grabbed the rope. It was slippery but held. He tried to pull himself higher and nearly lost his grip as an angry stabbing pain shot through his injured side.

Several zombies jumped at Michael, forcing him to pull his legs up each time to avoid them. His arms began to burn with fatigue and he only had seconds before he'd fall to his death. Michael desperately lifted his legs and kicked towards the tree, catching a thick branch with his heel. Using it as leverage, he pulled himself over to the trunk and caught hold of another branch. He pulled himself onto the platform and collapsed as his strength gave out.

He fell on his back, gasping for air as cold rain pelted his face. His body had been pushed to its absolute limit and every muscle burned with exhaustion. He could feel his heart beat in his wrist as it throbbed with pain. The zombie bite! Panicking, Michael pulled his sleeve back and looked at his injured wrist. It was deeply bruised, but the skin appeared whole and unbroken. Relieved, he fell back against the platform and...

Michael must have passed out because as he blinked, the sky darkened and the zombie's screaming cut off. The temperature was noticeably cooler. That wasn't good. If he hadn't awakened, he would have died from hypothermia. He needed his pack.

Michael rolled to the platform's edge and whistled at what he saw. Hundreds of zombies surrounded the tree. Soon as they saw him, they started screaming and jumping at the platform. One zombie launched at the rope forcing Michael to yank it out of reach. The zombie barely missed the rope, disappearing into the crush of undead below.

He rolled to the center of the platform and lay as flat as he could, hoping the zombies would calm down if they didn't see him. After a few minutes, the screaming died down and he could think clearly again.

He was safe from the zombies for the moment, but now his main concern was hypothermia. The wind and rain were picking up, bringing with them a promise of cold death if he didn't find shelter soon.

Michael sat up and folded his legs under him so that the

parka protected them from the rain. Not much use as he was already drenched. He shivered as he considered his options. He immediately dismissed the farmhouse. It was too far away, and there were too many zombies below. He also didn't like the idea of going blindly into a dark, unknown building where there could be more zombies or something else waiting for him. It also could be locked.

The barn was closer, though it was as much of an unknown as the house. Its front doors were open, and there was a good chance that some of the zombies may have wandered into it. However, it did have a roof and, if he was lucky, some dry hay. Maybe he could even get up into the loft. Still, it was as useless to him as the farmhouse unless he found a way through the hundreds of zombies below.

Lastly, if Michael could somehow get to his pack, he could set the tent up on the platform but he was forced to dismiss that idea. The platform was too small for the tent. It also was too much in the open, leaving him exposed to anyone or anything wandering by. Time was running out and he had to make a decision. Right now, the platform and the house were too dangerous, leaving only the barn as an option.

Michael crept closer to the platform's edge and tried to look down again without the zombies seeing him. No screams came from below. So far, so good. From what he could see through the scattered zombies there wasn't much in the yard to be of use. An old swing set sat next to an ancient rusted truck hulk. A makeshift charcoal grill was next to a broken picnic table. The metal silo towered over the barn with a rusting farm tractor beside it. Not much to work with.

A zombie howled below went into a frenzy as it saw

him, tearing at other zombies to get to the tree. Michael cursed and rolled back out of sight, feeling grim about his situation. His shivering was worsening, and his extremities were turning numb—the beginning stages of hypothermia.

Michael forced himself to his feet and took another look at the yard. The zombies below rioted as soon as they saw him but he ignored them. Everything was still where he had left it minutes before: swing, old 1950 Chevy truck, grill, picnic table, barn, silo, John Deere tractor, hundreds of zombies. Same dead-end options.

Dispirited and beyond exhaustion, Michael collapsed on the edge of the platform and looked down at the tree trunk. The pack was still there, with the pistol lying a few feet away. Several zombies began jumping up at him, falling just short of the fifteen-foot-high platform. Michael's eyes wandered over to the John Deere, and a desperate plan suddenly came to him. It was a long shot, but that's all he had left.

Michael emptied his coat pockets and took inventory. Lighter, cattail fluff in a watertight bag, multi-tool, paper clip, three fishing hooks in a plastic container, and a spindle of ten-pound line.

He unraveled the fish line as fast as he could with numb fingers. Once he had twenty feet of line, Michael cut it and repeated the process five more times until the line ran out. He tied one set of ends together and then tied the other set to the hook.

He figured that his pack must weigh between forty and fifty pounds. A ten-pound line would snap if he tried to lift the heavy pack with it but he hoped that by using five lines together their combined strength would lift fifty pounds. That still may not be enough to lift the pack but he had to try.

Michael crept back over to the platform's edge and fed the line over the edge until he was sure the hook was close to the ground. Looking down, he saw that the area around the pack was free of zombies. He quickly flicked his wrist, and the hook caught the edge of his pack.

Michael ducked back from the edge and began to pull on the line. It went only about a foot before there was a noticeable vibration. Michael paused and the vibration lessened. He slowly began to draw it again, hoping not to jar it. Halfway up, one of the lines went slack as it snapped, and vibration increased on the other lines. Cursing, Michael leaned over the edge and grabbed the line as far down as possible. The zombies went into a frenzy again as soon as they saw him, their screams deafening, but all Michael saw was the pack only a few feet below.

Using smooth, fluid motions, Michael started pulling the pack up again, hand over hand. It rose another two feet, then another line snapped. Michael yanked as hard as he could and the rest of the lines snapped as the pack shot up. Holding on to the ledge with one hand, Michael leaned out and grabbed the pack just as it reached its zenith. He screamed as pain tore through his side but didn't let go. Gritting his teeth against the pain, Michael pulled the pack over the edge and collapsed on top of it, exhausted but relieved. Maybe there was hope yet. The next part would be far trickier, however.

Numb hands shaking from the cold, Michael cut the longest line free from the others with his multi-tool. He futilely wiped the rain from his eyes and tried to feed the line through the eye of another hook. The storm was building again, and Michael knew he couldn't function much longer. The hook slipped from his numb fingers, and as he fumbled to pry it up from the wet wood, it fell through a crack and was gone. Michael screamed and punched the platform as hard as he could.

He took a deep breath and forced himself to calm down. Anger would do nothing to help the situation. He removed the last hook from the container and cradled it in his hand. He picked up the fish line again and cried out in relief when he got it through the eyehole on the first try. He tied a messy knot with fingers that refused to bend and tossed the hook over the edge.

He glanced over the edge when he was sure it was close to the ground. The hook was dangling within a foot of the pistol. He flicked his wrist back and forth, trying to catch the gun's finger guard before the zombies saw him. The hook danced around the guard and Michael swore silently again. Just as a zombie was about to walk into the line, the hook caught.

Michael pulled the line up as fast as he dared. The zombie, a foot taller than the others, seemed to watch with curiosity as the gun levitated in front of its face. Its red eyes followed the gun up until they saw Michael. Snarling, it leaped up at him, and its arm hit the gun, causing it to spin away. There was a hard thump as its hand caught the platform. The zombie began to pull itself up, baleful red eyes never leaving Michael.

Michael snapped on the line and rolled away. He grabbed the pistol as it flew towards him and winced as the hook sunk deep into his hand. Michael juggled the gun for a moment and almost lost it over the edge.

The zombie's head rose from below, hissing when it saw him. Michael tried to shoot it but his frozen fingers refused to work. Using a finger from his other hand, he jammed it into the trigger and pulled back with his arm. There was a satisfactory pop and a hole bloomed on the zombie's forehead. It sighed and let go, disappearing into the screaming throng below.

Michael was shivering violently now and couldn't stop his teeth from chattering. He crawled across the platform on his knees and tried to aim the pistol at the tractor's gas tank. The gun jumped wildly in his shaking hands, forcing him to rest them on the platform to steady his aim. *One bullet left.*

For a moment, Michael entertained the idea of the gas tank going up in a huge explosion like in the movies. He aimed for the gas tank as best he could and pulled the trigger with both hands. The bullet tagged the bottom of the tank. If it had been a millimeter lower, it would have missed. Gas began to pour out onto the ground next to the silo. Definitely not like the movies.

Michael pulled a flare from his pack and slammed it on the platform. Its blue flames spat angrily in the rain but didn't go out. He held his hand near the flame, the heat feeling alien to his cold fingers.

He lifted the flare and threw it toward the tractor. There was a *fwump* sound when it landed and a bright flame kicked up. The zombies around the tractor jumped back, throwing their arms up and shrieking in fear. The flames slowly licked up the side of the tractor and there was a loud pop as the tank caught. Burning shrapnel shredded the side of the silo and several zombies ignited despite the rain, spraying sparks.

Now for the last miracle. Michael slipped on his pack and figured it was now or never. Sitting on the platform's edge, he adjusted his pack and then picked out a zombie to crash down on.

Suddenly the silo exploded, a massive mushroom like cloud erupting from its shattered shell. The shock wave blasted the rain sideways and Michael barely caught the edge of the platform to keep from being blown off. Then the heat from the inferno hit him and steam began to rise from his parka as it melted onto his coat.

The screaming zombies below erupted into millions of green sparks in a rapid chain reaction, far better than any fireworks Michael had ever seen. Some exploded into shimmering dust; the motes quickly swallowed up in the returning rain. A strong smell of sulfur dominated the air.

Flaming debris began to rain down around the platform. Michael shielded his head with his hands, watching with alarm as several burning chunks landed on the barn. "No, no, no!" He yelled. His dismay turned to relief as the heavy rain pummeled the fire, quickly putting it out, leaving only a few smoldering spots.

The remnants of the silo continued to burn, shooting a tower of flame high into the air. *What the hell had been in there?* Michael had heard stories of silos sometimes exploding because their contents had caught on fire. *But would they have caused that big of an explosion?*

The air began to cool again, prompting him to get moving. Looking down, this time he did not see any zombies. The way to the barn now appeared clear. The plan had worked a little too well but it had worked.

The still burning silo worried Michael. It would be a beacon to anything on the prowl. The fire illuminated the surrounding fields and he watched them for a moment but didn't see anything in the light's radius. He knew he should get away from the area as quickly as possible but he wasn't in any condition to travel, especially in the freezing rain. No choice but to head to the barn.

Michael pulled off his pack and looked it over. It was a little more singed than before and had bits of parka melted onto it. Otherwise, it was in good shape. He dropped it to the ground below and then slid over the platform's edge. He held on only for a second before the pain in his side forced him to let go. He tried to bend his knees to cushion the impact but his legs collapsed, slamming him hard into the muddy ground.

Lying still in the cold mud, Michael wondered if he had broken his legs. He carefully shifted one leg, then the other, and was relieved to find them whole. The mud had absorbed most of the energy from the fall. He slowly got to his feet, his tailbone feeling a little bruised. Just like everything else, he thought without humor.

Michael began limping towards the barn, dragging the pack with one hand and holding the empty pistol in the other like a club. He paused at the barn door and peered inside. Light from the burning silo flickered through the slats, illuminating the interior and casting dancing shadows in the back of the barn. The ladder to the loft was off to the side. Michael walked towards it, never taking his eyes off the undulating shadows.

Michael froze when he reached the ladder. Had he heard something? Was something in here with him? He wasn't in any shape to do anything about it if there was. The sound did not repeat itself so Michael slipped his pack over his shoulder and climbed the ladder as fast as his shaking legs would allow.

Once he reached the loft, he collapsed on the hay as the last of his energy played out. The interior of the barn was heaven compared to the exposed platform. The burning silo had heated the air and the structure blocked most of the wind and rain. The hay was soft and warm, and soon Michael found it difficult to keep his eyes open. Exhausted and shivering, he wished he could pass out, but there was one last thing he had to do.

The ladder was attached to a clever pulley system that allowed it to be easily raised and lowered. Michael grabbed the rope and pulled the ladder up until it was parallel to the ground. Then he tied it off on a beam and pulled up the excess rope from below. Now, there was no easy way up to him.

He crawled over to the largest pile of hay and burrowed deep into it. His coat and clothes were still wet but he didn't care. Covered with warm, dry hay, his injuries faded away as sleep took him. The shattered wreck of the silo burned for the rest of the night, keeping the boogeyman and bad dreams away.

# CHAPTER SEVEN

**M**ichael drifted in a dreamless limbo for an unknown time. When he finally awoke, it was a gentle transition that built until he was fully conscious. Aside from some stiff muscles and a parched mouth, he felt surprisingly well rested. His side was still tender but seemed to be on the mend as well. How long had he slept?

He lay in the straw and listened for a while to the sounds of the barn. The building creaked and groaned, and the door nudged its frame every so often when the wind whipped up. The world sounded peaceful and safe, but he knew that to be a bitter lie.

Michael slowly dug his way out of the hay. Weak light greeted his eyes and he had to take a minute to let them adjust. He crept to the loft's edge on stiff legs and looked down into the barn. Sunlight streamed through the doors and Michael was relieved to see that there weren't any zombies below. He needed to check outside before heading down.

Picking the hay from his hair, Michael crouch-walked to the loft window and peeked out. From his vantage point, the yard was empty of zombies. A thick gray slurry circled the oak tree where their ashes had mixed with mud. Michael looked down and noticed he was covered in the same grey mud. He felt a lurch in his stomach.

A fetid smell came to the foreground—sweet, burnt, and rotten—that he had become desensitized to while sleeping. Suddenly nauseous, Michael gagged as he shrugged out of his ruined coat as quickly as possible. Unfortunately, that did not do much to improve the smell. He definitely needed a bath and a change of clothes.

Michael shoved his disgust into the background and rechecked the surrounding area. So far, it looked safe to venture outside the barn. Maybe he had been lucky and nothing had been drawn to the burning silo while he had slept. Maybe there was something out there waiting for him. Only one way to find out.

Michael checked the yard a final time, strapped on his pack, and climbed down the ladder. He quickly swept the barn, searching for anything of use. A brand-new machete in a weatherproof sheathe was hanging on the wall by the main door. Michael strapped it to his belt then pulled out the machete and did a few practice swings. It felt flimsy and had a horrible balance, but it would have to do until he could find something better. Holding the machete ready, he went to the door and looked out. The yard still appeared clear.

Michael ventured a step outside and stopped. His eyes scanned for any movement, but all he saw were the trees and bushes moving in the wind. Then he walked around to the back of the barn to get a closer look at the silo. The remnants sat dark and silent like some volcano that had long fallen asleep. A thin reed of smoke trailed up into the sky. The ashes appeared to be dry. *Must have slept a lot longer than I thought.*

He picked his way around the edge of the silo, looking for

clues to the source of the explosion. The fire had been absolute and whatever had been stored there had been consumed. Michael considered himself lucky that he hadn't been closer to the explosion.

Michael made his way over to the house, keeping a wary eye on his surroundings and the machete loose and ready in his hand. Just because it was day didn't mean it was safe. The house had a small porch with steps leading up to the back door. Four large windows overlooked the yard. Michael watched them closely as he approached. Nothing moved. Two windows had blinds that were closed but the other two were open. He walked closer and peered into each open window to see if the rooms were zombie free.

Through one, he could see a simple half bath, the décor heavy handed with a feminine slant. Through the other window was a large country kitchen. The owner must have liked apples because the theme was everywhere, from the wallpaper to the plates hanging on the wall. It gave the kitchen a cozy, lived in feeling. It reminded Michael of when he visited his grandma's house as a child.

It appeared safe, but appearances were often deceiving in this new decaying world. Holding the machete ready, Michael tried the back door and found it locked. He had lost his lock picking kit in town when he and Rachel... He looked around carefully one more time to see if anybody was watching and then kicked the door in with a crash. That should draw attention, if anything were in the house—zombie, human, or otherwise. If there was a geist, well, he wouldn't know until it was too late. He stepped off to the side so that he could peer through the kitchen window and watched for several minutes. Nothing stirred, so he took a deep breath, tightened his grip on the machete then walked inside.

The kitchen was larger than it had appeared outside. Various apple themed knick-knacks monopolized most of the open spaces. A huge latch door fridge dominated the wall on one side and a wide, claw foot stove on the other. The appliances looked to be circa the nineteen sixties, if not older. A well-used cutting board island with a scarred white sink centered the room. A small pantry door sat next to a standard size door on one wall. At the end of the room was an open doorway through which he could see a dining room.

Michael's stomach grumbled, reminding him that he was hungry, but for the moment, he ignored it as ensuring the house was safe was a top priority. After dropping his pack by the back door, he walked over to the second window and opened the blind to allow more sunlight into the room. He then walked over to the dining room door and made sure it was clear of zombies. He placed one of the stools from the island in the doorway so that it leaned against the frame. Now he felt a little safer exploring the kitchen.

Michael opened the cupboards one at a time, not bothering to close them before moving to the next. They contained the usual kitchen supplies, most following the apple motif. Unfortunately, there wasn't anything really of use unless he felt like braining a zombie with an apple shaped ceramic frying pan.

He grabbed his pack and dragged it over to the fridge. On the door were several photos of smiling children, each one held up with an apple magnet. Next to the pictures was a grocery list, a business card for car insurance, and an auto part supplier.

There was also a note written in impeccable cursive:

*Father, my fruit jams are now in the fruit cellar. I put a few in the pantry for later. You are not to lay one finger on them without my express permission. –Mother*

Michael smiled briefly, feeling tempted to find the fruit cellar. The smile faded as he realized the cellar would likely be windowless and pitch black. Not worth it. He sighed and opened the fridge instead and instantly gagged at the stench. He took one quick look and then closed it. Only mold and rot lay on the shelves.

He then dragged his pack over to the pantry and opened the door. It was a deep walk-in pantry, with thick wooden shelves filled with jars of fruits, vegetables, jerky, baking goods, and various jams and preserves. Enough to feed him for months!

Michael's smile returned as he reverently picked up a peach jam, a favorite from his childhood. He admired its golden color and was tempted to open it immediately. No, there would be time for that later. With a sudden inspiration, he slipped it into an apple oven mitt before adding it to his pack. Michael also added some deer jerky, a jar of green beans and peas, and some pickled carrots before regretfully turning away. He had to travel light and fast. It wouldn't do to overload on food if it slowed him down and got him killed. He didn't trust the area to be safe after the pyro technics during the night—or the night before, depending on how long he had been out.

He closed the pantry door, opened the full-size door next to it, and looked down into steps that faded quickly into a black maw. The basement, just as he had thought. He shut the door quickly and stuffed a chair under the knob. He studied the door and the propped chair. It seemed like a ridiculous and yet, at the same time, inadequate precaution. He considered moving the fridge against the door instead, but it was too massive and heavy to move in his weakened state. He took some assurance that at least the door was in full sunlight.

Michael left the kitchen for the dining room, carefully maneuvering around the chair he had propped up in the door. The room was long and narrow, with two large, heavily curtained windows along the outside wall. An antique buffet sat between the two sills. A stretched oak wood table centered the room, blazoned with a bright apple tablecloth liner. Michael opened the curtains and quickly searched the room, finding only a few wooden matches and some candles in the buffet. He added them to his pack and moved on to the family room.

He paused at the threshold and listened to the house momentarily before stepping into the room. The feminine persuasion ended abruptly here, juxtaposing with an ugly, drab avocado-green chair sitting in one corner. Its armrests were covered with various green patches where the fabric had worn out. In front of it sat a wooden monstrosity of an old television set. Opposite Michael was a staircase leading up to the second floor. It felt like he had stepped into an earlier decade, circa the sixties or seventies.

Hanging on the walls was an eclectic mixture of hunting trophies and religious symbolism. Below a moose head was a painting of Jesus. A black bear rug lay in front of the fireplace, and on the table next to it was a large print bible. There was an old electric organ with a yellowing book of hymnals against one wall. A gun cabinet was tucked away in a corner, it's glass door covered with a fine layer of dust.

Michael walked over to the cabinet and wiped the dust off

the glass with his coat sleeve. Inside, he could see six old but well-maintained rifles hanging on the racks. He tried the door to the case and found it locked. Michael felt along the top of the cabinet but didn't find any keys. Not seeing any other option, he smashed the glass with the machete's handle. The glass landed inside the case with a loud tinkling crash.

A loud "SHHHH" came from directly behind him.

Michael spun around, raising the machete to strike, only to find no one there. He scanned the room and even the stairway but didn't see anyone. He could have sworn the sound had come directly behind him. There was a faint smell of tobacco in the air.

He jumped as the TV clicked on with a pop, hissed with static for a moment, then switched back off. The hair on Michael's neck stood up, and goose bumps rose on his arms. The house was spook central! He carefully started walking towards the front door. Forget the food and the guns; they would be worthless if a geist ripped him apart.

"Hey!" A loud voice said behind Michael. Michael spun around again and again saw nothing. A slight movement by the recliner caught his eye, and he watched as it began to rock on its own. He took another step back towards the door and froze as an elderly man materialized in the chair. He was working at a tobacco pipe with his mouth, his pale blue eyes fixed directly on Michael.

Not a geist as Michael would have already been dead, but a ghost instead, though his relief was limited. A ghost could probably do damage as well.

The old ghost pulled the tobacco pipe from his mouth and jabbed the pipe stem towards Michael and then the gun case several times. He nodded as if granting permission, then faded away. The chair's rocking slowed to a stop. Michael was at a loss for what to do. Part of him wanted to immediately flee out the front door and never look back. Yet oddly, the place didn't feel wrong at all. It felt cozy, safe even. Was a poltergeist playing tricks on him, or had he actually found a benign, perhaps even benevolent spirit instead?

He watched the chair for a long moment and it didn't move again. The ghost or ghosts seemed to be gone, though the sweet smell of tobacco and apple pie remained in the air. Michael felt in his gut that the house was safe. Low on supplies and desperate, he decided to trust it and returned to the gun case.

He pulled out each of the six rifles, pausing to admire the beautiful artisanship of each custom gun. Scenes of lakes and various animals were carved into each rich wood stock with exquisite detail. One even had what appeared to be Native American designs cut into the barrel. The guns weren't only meant for show; each, while well kept, also showed subtle signs of use.

Michael argued with himself for a moment over which gun to take and finally decided to go with function over form. He chose a rifle that, while plain in comparison to the other rifles, was still beautiful with infinity signs scrolling up the barrel and several running wolves carved into each side of stock. More importantly, it had a scope and held more ammo than the others. He carefully put the other rifles back into the case, then picked up several cartons of ammo and put them in his backpack. He replaced his nearly worn-out gun cleaning kit with one he found in the bottom of the case. Finally, Michael rolled up one of the soft gun cases and tied it to the edge of his pack. With winter coming, it would be good to keep the rifle as dry as possible.

Michael slid the machete back into its sheathe and loaded the rifle. He now felt a little better about checking out the second floor. He debated for a long moment whether it was worth it to explore the upstairs. While he had food and a rifle now, obviously the most important things, his clothes were ruined with foul-smelling zombie ashes, and he was pretty rank himself. He needed a bath, or at the very least, a new change of clothes.

He looked at the ugly green chair and, after a moment's hesitation, inclined his head in quiet thanks. He couldn't help but think it would be ironic if the old man's ghost helped him downstairs, only to have his zombie attack him upstairs. He slowly crept up the stairs wincing at each creak or groan the wood made. He paused each time to see if anything reacted before continuing.

At the top of the stairs was a long hallway with several closed doors that ran the length of the house. It was only lit by small windows on either end, making it darker than the first floor. Despite this, the house still didn't feel wrong. Michael decided to go with his gut, though there was a small yet very vocal rational voice in the back of his head screaming for him to get out. He pressed on. Maybe he just wanted to believe something was still good in the world. Maybe he needed a short reprieve from the harsh reality of survival. Or, more likely, he was an idiot and was walking into a trap. Anyway, he was about to find out.

Michael turned right from the stairs and silently walked past the closed doors until he reached the window. He pulled on the blind's drawstring and it jumped from its holders, falling to the ground with a loud thud. Michael winced and waited, half expecting to hear some admonishment from the ghost or, worse, a zombie grunt. The house stayed quiet so he moved on. He stopped at the first door and placed his ear against it. He didn't hear any scraping or groaning noises, so the room was most likely zombie free. Still, he held the rifle ready just in case and opened the door.

It was a full bathroom, and the woman's touch was evident again. On top of a linen cabinet were folded washcloths and towels arraigned around a basket filled with scented soap shaped like roses. They were only for looking and not using, which he had always found to be a bit odd. If the male ghost was below, then where was the female spirit?

Opposite the sink was a large clawfoot tub covered with a tarp. He reached down to pull it aside, then stopped. Is this where he would find the farmer's body? He grabbed the tarp and flung it aside, relieved to see the tub filled to the brim with water. When things went south, the old farmer had probably filled it for a temporary water source. Michael ran his fingers through the clear liquid and watched the ripples reflect off the enameled sides. It felt cold to the touch and he cupped some in his hand, took a sip, and grimaced. It tasted like bath water, soapy and a bit metallic. It would probably give him the runs if he drank too much.

Michael absently swirled the water with his fingers again and decided that even though it was cold he probably could bear bathing in it. The first order of business, however, was to find new clothes to wear, as there was no point in bathing if he was going to put the same disgusting clothes back on. Maybe he'd find something in the farmer's closet, but he doubted it. The old man's ghost he'd seen sitting in the chair looked to be quite a bit smaller than Michael was.

Michael caught his reflection in a mirror and saw a gaunt, filthy stranger looking back. He appeared destitute with his wild beard and long, greasy, unkempt hair. No wonder Rachel had been scared of him. Hell, he frightened himself, to be honest. Michael could only bear to look himself in the eye for a half second before looking away. The pain there was too raw and he didn't need a reminder of it. He felt it every waking moment.

Michael left the bathroom and went to the door across the hall. After listening for zombies, he opened it and found the master bedroom. The blinds were open, illuminating most of the room. The room smelled faintly of cedar and mothballs. He half expected to see the elderly couple's bodies lying on the bed in some kind of suicide pack, but it was empty and the blankets and pillows were perfectly made up. Where were their bodies? Out in a field? In the basement?

He walked past the bed to the closet, opened it, and sighed. Just as he feared, the farmer's clothes were too small. To the right of the everyday clothes were several vestments and a white collar. So, the old man was a preacher as well. That may explain the friendly ghost and why the house felt safe.

He left the master suite and went to the next door down the hall. Michael again put his ear against it and, again hearing nothing, opened it up to find another bedroom. It was half the size of the master and only had a twin bed. He walked over to the blinds and opened them. Opening the closet, he couldn't help but smile in relief at what he saw.

Crammed from one end of the closet to the other were a variety of large men's clothes that looked to be about twenty years old and some camping gear that probably had belonged to a son or grandson. The clothes were mostly plaid and smelled strongly of mothballs, but that didn't matter. Michael pulled out a shirt and held it to his chest. It looked to be a good fit. If anything, it appeared to be a size too large. Perfect!

He picked out a pair of jeans that was also a couple of sizes too large. Nothing a belt couldn't fix. There were even several heavily insulated camouflaged winter coats made for hunting. He left them alone for now, grabbed some yellowed thermal underwear along with the jeans and shirt, and headed back to the bathroom.

Michael picked up the ornate garbage can next to the sink, pulled out the bag, and then walked over to the tub. He scooped out some water with the can and set it aside for rinse. He then dumped a half bottle of body soap into the frigid water and stirred it with a cupped hand and forearm. He left the decorative soaps where they were, not out of concern of offending ghosts, but because strong scents made him trackable.

He removed his clothes and made himself look in the mirror. His skin was covered in grime and was pale, almost translucent. His muscles hung loose on him, and he was gaunt to the point of looking emaciated. New and faded bruises covered his body with a muted, surreal tapestry.

Michael propped the rifle against the tub and then closed and locked the door just to be safe. He hiked one leg into the tub and gasped as the cold water hit him. He quickly swung the other over the rim and slowly lowered himself into the water, hissing through clenched teeth as some water splashed over the rim. He grimaced in pain as the muscles in his injured side locked up.

After a few minutes of painful shivering, he acclimated to the water, and his side relaxed enough that he was able to lay back. He agitated the water with his arms and legs until there was a thick layer of bubbles on the surface. Taking a deep breath, he plunged his head and torso under the water, splashing some over the edge, and began scrubbing his hair and beard as quickly as possible.

A long moment later, Michael sat back up, gasping for air and splashing more water over the edge. The water was now charcoal brown, and he couldn't see the tub's bottom. He scrubbed his hair and beard with more body soap, then pulled the plug. As the muddy water swirled down the drain, he began to shiver with cold again.

Once the water was gone, Michael stood up on trembling legs. Bracing himself, he picked up the garbage can filled with rinse water and promptly dumped it over his head, washing off the remaining soap. He quickly jumped out of the tub and wrapped a towel around his waist. The terry cloth felt warm and soft next to his skin. He grabbed another towel from the linen cabinet and began wringing out the water in his hair and beard.

The house felt warm and safe. He was tired of being on the run during the day and freezing at night. He was tired of starving. If he stayed for just a few days, he could rest and his injuries would heal faster. He could fill up on food. At the same time, Michael doubted he could sleep in a haunted house, even one with a friendly ghost. The still smoking silo would be a beacon for miles around. No, he couldn't chance it. "Need to leave," Michael whispered, letting out a long sigh.

After getting dressed and now smelling faintly of mothballs, Michael grabbed the rifle and returned to the guest bedroom. He slipped on a leather belt and then pulled a metal framed hunting backpack he found in the back of the closet. He quickly transferred the contents from his old pack to the new one, except for his dirty and worn clothes. Those he left on the bed, replacing them with clothing from the closet.

Michael selected a heavy down filled winter coat from the closet and shrugged it on. He put on a knitted winter hat and worn thin gloves then tied an old weatherproof sleeping bag in the new backpack. On the top shelf of the closet, he found a new half-filled oil lantern and hooked it to a carabiner on the pack. Michael adjusted the straps, slid the backpack onto his shoulders, and snapped it into place. He tied the machete to his new belt, picked up his rifle, and looked at his reflection in the mirror. He made a statement though it definitely wasn't fashion. He'd take function over form any day.

Michael headed back downstairs, keeping a close eye on the green chair as he passed, but it didn't move. He stepped into the dining room and froze. The stool that he had placed in the kitchen doorway was missing. He was not alone!

# CHAPTER EIGHT

**M**ichael pulled the rifle from his shoulder and crept through the narrow dining room towards the kitchen. He heard a faint humming and a shuffling sound. A few seconds later, the smell of freshly baked apple pies came wafting from the kitchen. Maybe it was the old ghost's spectral wife or another survivor. Perhaps it was something far worse and he was walking into a trap. Suddenly, the humming cut off as he reached the kitchen doorway. Michael's jaw dropped at what he saw.

The mess he had left behind had been cleaned up. All of the cupboard doors he had opened were closed, and the empty jars had been put in the sink. Even the glass from the broken door was gone. Stacked on the island were more jars of food. The smell of freshly baked apple pie and cinnamon lingered in the air.

"Okay, that is just... spooky," Michael said to the empty room, feeling foolish as he said it. "Sorry, I don't mean any disrespect lady, err ma'am... I just wasn't expecting... I appreciate it and I'm sorry for the mess." Feeling foolish, he shook his head in disbelief. Here he was apologizing to a ghost, worrying about hurting her feelings. And yet, somehow, it felt appropriate.

The apple pie scent grew stronger for a moment and then faded. Michael quickly stuffed the proffered food into his pack and swung it on his shoulders. He looked over at the splintered back door and a sense of sadness came over him as he realized that the elements would now be free to come inside the house. Maybe they could also fix the door since the wife's ghost had cleaned up all of the broken glass and set the kitchen right. Maybe.

A sharp crack off to the side made him jump. He looked up and saw that the apple cookie jar on the shelf above the stove had split in half. The two halves fell away, revealing another jar of golden peach jam. Michael forgot his worries for a moment, a grin cracking his worn face. He reached up and reverently brought the peach jam down. He had it sitting in an oven mitt next to its twin in the pack in no time. Michael inclined his head towards the center of the kitchen and said, "Thank you ma'am, for your kindness."

Michael was filled with a sense of wonder as he left the farmhouse. This was the first time since the world ended that he had found a house haunted by good spirits instead of bad. *Maybe things are getting better,* he thought momentarily before his pessimism kicked in. No, he thought shaking his head. This was a one off, and he would not let his guard down again.

A narrow footpath led away from the house and followed a rolling hill down into the woods. A brief cold breeze hit Michael as he considered the trail. He looked at the sun, surprised to find it setting behind the mountains. Time had gotten away from him again. He was not looking forward to another freezing night outside.

He looked back at the Barn. Maybe one more night in the loft wouldn't hurt. The house was a little too crowded for his tastes. He looked back at the trail and wavered for a moment before deciding to move on. He shifted the heavy pack on his shoulders and took a final look at the barn. Michael sighed and began to follow the trail down the hill. It was best that he kept moving. If he lingered, death would be that much quicker in finding him.

The light began to wane as the sun set behind the mountains. Michael shivered as a cold wind wrapped around him, enticing his body heat away. He felt his legs begin to weaken and his side tighten up but forced himself to keep walking. By the time he reached the bottom of the hill a quarter hour later, he was questioning his gut feeling to leave the farm. It had been wrong about Rachel. Maybe it was wrong about this too. He pressed on, not wanting to consider the alternative.

When Michael came to a stop below a big oak tree sometime later, his legs were shaking so badly that he fell against the tree. He slid down to a sitting position, holding his side with his hand. He tried to breathe past the pain but only managed short, agonizing gasps.

He was in no shape to spend another night in the woods but there was no way he could make it back up the hill to the farm. The only choice was to continue and hope that he came across shelter soon before he died from exposure. After a few minutes, his breathing became easier as his side calmed down. He needed to keep going. Grunting against the weight of his pack, he somehow managed to get to his feet.

Michael continued down the trail, holding onto the slim hope that his gut wasn't wrong and that it would lead him to shelter. His progress was slow and frustrating, as he had to rest often. The woods darkened as the sun slipped behind the mountains, filling him with cold dread. He pushed on, fearing the worst. Other paths began to intersect with Michael's, combining into a larger trail. If he were lucky, it would lead him to some kind of shelter. If he weren't then it would lead to something useless like a popular swimming hole. As he came around a bend in the trail, he sighed in relief at seeing a steeple outlined against the dark sky. The feeling had been real. He had found the old man's church.

It was a modest sized building with white tongue and groove siding and a red brick foundation and tall windows with what looked to be stained glass covering the facade. The church was surrounded by open fields while the front had a long winding driveway. He could not make out the denomination but that didn't matter as long as it was safe.

Michael made a slow approach, rifle at the ready, constantly shifting his eyes between the church and the surrounding fields. When he got within a few feet of the building, he watched the windows for any sign of movement. Nothing moved in the blackness.

Michael walked up the stairs and found the front doors unlocked. He opened one a crack and looked inside. It was too dark to make out any detail so he untied the oil lantern from his pack and lit it. He knew he was taking a considerable risk of the light being seen from the road but there was no way he was going to explore the building in the dark. Holding the lantern aloft in his left hand, he pushed the door open with the rifle and peered into the structure.

There was a small foyer area with bathrooms on both

sides and a place to hang coats. Through another set of open doors was the main room, the weak lantern light only hinting at what it contained. Michael stepped into the foyer and stopped as a familiar feeling came over him. The building felt clean and safe, just like the farm! Feelings aside, he was going to search the building to make sure. The only reason he had survived this long was that he didn't trust anything.

Michael cleared the bathrooms and then moved onto the nave. He approached the threshold and raised the lantern above his head so that light would shine to the back of the large room. A center aisle split at least a dozen rows of pews. Past the pews was a low wall with a raised pulpit mounted behind it. Beyond the pulpit lay a staired choir section. Stained glass windows lined each side of the room, their colors muted and liquid in the dim lantern light.

Michael made his way down the center aisle, checking each row of pews as he passed them. Nothing but hymnals and the occasional bible. The area behind the low wall and pulpit was clear as well. There was a stairway on either side of the choral section, one leading to a locked outside door and the other led down to what Michael guessed was the basement. That could wait until sun up so he locked the door and went back up the stairs.

Satisfied the building was relatively safe, Michael decided it would be best to camp out behind the pulpit. The stained-glass windows or the back door would offer a quick escape if necessary. He pushed past his exhaustion and walked around the building, ensuring all doors were locked. Michael unrolled his sleeping bag between the first and second rows of choir seats. The bag was very similar to one from his childhood, down filled with an army green shell lined with a red interior depicting deer at play.

Michael looked out at the empty pews, wondering if any of the church members had survived. The pews didn't offer any answers, so he put the lantern out and snuggled down into the warm sleeping bag. He left the side unzipped so he could easily access the rifle laying along his side. He lay back and was out as soon as his head hit his hard backpack.

He woke once during the night in a silver moonlight drenched room. Michael sat up, panicking for a moment before remembering where he was. What had awakened him? He remembered dreaming about some place that seemed familiar and yet somehow wasn't, with people singing hymnals. The odd thing was he could have sworn he had still heard the singing when he woke up, though it had faded quickly.

He listened for a while, but the singing never came back. Maybe the church was haunted by good spirits like the farm, or it all could have been simply a dream. He settled back down in the sleeping bag, checked again to make sure the rifle was still at his side, then fell into a dreamless sleep.

It wasn't until midafternoon the next day that Michael woke, his mouth dry and stomach grumbling loudly. His side was still sore but felt much better than the night before. He sat up and peeked over the row of chairs before him. The nave was awash in vibrant colors as the sun glowed brightly through the painted glass.

Satisfied he was alone, Michael laid back down and considered his situation. He had come very close to dying last night as he had made his way to the church. Maybe the mountains wouldn't be a haven after all. If September was this bad, he could only imagine what it would be like when winter arrived. As much as he hated to admit it, he needed to head south, out of the mountains. What was the point of avoiding the monsters if the weather killed him instead?

Michael's stomach began to rumble, complaining loudly about the past several meals he had missed. He slid the pack closer and pulled out a jar of peach jam. Admiring its golden color, he unscrewed the metal band and popped the lid with his pocket knife. A delicious aroma of peaches engulfed his nose, and Michael took a moment to savor the scent. He carefully scooped up a little of the jam with a spoon, careful not to drip one precious bit.

He lost his self-control as the first drop of the jam hit his taste buds, quickly jamming the whole spoon in his mouth. Amazing! Michael quickly scooped another large bite and slurped it off the spoon. He could only imagine what it would taste like on a thick slab of homemade bread slathered in butter. He wouldn't be surprised at all if the old woman had won awards for it.

Michael took several more bites, savoring each one before making himself stop. The jam was too good to eat up in one sitting. Instead, he would ration it out, one bite at each meal. The two jars should last him a few weeks if he were careful.

He screwed the lid on the jar and placed it carefully back into its protective oven mitt. He then pulled out a can of mushroom soup, popped the pull-top lid, took a bite, and grimaced. The soup tasted gross after the jam but he made himself finish it. It was tempting to chase the soup with another scoop of the jam, but he somehow resisted.

Several indolent days passed as Michael remained at the

church. The idea of leaving felt wrong and he wasn't about to argue with it. Six months of relentless fear and constantly being on the move had worn him thin. Sleeping with a roof over his head was a rare luxury.

One morning, it started raining, and the storm continued for several days. Michael spent the time convalescing and catching up on sleep. He cleaned the guns with the new kit, reorganized his new pack, and played solitaire with a deck of cards he had found in a closet.

He even braved the basement once and found a large room with several rows of wooden tables surrounded by metal chairs. No doubt the congregation came down after service to eat cake, drink coffee, and fellowship together. A large commercial sized coffee pot sat on a small card table at the end of the room. There was a small kitchen in the back, though it had little to offer except a few cans of coffee and expired condiments. He found several plastic bowls of various sizes in a cupboard and plastic utensils in a drawer.

Michael brought the coffee and the bowls upstairs and set the bowls outside to collect rainwater. Tonight, he would start a fire and have hot coffee to go with his hot soup and another spoonful of peach jam for dessert. A small bit of heaven in a world filled with hell.

He walked over to one of the stained-glass windows and looked out. Though the clouds were multihued from the glass, he could see the sky lightening up a little. The rain would most likely end tonight, if not in the morning. A familiar feeling came over him then and Michael sighed. It was time to move on. He would stay the night and-. His head whipped towards the double doors a moment before they flew open with a crash.

Michael ducked behind the choir seats as two large men entered the doorway. They were dressed like bikers, and each carried a rifle over their shoulders. A pregnant Latino woman in her early to mid-twenties followed on a leash unsteadily behind them, arms tied behind her back. Three more bikers followed her, laughing as she fell to the ground.

# CHAPTER NINE

"Okay boys, it's time to party. Is the guest of honor nice and comfy?" A short man with spiky peroxide blonde hair asked, laughing. It was an ugly laugh, heavy with the ghosts of unfiltered cigarettes and hard liquor. The tallest biker, muscle gone to fat with an impressive beer gut, kicked the pregnant girl and laughed as she cried out in pain. "Looks like she is, Blondie." The man named Blondie laughed again and then called out. "Jericho, where you at?"

Michael heard a gun cock next to his head and froze. "Come see, boss." A voice said behind him. A pistol was shoved hard into Michael's jaw, forcing him to stand up. "Good thing I decided to check out the back 'cause we have an audience, and I'm pretty sure he didn't pay for the show!" As soon as Michael was on his feet, Jericho pistol-whipped him to the floor.

"We'll have to make sure he pays up then," Blondie laughed. "Grab him."

Michael spat out blood and glared up at Jericho as the biker held the pistol on him. He was small and wiry, but still taller than Blondie.

"Upset I snuck up on you, big baw?" Jericho asked with

a smirk. There was an odd singsong cadence to his speech that sounded Cajun. "Don't be, sweetheart. I was in special forces before the world hit the fan. Granted me special powers. Hell, once I even snuck up on a fawn in the woods. The little guy didn't even know I was there until I slit his throat." Jericho kicked Michael hard in his uninjured side and whispered, "You're not going that easy."

The Cajun nodded, and two bikers roughly picked up Michael by the elbows and threw him into a choir seat. "You might as well enjoy the show before we get our pound of flesh out of yah," Jericho said, and the others laughed. He casually leaned toward Michael's face and said. "What I mean, just so we're clear, is that after this fais do-do—that's a show and dance for your unlearned ears—we're going to kill you." Jericho looked over at the pregnant girl and grinned. "Woohoo, isn't she a beaut. A little too ripe for my taste, but I'm sure there is some sweetness left in her." The girl snarled at him and Jericho chortled. "Fierce little thing, aren't you, che?" He smacked the top of the pulpit with his palm. "I think I'm in love!"

The girl met Michael's eyes at that moment, and Michael saw anger and defiance in her eyes before she dismissed him. No, she was not the type that would go quietly. Not that would do them much good, as outmatched as they were. They needed a miracle. He looked around the church frantically, trying to think of a way out of the situation. He took a deep breath and let it out slowly to clear his mind. There had to be something he could do.

Jericho turned while laughing and, in one quick motion, cracked Michael across the face with the pistol. "Don't like that expression on your face, big guy." He said with a smile that didn't reach his eyes.

Michael spat blood on the floor and glared at the little man.

Jericho's smile broadened, but his eyes became wary. "You gonna make a move? Well, take your shot then, crouyon. I welcome the entertainment." He drew in close to Michael's face again and said. "You're dead anyway." The man's breath smelled rotten, and his eyes were an unholy shade of bloodshot, almost like a zombie.

"But first, some play, boys," Blondie smirked as he removed his belt slowly, an evil light shining in his eyes. The bikers began to whoop and yell as their leader approached the girl. The girl screamed in fear and tried to back away from him. Michael looked at her sharply. The girl's reaction was not congruent with the defiant look he had just seen in her eyes.

Jericho kept his eyes and weapon on Michael, a knowing look in his eyes. Cocking the pistol, he yelled, "Get you some boss! Laissez les bon temps rouler!"

Blondie grabbed the girl by the hair, forcing her to look at him. "Now you be a nice little foxy, and it will go good for everyone." The girl closed her eyes tightly and nodded.

Blondie laughed and looked up to see his men's reaction, and that's when the girl struck. Her head shot forward like a viper, and she clamped her mouth down hard on Blondie's groin. He made an impossibly high squealing noise, his face turning white with pain.

"What the...?" Jericho asked. He looked away from Michael and then quickly turned back, realizing his mistake too late.

Michael jumped up from the chair and swatted the pistol into Jericho's leg. The angle forced the man's finger against the trigger, and the gun went off into the man's thigh. At the same time, Michael punched the biker in the throat with his other hand, causing Jericho to choke on the agonized scream from being shot.

Sensing movement in his peripheral, Michael spun the dazed man before him as the biker with the large beer gut fired his shotgun. Jericho took the brunt of the blast to his chest and slumped in Michael's arms. Michael let go of the body and dove behind the pulpit as another biker let loose with his shotgun, shredding the top of it to bits.

Across the room, Blondie had stopped squealing, though the girl still had his bits firmly in her mouth. "Do... something," he gasped in a hoarse whisper to the two men next to him, but all they could do was stare at the girl in horror. Desperate, Blondie tried to shove the girl's head away and shrieked in agony as the pain intensified. He then passed out with a low, anguished groan and fell forward over the girl, his jaw bouncing off the floor with a crunch.

The girl finally let go and crawled out from under Blondie. She spat blood out of her mouth and spun around on her knees to face the two bikers as they walked cautiously towards her, rifles aimed at her head. The girl flashed her bloody teeth and snarled, ready to fight to the death.

Michael, peeking over the low wall with Jericho's gun in his hand, saw the two men approaching the girl. At the same time, Beer Gut roared and charged towards him, apparently out of ammo. Hoping to give the girl a chance to get out of this, Michael quickly stood and fired at the two men until the pistol clicked empty. Both bikers collapsed under the hail of bullets, one falling on the girl like a landslide.

Michael turned to catch the big man barreling down on him but was a split second too late. Beer Gut slammed into him, and together they smashed the pulpit into kindling. Michael's almost healed ribs screamed in agony again, the impact causing his back muscles to writhe uncontrollably. Beer Gut threw an arm around Michael's throat and yanked back, causing the pain to crescendo to an almost ecstatic level.

Bright sparks and black motes floated like flies in Michael's vision, and the room dimmed. The pain fell to the background, and he felt himself begin to drift into unconsciousness. Michael looked out into the pews and saw shadow people sitting there, the congregation still and solemn as if they couldn't see the battle around them. They were all looking at him.

The black motes began to coalesce into a dark spot above Jericho's body. Michael watched as it took on a form similar to the one he had encountered in the hardware store. The thing turned to face him and the biker, opening its mouth to show an incredible display of teeth. Fear giving him new strength, Michael grabbed the arm around his neck with both of his and forced it away. He jabbed back with an elbow, catching the big man in the throat, then dove away.

The black monster slammed into Beer Gut, and they went down in a bloody spray behind the now empty choir seats. It turned, growling like a large cat, and began to stalk towards Michael. He backed away slowly, in sync with the creature's steps. Beer Gut's shotgun and Jericho's pistol were used up. His only chance was to try to make it to his rifle in the choir section, but there was little doubt in his mind that the cat thing would reach him first.

The last biker saw the monster and screamed, then made

a break down the center aisle towards the foyer. The cat thing hissed as it jumped over the wall, then vanished under the pews. The biker only managed a few steps before it jumped up and hurled into him with shocking speed. They disappeared between two pews, leaving a bloody mist in the air. *Greedy monster*, Michael thought. It obviously didn't want any of them to escape alive.

The pregnant girl finally pushed the dead biker off her and climbed unsteadily to her feet. She took a step towards the open doors, and Michael yelled, "Don't move!" She froze, turning to look at him with huge, panic filled eyes. "Stay there," Michael mouthed to her, and the girl nodded.

A chittering sound came from somewhere in the pews between the girl and Michael. Keeping an eye on the pews, he began to back away towards the choir seats, hoping to get to his rifle. Suddenly, the chittering sound came from that direction as well. Were there two of these things, or was the thing that fast? Cursing silently, Michael began to back away, his mind racing on what to do next. He was running out of options.

Across the room, Blondie stood up with a pain-filled roar. Seeing the girl only a few feet from him, he began to limp slowly to her, sobbing in agony and rage. The girl took another step towards the door.

"Stop moving!" Michael yelled, and she froze again, clenching her small hands into tight fists. Blondie closed in on her, gibberish and bloody drool pouring from his ruined mouth. The girl's eyes seemed to be going into the back of her head in an attempt to see the man approaching her.

The chittering suddenly stopped behind Michael, and he figured that the creature was on the hunt again. With all the noise coming from across the room, he had a good guess on who it was hunting. Taking a desperate gamble, he jumped over the choir seats, grabbed his rifle as he rolled, and came up ready to fire. Only his pack greeted him, and he exhaled loudly with relief.

Switching the safety off, Michael looked over the seats to see a slavering Blondie reaching for the girl's shoulder. As Michael took aim at the peroxide biker, a furious black ball of claws and teeth crashed into the biker, knocking him down in another spray of blood.

"Run!" Michael yelled.

The girl tore towards the foyer, cradling her pregnant belly with both hands. The black form leaped at her from where it had taken Blondie down. Michael, anticipating the attack, fired and knocked it off course. The cat thing rebounded off the wall with a roar and scrambled under a pew, hissing and spitting.

The girl ran through the doors without looking back. Michael didn't blame her. Hunkering down, he reached for his pack, and a chittering sound came from the basement stairway. Another cat thing crawled up from the stairs, its red eyes staring at him with dreadful malevolent intent. Michael slowly backed away from the pack, rifle at the ready. He doubted he could kill the thing but maybe slow it down enough to escape.

Then he noticed in his peripheral another black form crawling on top of the pews towards him. Michael changed his direction slightly to encompass both creatures, hoping still to make it to the stained-glass window. Suddenly, another form appeared from under the pews in that direction and began stalking him. Michael knew then that he was a dead man.

The pregnant girl ran back through the doors, her arms

now untied, a burning Molotov in her hand. "Run!" she screamed, throwing the flaming bottle towards the center of the room. She was back outside before it landed.

The Molotov shattered on the floor with the tinkling of breaking glass, followed by a loud *whoompf* as the alcohol caught fire. The three creatures jumped away from it, screaming in fear. Michael reacted too, throwing himself through the nearest stained-glass window and falling to the ground below in a shower of colored glass.

He landed hard, the impact knocking the rifle from his hands. The girl was at his side in an instant, scooping it up before he could grab it. "Come on!" she said, tugging at his arm, "There isn't enough sunlight."

One of the windows shattered as a black form hurled through it at the girl. She screamed and braced for impact, but the creature exploded in a shower of bright red sparks before it hit her. Michael and the girl stumbled back, watching as the sparks flashed bright and then burned away to grey ash. Its shape hung in the air for a moment before being carried off by the wind. Growling and hissing came from the two remaining creatures in the church.

"What... why did that just happen?" The girl asked, looking up at the darkening sky. "It isn't sunny enough."

"I don't know," Michael replied. Nothing made sense anymore. The flames grew higher as they consumed the church. A series of loud popping noises started as the ammunition inside his pack went off. A bullet tore out of the wall near the roof. The creatures roared from within. "We better get away from here," Michael said, ducking. He turned to find the girl already halfway down the driveway, walking briskly with his rifle slung over her shoulder.

# CHAPTER TEN

"Hey, hold on!" Michael yelled, running down the driveway after the girl. "Wait!"

She ignored him, continuing her furious pace towards the dirt road. "I want my rifle back." He demanded when he caught up to her.

"Nope. Sorry. Need it." The girl said, her head down and a determined look on her face. She was surprisingly fast despite her large pregnant belly.

"Why?"

"My brother Roman. They have the idiot."

"Who does?"

She stopped so suddenly that he almost bowled her over. "Does it matter? I need to save him."

"I think I'm owed a few answers after saving your hide back there," Michael growled, his temper flaring.

"Well, I saved yours, so we are even on that." She replied in short, clipped words.

"That doesn't entitle you to take my rifle."

"My brother's life is in danger, and that *entitles* me to the rifle. He could be dying right now, and here you are, asking me stupid questions." She started off again, doubling her pace.

Michael stared after her, lost for words.

"If you want your rifle back, you better keep up," The girl called over her shoulder.

Michael muttered a curse and ran until he caught up to her again. "Can you at least tell me what we are walking into?"

"The bikers have a camp down the road." She replied, breathing hard. "They were building a fire when they took me away. I was to be the dinner entertainment, my brother the main course."

"Cannibals." Michael spat, suddenly remembering that Jericho had said something about taking a pound of flesh out of him. The practice horrified and disgusted him. There was no need for it if you were clever enough. There were plenty of food supplies in houses and buildings to last decades. Cannibals did it out of cowardice, laziness, and worse-- enjoyment. They were similar to cats; they liked to play with their food first, deriving some sick pleasure from someone's misery and pain. Could he leave anyone to that fate? His gut told him no, so his decision was made for him.

"Are you any good with a gun?" Michael asked, already sure of the answer.

The girl shrugged as if it didn't matter. "I'm good enough."

"Had any training?"

"No. Why?" She asked, looking at him from the corner of her eye as she kept up the brisk pace.

"I have."

She stopped again, breathing heavily. "Where are you going with this?"

"Simple. If you want to save your brother, give me the gun."

The girl snorted and said, "How do I know you won't just shoot me or walk away?"

"You don't, and you don't have any choice if you want your brother back alive."

She glared at him, apparently indecisive and not happy about it.

"Well?"

"As you said, I don't have a choice." The girl snarled. She whipped the gun off her shoulder and tossed it to him hard. Michael was forced to catch it with both hands to keep it from smashing him in the face. The girl watched him nervously as he checked it out of habit and looked relieved when he motioned her to lead on. She started up again in the same direction without a word.

"How many are there," Michael asked as he followed behind.

She looked back at him and said. "Six at the camp with a lot more expected tonight."

There were fourteen rounds left in the clip, plus a handful loose in his coat pocket. Michael wished he had been able to grab his pack back at the church. There had been over a hundred rounds in it. Still, if they were lucky, the twenty or so rounds he had left should be enough to take care of the six bikers before their main force showed up. "When are the others due?"

The girl looked at the setting sun and said, "Nightfall."

Anytime then. "How are the ones at the camp armed?"

She was silent for a few seconds and then said, "Several have guns and the others... I'm not sure. It was dark when they ambushed us last night. They kept us blindfolded." She stopped, staring at the road ahead. "We're getting close, so we need to be quiet."

Together, they cautiously walked down the dark road, and after a few minutes, they could make out faint sounds from the camp. As they got closer, the dissonant sounds resolved into rowdy cries and drunken singing. A flicker of light appeared in the distance and the girl froze at the sight. A gust of wind hit them, bringing with it the smell of wood smoke. "Oh no!" The girl gasped, panic giving her voice an odd reverb. She turned to Michael. "They already started the fire!"

Michael felt himself grow calmer as his sniper training kicked in. In the dying light, he could make out a steep hill to their left, overlooking the camp. That was where he would go. Pointing out the hill to the girl, he said, "I'm heading up there. You stay here, slow count to thirty, and then scream as loud as you can."

"That's your plan? We don't have the time. He could be burning already!" The girl whispered harshly, tugging at his arm. He needed to calm her down before that panic pushed her into an early labor.

"What's your name?"

She looked at him in confusion. "What? Oh... Lucia. It doesn't--"

"Lucia, we're going to get your brother back, but I need you to calm down first."

"No! I've gotta..." She took a step towards the camp, and he grabbed her by the arm and spun around so that she was looking at him. She flinched and tried to free her arm, but Michael held on tight.

"Calm...down!" He told her in a harsh whisper. "If you don't, then your brother will die, you will die, and so will your baby. Do you want that?" Lucia stopped struggling and shook her head without looking at him.

Michael let go of her arm and said, "We're going to save him, but only if we keep...calm."

"Promise?" Lucia asked, sounding very young.

"I promise." He would say whatever he had to now and pay the piper later if he had to. His gut had only told him to try to save the girl's brother. Nothing about it had suggested that Michael would be able to. "Are you calm now?"

Lucia shook her head for a second, then paused and nodded yes. Michael read that as no, she wasn't calm, but yes, she would do what he had said. "What's your name?" She asked.

"Michael. Now slow count to thirty and then scream bloody murder." He waited for her to nod again and then made his way up the hill as quickly as he could, hoping the racket from the camp would mask any sounds he made. He fast counted to thirty silently in his head as he climbed, figuring the panicking girl would do the same.

Michael reached the top of the hill, breathing hard from exertion, his side nearly twisted in agony. He still hadn't recovered from the fight in the church. Ten counts. Choosing a large pine for cover, he dropped to his knees next to the trunk and took a slow, deep breath to control his breathing. He let it out slowly, brought the rifle up, and looked through the scope at the camp below.

It was getting dark, but there was still enough light to make out detail. He could see several tents in a semi-circle beneath the tree canopies. A young man in his late teens or early twenties was tied to a spit over a small pile of wood in the middle of the camp. Twenty counts.

A bald, chubby biker was on his knees next to the pile, blowing on a spot that smoke was pouring out of, the coals illuminating his harsh face briefly with each puff. He must be having trouble getting the wet wood lit. Two other bikers critiqued his fire-starting skills with chortles and crass insults.

Michael was appalled to see that one of them was female. He lowered his rifle for a moment. Steph and Rachel flashed through his mind before he could stop them. Forcing his mind clear, Michael raised his rifle again and made himself aim at the female biker first. She was a cannibal, he reminded himself, a monster. She had decided to go down this evil path, and Michael would do what he had to do. The girl grinned in the dying light, flashing sharpened teeth. Thirty counts. Any time now.

Seconds passed and Lucia remained quiet. The girl must have been calmer and counted slower than Michael had thought possible. One of the bikers picked up a bottle of whiskey, hefted it in his hand for a second, and then whipped it into the woodpile. Flames shot up and the biker that had been blowing on the coals fell back with a yelp. The two onlookers roared with laughter. Roman started to struggle and the female biker kicked him hard in the side.

A second later Lucia started screaming. The bikers went silent and turned towards the sound with their mouths agape. The whiskey thrower fumbled with his shotgun for a moment, then pushed the woman towards one of the tents. Michael followed her with the rifle and just as he was about to pull the trigger, the sound of Lucia's screams began to move.

Surprised, Michael hesitated for a split second and the female biker disappeared into the tent. Cursing, he swung the rifle's scope toward the direction of the screams and saw Lucia's dark form running towards the camp. "Stupid, stubborn...."

As Lucia passed a tree, a huge hairy brute of a man stepped out from the shadows, wielding a fire axe. He swung hard at Lucia's pregnant belly as if trying to hit a baseball. Michael sighted and fired in one motion. The hairy biker spun to the ground in front of the girl. Lucia's screaming cut off in a yelp as the axe just missed her. She looked at the dead biker for a split second before she started running towards the camp again, screaming even louder.

Stupid girl was going to get us both killed, Michael thought and then forced himself to calm down. He led Lucia with his scope, trying to see any dangers that lay ahead of her. Two bikers ran out of the dark brush, one carrying a rifle, the other packing a shotgun. Michael fired twice and they crumpled. Lucia tripped over one in the dark, her scream cut off abruptly as she scrambled to keep her feet for a moment, then continued running quietly for the camp.

Three down, three to go. Michael swung the scope back to the fire and spotted two of the remaining bikers crouching behind Roman. The fat bald one and the tall skinny one that had thrown the whiskey. The flames were higher now, and the boy struggled desperately against the bindings. He would die soon if they didn't free him.

The fat biker's bald head swung back and forth between the hill and Lucia's direction, terror apparent on his ugly face. The skinny one was glassing Michael's direction with binoculars, though the firelight had to be messing with his night vision. Still looking through the binoculars, he tapped the fat biker's shoulder with his shotty and then pointed up the hill with it. The other biker turned his attention to the hill and began scanning it with the scope of his rifle. Michael knew that if he fired another shot, they would have a fix on his position.

Lucia started screaming again as she hit the edge of the camp. The two bikers spun around and started firing wildly in her direction. Lucia's scream cut off as she fell hard behind an old tree stump, curling up to make herself as small a target as possible. The bikers stood up to get a better angle, giving Michael a clear shot. He took aim and fired. A red plume sprayed from the side of the fat biker's head. The other biker dove to the ground as Michael shot at him. Michael cursed. He wasn't sure if it was a hit, so he fired three more shots where the man had fallen, hoping to finish him off. Seeing a break in enemy movement, he quickly reloaded the rifle.

Lucia crawled to her feet and ran towards her brother again, limping hard on her right leg. It was hard to tell whether the girl had been shot or if she had injured her leg when she fell. Lucia slammed hard into the branch tripod near her brother's feet, and it snapped apart. The spit fell to the side, lowering Roman's feet away from the fire and his middle almost directly into the flames.

Roman tried to lift his body above the fire, screams muffled by a dirty rag stuffed in his mouth. Lucia grabbed the spit near her brother's head, wrenching it back and forth, trying to break it free from the tripod. The branches were thicker and she couldn't budge them. Frantic, Lucia looked at the hill and screamed, "Help me!"

At that moment, Michael spotted the female biker coming up behind Lucia, running fast and low to the ground with a machete in her hand. Having no time to think, Michael let his instincts take over. *Crack!* The bullet shattered the tripod, and it broke apart as Lucia pushed on the spit. Roman fell into the fire and rolled away, screaming as his clothes ignited. Lucia chased after him, trying to beat out the flames with her bare hands.

The skinny biker popped up from his hiding spot and fired at Michael with his rifle. The ground kicked up in front of Michael, but he ignored it. *Crack!* He winged the female biker just as she reached Lucia. She fell to the ground with a squawk but continued to crawl towards the siblings with the machete in her good hand, the other arm dragging limply on the ground behind her.

Lucia tugged vainly on her brother's feet, trying to pull him away from the biker, but the boy was too heavy. *Crack!* Michael took out the skinny biker as the man popped up and fired at him again, shooting him in the head to make sure this time. *Crack!* Michael finished the female biker just as she hauled herself up and was about to split Roman's skull. Though it seemed like thirty seconds had passed between the first and last shot, Michael knew they were nearly on top of each other in the space of about ten seconds.

Michael wiped the sweat from his brow and scanned the camp for more targets. When none presented, he quickly descended the hill to the two siblings, holding his rifle ready just in case. Sound traveled fast and far at night, and there was no doubt that the other bikers had heard the shots as well as anything else in the area. They needed to leave as soon as possible.

The boy was struggling against his bonds and yelling something unintelligible through the dirty rag stuffed in his mouth. Lucia was fighting against her brother's movements, trying to cut the rope with the rusty machete the female biker had dropped. Exasperated, she grabbed his hair and jerked his head back. "Roman! Stop moving!"

Roman went still, glaring at his sister as she cut his bonds. When his hands were free, he shoved Lucia back and ripped the rag from his mouth. He went into an epileptic fit of spitting and wiping his tongue with both hands, then turned to his sister accusingly. "I was yelling to remove the rag first!"

"I left it last for a reason." Lucia said, grunting as she slowly climbed to her feet, one hand holding her belly.

"Ha ha, very funny," Roman said, then gestured to his bound feet. "Well?"

Lucia made a disgusted noise and threw the machete near her brother's feet, the blade quivering in the ground. "Cut them free yourself." She said, turning away. Roman snorted and started sawing on the rope. Looking off into the night, Lucia wiped her eyes and said quietly, "I should have left you to burn."

Roman chuckled as he cut his feet free. "Ah, but you didn't, sis. Means you still love me."

Lucia spun around and backhanded her brother hard across the face. "It's not funny, Roman!" she yelled as he stared up at her in shock. "You're stupid, obstinate arrogance nearly got us all killed." She cradled her belly and said softly, "No more. I won't let you get my baby killed like you did…"

Roman shook his head in frustration, and that's when he saw Michael. He quickly jumped to his feet, shoving his sister behind him. "Come any closer, and I'll gut you," he threatened, brandishing the rusty machete.

Lucia pushed his arm down and stepped between them. "Stop! That's Michael. He was the one doing the shooting. He just saved your ass."

Roman spat on the ground. "More like dropped my ass in the fire." He sneered at Michael and added, "Don't expect thanks." He took in Michael's dated hunting outfit. "Where did you find Jeremiah Johnson here?"

"I wasn't," Michael said and turned to Lucia, his decision made. Feeling or not, he just wanted to be rid of them. "You've got your brother. I've got my rifle. I'm going."

Panic shot across Lucia's features. She looked out at the dark woods beyond the camp and said, "Wait, it's night now, and the rest of the bikers are coming. At least stay with us until we're safe."

"No," Michael said, turning to leave.

Lucia grabbed his arm and said, "Please."

He pulled his arm free. "I said no."

"Let him go, sis. We don't need him." Roman said. He lifted his charred shirt to look at his side and whistled softly. "That's going to leave a scar."

"Why?" Lucia asked, rubbing her belly. She sounded very young again, and Michael wondered if she was doing it on purpose. She was wasting her time if she thought she could manipulate him.

"You don't listen, and your brother is an idiot."

Lucia nodded as tears filled her eyes. She absently started rubbing her swollen belly again, looking lost and frightened. Michael forced himself to look away. Leaving was the right thing, the smart thing to do, he reminded himself. *If so, then why do I feel so horrible about it?*

Roman's eyes narrowed, and his knuckles went white on the machete. "What did you call me, son?" He asked in a quiet voice.

Michael ignored the posturing and tried to assuage his conscience by giving the girl some advice. "Get out of the area as fast as you can. The rest of the bikers will be here soon. Stay off the road and keep moving, and you might make your way free of them." Michael turned without waiting for a reply and started walking away as fast as he could.

"Hey, I'm talking to you!" Roman yelled after him, his voice breaking with anger.

Michael kept walking, wanting to escape before the guilt changed his mind. This was *precisely* why he had chosen a solitary life. People always complicate things, and he was done with them.

"Keeping walking hero," Roman called after him.

"Go get your idiot self killed," Michael replied.

The only warning he got was the sound of feet running through the damp grass. He continued to walk until he heard Roman grunt as he swung his machete. Spinning to the side, Michael grabbed the boy's arm as it swung past him and pulled hard, using Roman's momentum against him. Off balance, Roman fell forward and Michael yanked back hard on his wrist, forcing him to drop the machete.

Roman cried out in pain and fell to the ground. Michael dropped down on top of him, grabbing the boy's arms. He wrenched them up behind Roman's back and sank his knee into the boy's neck, forcing his face down into the grass. Roman screamed and struggled against the submission hold, but Michael was in complete control.

"Don't kill him!" Lucia cried; her eyes wide with fear.

"Why shouldn't I?" Michael growled. Roman's struggling increased, so he pushed his knee down on the boy's neck until he stopped. Roman's body went rigid, and then he collapsed and began sobbing into the ground.

Lucia grabbed Michael's arm and then let go when he turned. "Please stop."

"He tried to kill me."

Lucia nodded fast and said, "Yes, he did. He's afraid, we're both afraid." She put her hand on Michael's arm again. "Please, he's my brother. He's all I have left."

Looking into those tear-filled, frightened eyes, Michael felt the anger slowly drain from his body, leaving only exhaustion in its wake. Keeping a wary eye on Roman, he let go of the boy and stepped back. Lucia knelt next to her brother and laid a hand on his head. Roman flinched away and curled up into a sobbing fetal ball.

As Michael looked down at the siblings, he felt a familiar feeling come over him. He sighed in frustration, certain that the two would be the death of him.

# CHAPTER ELEVEN

Lucia looked helplessly at her brother as he lay crying on the ground. Roman was usually inconsolable when he got like this. Usually, the best thing to do was to let him cry it out and give him time to calm down. Unfortunately, time was the one thing they lacked, as the rest of the bikers would be here any moment. The only way to calm Roman down quicker was to let Michael leave. "You said you were going to go, so go," she told Michael, tears filling her eyes. She *hated* being pregnant. Everything seemed to make her cry.

"I'm staying," Michael said, watching Roman with an unreadable expression.

"What?" Lucia asked in surprise, walking over to confront Michael. His haunted blue eyes fixed on her, and Lucia found again that she had a hard time meeting them. They were so filled with pain and misery that they seemed to manifest a fey energy. She found that she somehow shared some of that pain when she looked into them. Regardless, none of that was precedent at the moment. She needed answers. "What changed your mind? Did your moral compass tell you that abandoning a pregnant woman may not be good for your karma?"

Michael bristled in response, then his head abruptly

whipped to the south. "We need to leave now!" He whispered between clenched teeth.

Lucia hadn't heard anything but saw no point in arguing. First things first, though. "I need a moment to talk to my brother."

He looked back at her, blue eyes now electric with anger. "We don't *have* a moment."

Lucia flinched under that gaze, but her anger rose to meet his in turn. "I said I need a moment!" She could feel Michael's eyes on her back as she walked over to her brother.

Roman was sitting on the ground with his arms wrapped around his knees, his nose and lips bloodied, with pieces of grass in his hair. He wasn't crying anymore, but she could tell instantly that he had his obstinate wall up, something that she was all too familiar with. She didn't have time to talk him down gently, so she decided to be very direct.

"Roman--no Roman, look at me." She grabbed his chin when he tried to look away, forcing him to look at her. His puffy red eyes met hers, angry and flat. "Roman, we need to leave now."

Her twin pulled away from her grasp. "Is he coming?"

"Yes."

Roman's eyes widened. "But he tried to kill me!"

"You tried to kill him first. You had it coming."

Roman gave her a surprised look. "I-I had it coming? Yeah, you would let that Neanderthal kill me, wouldn't you."

"He's staying. End of story."

"End of story? End of story?"

"Roman, enough! We don't have time to argue about this. We need to get out of here!"

"Well, I'm not going with him. For all we know, he could be

one of those… those things!"

"Roman!"

"Guess we will know by morning." He sneered. "Oh, wait, we'll all be dead!"

Lucia's temper flared, and she reached down, grabbed Roman's ear, and hauled him to his feet. Roman squealed in pain and tried to pull back, but she squeezed harder. She may be nearly a foot shorter than her brother, but she knew exactly how to cut him down to size. Now, only if she could get him to listen to reason! Lucia yanked his head close to hers and turned it so she could speak into his free ear. She was so angry and afraid that she was tempted to bite it out of spite.

"Now you listen and listen well. I don't have time for your childish, whole 'angry with everybody and the world' routine. "My baby is in danger, and I'm leaving now, with or without you. Family doesn't abandon family, but I'm leaving to protect my baby. If you don't come along right now, then it is you that has abandoned me. Understand?"

"Sis, the ear." Roman groaned.

Lucia tightened her grip and twisted hard. "Understand!" This time, it was not a question but a statement of fact—a declaration of will. She would make him go with her through force of will alone. She had decided back at the church as the bikers dragged her inside that if she somehow survived, she would never allow anyone to jeopardize her baby again. Especially Roman, with his inclination towards immature stupidity.

"I understand, I understand, I understand!" Roman squealed, and Lucia let go. He stepped back away from her reach, rubbing his ear. "We don't need him." Roman began again.

"Yes, we do!" Lucia furiously stepped towards her brother, and he stepped back quickly, cupping his ear protectively.

"You'd choose him over your own blood?"

"Yes."

Roman's eyes widened in disbelief. "Why? You pregnant crazy or something?"

Enough, Lucia decided. Time for some brutal truths. "Because you've proven to me that you can't protect us. Because you're arrogant, immature, and just a plain stubborn-stupid ass. Because you nearly got the baby and me killed. Just like Dominic." Lucia added softly, consequences be damned. Tears welled up in her eyes again, but she ignored them.

"That wasn't my fault," Roman said in a small voice.

"Wasn't your—you know what I'm done with you! You hear me? Done!" Lucia screamed and turned to tell Michael that they should leave. He was gone. "Oh no!" She gasped, looking around, desperately trying to find him in the surrounding darkness.

"So much for the hero." Roman snorted.

There was an instant feeling within Lucia of falling down. Michael had left them... left them to die. She felt a strong urge to sit on the ground but fought it. They needed to go.

"You always had great taste in men," Roman said.

Lucia turned to slap her brother and froze. Two bikers were standing behind Roman. He saw her expression and spun around to find a shotgun in his face. He threw his hands up and gave Lucia a fearful look over his shoulder.

"None of that." The man holding the shotgun said, his voice dry and emotionless. His partner trained his rifle on Lucia, giving her a toothy smile over the scope. He looked like a scarecrow, his arms and legs jutting out of clothes several sizes too small.

Lucia quickly compartmentalized the terror she felt, as she often did, and kept it separate from her baby. Instead, she directed only happy thoughts and love towards it. Her child did not need to know fear in its womb; it was supposed to be a safe haven. There would be too much of it after he was born. *If he were born.* She thought as she fearfully eyed the bikers.

The biker with the shotgun eyed the corpses on the ground. "Did you do this?"

"No, a-a man came and killed them." Roman stammered, swallowing hard against the gun barrel under his chin.

The biker looked around. "Where is this 'man'?"

"Gone."

The man stared at Roman for a long moment before nodding. He looked at the bodies on the ground again and shrugged. "Means more food for the rest of us."

"Sure does," The other one said, his salacious gaze never leaving Lucia.

Lucia would have been furious with herself if she hadn't been so scared. She was such an idiot for arguing with Roman so long, and she couldn't blame Michael for abandoning them. Well, she could a little, she thought, hand on her belly. The biker watching her grinned, his eyes filling with a dreadful intent, like a cat upon seeing its prey. Lucia glared defiantly at him. She wasn't some timid mouse, and she would fight to the death for her baby if it came to it.

There was a muffled sound in the distance, followed by a sharp snap. Both bikers looked towards the sound.

"What was that?" The one with the rifle asked, looking

around, scared.

The other biker scanned the darkness. "Chubbers, that you out there?" Silence. The biker turned back to Roman, his eyes narrowing. "I thought you said he was gone, boy."

Roman's face turned white. "He is, I swear it."

The biker looked at Roman for a long moment. "Doesn't matter. Get down on your knees."

"Please don't," Lucia begged him.

He glanced at her for a second and then said in a bored voice, "Kill her."

The other biker grinned and took aim at Lucia's belly. The other biker cuffed him on the back of the head and said, "No, you moron, don't waste a round. There are zombies in these woods."

"Oh, okay." He said, then raised his rifle to bash Lucia's skull in.

A blur slammed into the biker from the side, sending him crashing to the ground and the rifle flying into the brush. For a second, Lucia thought it was Michael until the zombie looked up at them, eyes flashing silver green in the firelight. Oh no! Things had gone from bad to worse.

The zombie let out a screeching hiss, its face covered with blood and gore from its victim. The fallen biker groaned and moved weakly. The zombie lashed out once with its fist, and the biker moved no more. Then it began to growl, its head moved side to side in small jerks as if deciding on its next victim.

The other biker stared at the zombie in astonishment. His gun dropped slightly, and that's when Roman made his move. Still in shock, Lucia watched as her brother knocked the shotgun away, then grabbed the barrel with both hands and slammed it towards the biker, the butt of the gun smashing the man's mouth. Roman hit him twice more until the bloodied biker finally let go of the gun.

Then Roman reversed it and aimed as the quickened zombie leaped at him, arms swiping furiously at the air. He fired as he fell back, blasting the thing as it flew over him. The zombie crashed to the ground, but its limbs scrambled on the grass, trying to right itself to attack again. Roman quickly rolled over and shot it until the thing lay still. Zombie howls rang out in the distance.

The bloodied biker pulled a magnum from his belt and aimed at Roman's back. "Watch out!" Lucia screamed. As Roman turned to face the biker, Michael jumped out of the darkness, swinging a machete. It sheared through the biker's arm and lodged deep into his chest with a sickening crunch. Michael jerked the machete free, and the biker fell dead to the ground. He turned to find Roman aiming the shotgun at him.

The two men stood still, staring each other down while the tension ramped up as more zombies began to howl nearby. Lucia could see Roman's face redden as his anger grew. Michael lowered his machete to the side, relaxing his grip so that he held it loosely. There was nothing provocative about him except the thousand-yard stare focused on her brother.

Roman's fingers tightened on the trigger, and Lucia screamed, "Roman, no!"

Betrayal flashed on his face for a moment. "Why shouldn't I kill him?" He demanded.

"Because we—" She changed tactics as Roman scoffed, "I need him. Because he just saved your life again."

"Actually, I was trying to save yours," Michael told her, his eyes not leaving Roman's.

"Shut up!" Lucia told Michael. He was definitely not helping the situation. Were all men crazy now?

Michael ignored her and said to Roman. "Everything within a few miles is on its way here, thanks to the noise you two made. You fire that gun again, and it will only pinpoint your location."

"One more won't matter, I think." Roman said, grinning. The grin faded, and he demanded, "Apologize."

"For saving your life or for trying to kill you?"

Roman smirked. "Both."

"No."

Anger twisted Roman's face, and his finger started to tighten on the trigger again. Lucia quickly stepped between them. "Enough, you two! Are you both insane?"

"Out of the way sis," Roman demanded, stepping to the side. Lucia moved to block him. "Roman, enough! I'm so sick of your stupid temper and your ego. When did you decide that was more important than me or my baby?"

Roman looked at her in shock and said, "No, I never said…"

"No? That's not what this is about, then? What exactly are you endangering my baby and me for?"

Roman started to stutter some response, and she spoke right over him. "There are zombies out there." She said, gesturing to the woods around them. "Bikers too. Either will be here any moment! We should already be running. We should be long gone. In fact, I am leaving right now." She walked a few steps away and then turned back to Roman. "You decide right now what's more important, your precious pride or my baby's life."

Lucia walked away, her shoulders flinching every few

seconds in anticipation of the gunshot. It seemed inevitable. Finally, unable to resist any longer, Lucia looked back to see what would happen.

Roman's face was a livid red, and the shotgun trembled in his hands as his body shook with rage. He lowered the gun, quickly raised it, and then lowered it again. Emotions were stark on his face: anger, humiliation, confusion, and indecision all melting into each other. He took a step towards Michael, his eyes daring him to give him any reason to shoot. Michael remained still, expression never changing, hard eyes fixed on Roman. Oddly, he seemed resigned to whatever happened. Does he want to die? Lucia wondered.

Roman looked over at her for a moment, and then his eyes dropped to her pregnant belly. He looked back at Michael. "Remember this moment," he said and lowered the gun.

Michael stared at Roman for a few seconds before purposely turning his back to Roman and walking away. Roman snarled and took aim at Michael's back. Suddenly, he looked back at Lucia, and his face went calm as if he had flipped a switch. He gave her an exaggerated smile and lowered the gun as if to say, "See, I can behave myself." Roman then aimed his index finger and thumb at Michael's back and made a shooting motion.

Men! Lucia thought, though she breathed a sigh of relief simultaneously. Was she one of the few sane people left in this nightmare? Roman had always been a little crazy before the world had ended, but now he seemed borderline psychotic. Michael, unfortunately, didn't appear to be much saner. She wished more than ever that Dominic was still alive. She felt a sharp twang of loss at the thought and pushed it down deep. No time for the dead.

She looked down at her protruding stomach and rubbed it gently. *I will keep you safe, little one, I promise.* She wrapped her arms around her belly as best she could and gave it a little hug as she often did when she needed assurance. She may not be able to provide that for herself, but at least she could reassure her baby. *I love you.*

Off in the distance, a zombie screamed in fury, and a staccato of gunfire replied in response. The woods around them erupted with the discordant howls of zombies. Lucia felt a cold river of fear flood her veins. They were surrounded.

# CHAPTER TWELVE

"We're leaving now. Grab what you can." Michael told the siblings as he quickly wiped the machete on a dead biker and slid it back into its sheathe. His plan to silently take out the bikers had ended with Roman's lack of discretion. He pulled the rifle off his shoulder, checked it, and sighed. Nine rounds in the gun and another five or so in his coat pocket.

He looked up to find Lucia and Roman still exchanging looks. "Now!" Michael growled. Lucia flinched, then knelt and retrieved a pistol from a body next to her. She clutched the gun to her chest, searching the dark trees around them with frightened eyes. Roman gave Michael a lazy grin, casually strolled over to a dead biker, and picked up a bottle of whiskey and a machete. There was no doubt in his mind that the boy would be trouble, but unfortunately, there wasn't time to deal with him now. Michael just had to hope that it wouldn't come back to bite him later.

There were more screams from quickened zombies and frightened bikers in the distance, followed by more gunfire. The fools would draw everything in the area towards them. The sounds were coming from further up the road. Michael turned to study the road behind them. It would be faster and possibly safer than heading blindly into the pitch-black woods. The screams and the gunfire were getting closer so he decided to take the chance.

Michael looked back at the siblings to make sure they were ready. Lucia was watching him closely, looking frightened, but there was a determined set to her jaw. Roman languorously pocketed several shells from the biker who had tried to kill him and grabbed his sister's hand, giving her an excited grin. The boy was crazy if he thought this was going to be fun.

"Let's go," Michael said. He started down the road and stopped abruptly. The layered dark on the road in the distance seemed to be undulating, its movements furtive and amorphous. The moon's edge slipped out of the clouds, and the shadows resolved into a small group of zombies loping down the road. Upon seeing the humans, the ones in front instantly shrieked with rage and started sprinting towards them.

"Run!" Michael spun around and ran up the road toward the gunshots. The woods wouldn't be of any use now that they'd been seen. The zombies could see better in the dark and would have no problem navigating the trees and the brush. Their only chance now was to lead them to the bikers and hopefully slip through the ensuing chaos.

Looking back, he saw that the twins were slowly falling behind, and the zombies were quickly catching up. Roman was pulling Lucia along, but it was obvious that her pregnant belly was hindering her. Michael slowed down so that they passed him. "Faster!" He shouted at them. Roman gave him a nasty look, then yanked hard on Lucia's arm, nearly sending her sprawling.

Michael turned to face the zombies, letting the familiar

calm come over him as he aimed at the closest zombie. He fired, and his shot missed, so he took a deep breath and held it. He shot again, and the zombie's head snapped back, its body tumbling along the road. A zombie vaulted over the body, and Michael took advantage of its predictable arc, shooting it in the head just as it landed. Three more followed in its wake, their ruined forms running unbelievably fast. At least ten more followed close behind them.

Michael exhaled and started running again. He hadn't bought them as much time as he hoped. The flashes of gunfire and screaming were closer but still far too distant. He caught up to the siblings and saw that Lucia was limping badly now, and Roman was dragging her more than pulling. They weren't going to make it. "Keep going," he told them and stopped to face the zombies again.

Six shots left with no time to reload. After that, he would switch to the machete. And after that, he would die. Then Lucia and her baby would die. Hopeless, yet he would try to buy them as much time as possible.

Michael made himself calm again and then took out the three closest zombies. He fired the last remaining bullets into the horde as they closed in, hoping for a kill shot, and then automatically shouldered the rifle. He pulled the machete from his waistband and braced himself. They were only yards away and would be on him in seconds. Michael could now make out the dull metallic glow of their moonlit eyes, full of hate and promising a horrible death. He resigned himself to this fate. He didn't deserve any better.

Just as they were about to reach Michael, Roman ran up next to him, breathing hard. "Thirsty?" He yelled, then threw the whiskey bottle underhand at the zombies. He blasted it with the shotgun. There was an explosion of flame and heat and the zombies ran right into the fireball. They howled and fell to the ground, writhing as green sparks sprayed from their bodies like fireworks.

"Now we're even," Roman said as they watched the zombies burn. The moon hid behind the clouds again, making it difficult to make out the boy's expression in the weak flickering flame light but Michael was sure it wasn't friendly.

"Don't expect a thanks," Michael couldn't resist saying.

"Wasn't expecting one," Roman replied. The moon broke through the clouds, revealing a rictus grin on the boy's face. "Didn't do this for you." He looked down the road, and his grin vanished. "Uh-oh, round two, coming fast," he said as he took off running.

In the broken moonlight, Michael could make out dozens of zombies sprinting down the road and through the surrounding woods. He quickly ran after Roman as fast as his injured side would allow. Every hard breath was stoking the angry ember. This was all futile. The zombies would never tire and would run as fast as their rotted bodies allowed, which was faster than most humans.

They caught up to Lucia and grabbed one of her hands without speaking, pulling her after them. Lucia tried to keep up but tripped and fell, forcing them to slow down and pull her back to her feet. "This isn't working," Roman said as they started running again.

"I'm trying." Lucia gasped; her face covered with sweat.

"Don't stop," Michael told them, his mind racing, searching for any chance of survival. There wasn't any.

Rounding a bend in the road, He saw that the bikers were a short distance away. They were huddled together, forty or fifty strong, yelling and shooting at the occasional zombie attacking them. Several bikers took notice of Michael and the siblings just as the moon faded into obscurity again. There was a flash of light as one of them fired his rifle, and Michael felt the bullet whiz past his head.

"Stop!" Roman screamed in an odd, high-pitched voice. "It's Chubbers. Don't shoot me!"

"Hurry up your fat ass then!" A biker urged in a rough voice.

They ran blindly toward the bikers, and Michael could hear the zombie horde closing in behind them. A cold wind pushed them from behind, bringing with it the stench of rot and death. The zombies were close, a few steps behind. Holding tightly onto Lucia's hand, Michael didn't stop when they reached the bikers. He pushed right into them, pulling the girl behind him with Roman trailing behind, holding her other hand. Michael kept his head down, hoping it was too dark for the bikers to see that they were strangers.

Screams erupted behind them, followed by continuous gunfire and zombie shrieks. The bikers started jostling each other, some trying to escape, the others trying to see what was happening. It was getting harder to move through the throng, but Michael kept going, determined to make it through to the other side.

The moon broke through the clouds completely, revealing everything in silvery stark relief. Michael lowered his head further and kept pushing through. They were almost to the other side with only a few bikers between them and freedom.

Just as Michael tried to push past the last of the bikers, a huge beast of a man stepped in front of him. The massive biker yelled something unintelligible and lunged for him. Without stopping, Michael punched the man as hard as he could in the throat with his free hand. The biker fell to his knees, clawing at his neck and gasping for breath. A biker next to him took notice and yelled, "Hey!" Roman let go of Lucia's hand and punched the distracted biker hard in the ear, and the man also went down.

Michael plowed between two other bikers and finally broke free. They kept running, hunched down. No shots followed. Looking back, Michael could see why. The zombies were decimating the bikers. Those still alive were scattering into the woods with zombies right behind them. *Good riddance.* Michael thought. Luckily, none of the zombies seemed to be chasing them.

The moon disappeared behind a thick bank of clouds, and then they were running in complete darkness. The last human screams and gunfire faded behind them as the rest of the bikers were killed off. Michael kept going, ignoring the burning in his side. They weren't out of danger yet. He held on tightly to Lucia's hand as they ran, feeling the tension build in their grip as her strength played out. Roman was at his sister's side, holding her arm as she limped along. Finally, she collapsed, and they were dragging her again.

Michael stopped and reached down to check on Lucia, but Roman roughly shoved him aside and knelt next to his sister. Michael was very tempted to punch him in the back of the head but instead turned to watch at the black road behind them. The night was eerily silent now. The woods were crawling with zombies, and yet oddly, he heard nothing. He smelled them, though. The rotten stench seemed to come from around them.

He remembered how the quickened zombies had acted back at the farm when he had been up on the platform in the tree. They went crazy if they saw him but quieted down if he hid. They apparently went into a dormant phase unless there was some sort of outside stimuli. Maybe if the zombies couldn't see them, and they didn't make any sounds, they could sneak through and hopefully find someplace safe. Unfortunately, there was only one way to test that theory.

"She's fainted," Roman said in a low, frantic voice.

There was a sharp intake of breath a few yards away, sounding very much like an air of discovery. The zombie let out a low growl, and shuffling footsteps began to head their way.

Michael quickly hunched down next to Roman to explain his theory. The boy tried to draw back but Michael clamped his hand down on Roman's shoulder and jerked him closer. After he finished explaining, Roman was still for a moment, and then Michael could sense him nodding. Then Roman leaned over and whispered into Michael's ear, "Chair lift."

Familiar with the term from his time in the military, Michael located one of Lucia's arms, wrapped it around his neck, and then wrapped his forearm around her thigh and locked it with his other hand. He could feel Roman mirroring his movements and together they lifted Lucia off the ground. The zombie's footsteps were getting too close for comfort, so they started carrying Lucia's limp body blindly down the road, her head lolling back and forth between them. Michael could only hope that they wouldn't run into anything in the dark.

The lift left both of them at a sore disadvantage if anything attacked, but Michael couldn't think of any better way to move Lucia. He looked up at where the moon should have been and all he could see was a faint glow buried behind a deep wall of clouds. They should be safe if the moon stayed hidden and they didn't run into any zombies.

Michael scanned the formless black ahead of them, looking for any hint of movement, listening for a grunt or groan, or a dragging footstep to indicate where a zombie may be. Aside from the occasional gust of wind, the road and woods were unnaturally quiet. There seemed to be an ominous sense of waiting around them that Michael found very unnerving. The zombies were out there. He knew it. Felt it!

They almost walked into a zombie before they saw it; the only thing giving it away was the faintest shift of black on black. Michael and Roman froze mid-step The thing didn't groan like daytime zombies, and Michael wondered if they were being silent on purpose. *The better to hear you with, my dear.* A chill went down his spine at the thought. It had deeper implications that he couldn't afford to think about at the moment.

He felt a pull on Lucia's body as Roman moved left, and he followed suit, hoping the boy wasn't leading them into another zombie. There was a pause, and then Roman turned in another direction. A few steps later, he changed direction again. Though Michael couldn't see the zombies, Michael could feel them as he passed, the sense of something being there, similar to detecting a door in the dark.

Roman stopped again. Several seconds passed, and the boy remained motionless. Michael tried to see what was happening, but it was so dark he doubted he could see his hands if they were in front of his face.

After a few seconds of immobility, Michael pushed

slightly on Lucia's body and felt a nudge back a moment later. That way wasn't good then. The only option left was to head back and try to circumvent the other zombies they had passed. It was as if they were in a maze, except this one had invisible walls that could kill if touched. Michael stepped back and felt a pull and release on Lucia's body as Roman followed his lead.

Michael took one exaggerated slow step after another, straining his senses for any sign of where the zombies were. The air reeked of rot but he couldn't see anything. He was tempted to close his eyes, irrationally thinking the familiar dark in his head would be more helpful than the pitch black he was trying to see through now. He kept his eyes open though, and continued on, one slow careful step at a time.

He somehow sensed a zombie ahead of them and changed direction slightly, hoping his feelings were right. He almost walked into another one; the only thing giving it away was a small scrape of gravel as it adjusted its stance. Michael changed direction again, choosing at random. He felt turned around, and for all he knew, they were heading right back into the rotting arms of the mass of zombies that had wiped out the bikers. He thought he saw movement and changed direction again, though it may have been his mind playing tricks on him. They needed to get past the zombies soon. Lucia was deadweight and getting heavier by the second. He looked up at the moon. Luckily, it was still buried deep behind some clouds.

There was another loud scrape a few feet away, followed by rhythmic dragging sounds as a zombie started heading fast in their direction. Michael wasn't sure what had set it off. He didn't think they had made any noise but that didn't change the fact that the thing was coming towards them.

A slight movement revealed a zombie to Michael's left, so the only thing he could think to do was nudge Roman right and hope there wasn't one there, too. He pushed the boy through Lucia again, waiting precious seconds while the dragging sound drew closer. He felt another tug on Lucia's body and followed. Roman took two steps and stopped again, then pushed back again. No way to go! The dragging sound seemed to be right in front of Michael now. Acting on instinct, he turned sideways and pushed up his back against Lucia just as the zombie reached them. The dead thing's greasy hair brushed Michael's cheek and lips, sending shivers of revulsion and nausea through him.

The zombie limped past them, and Michael released a silent shuddering breath of relief. Lucia shifted in his grasp and grunted softly. The dragging sound abruptly stopped. Michael froze, heart pounding hard in his chest. He looked down at Lucia, hoping she would stay quiet and the zombie would move on. It didn't move, but Michael could swear he could feel it looking in their direction. Lucia's body tensed, and she let out a low, prolonged groan.

There was a loud hiss behind them, followed by the sounds of several sets of distinct footsteps heading in their direction. The dragging sound started in their direction again. *So much for finesse*, Michael thought as he lowered Lucia to the road. He pulled out his machete praying Roman would think to do the same.

Michael swung the machete at the nearest set of footsteps and felt it connect. He wasn't sure if it had killed the zombie, so he hacked at it again. It didn't make a sound so he must have killed it. Suddenly, there was a loud boom and a blinding flash of light as Roman blew the head off a zombie with his shotgun.

In the split second before the light died, dozens of illuminated zombie heads whipped toward them. A deafening shriek went up in the following darkness.

"Oops," Roman said as the zombies closed in from all directions.

# CHAPTER THIRTEEN

"Only use your machete!" Roman's voice came from somewhere nearby, its origin difficult to make out over the shrieking of the zombies.

Blinking against the painful afterimage burned into his corneas, at the moment the only thing Michael wanted to use his machete on was Roman. He felt a slimly claw clamp down on his arm and slashed down with the blade, hearing a chopping sound as the blade sheared through flesh and bone. He felt another hand pulling at his coat and hacked at it as well.

The dead kept coming and Michael kept swinging. He tried to keep his swings small to avoid hurting Lucia and hoped that Roman was being reserved as well. Near the edge of panicking, he fought hard to stay calm. Hundreds of zombies were coming at them in the dark, and a single bite from one of them was all it took to die. Michael could only locate them in the din if they touched him or when his machete connected. His fragile calm devolved into frantic slicing, punching, and kicking in all directions. He didn't see a way out of this. Why delay the inevitable by a few seconds? Why not just give in and succumb to his sins?

Something grabbed at his ankle and he almost slashed at

it before realizing the hand was warm. He grabbed the hand and pulled Lucia up to her feet. She clung hard to his arm, gasping, "There is something down there."

Michael swung his machete wide to the left and when it didn't connect with anything, he grabbed Lucia under the shoulder and pulled her over there. Taking her hand firmly so he didn't lose her in the chaos, Michael kicked around at the ground until his foot hit something solid. He hacked at it viciously with the blade and felt something claw at his back. He spun around and knocked another zombie away from him. "We need to get out of here!"

"This way!" Roman called out as several zombies screamed nearby.

"Where?"

The night lit up briefly as Roman fired another shot. The sudden bright light burned Michael's eyes again, the afterimage filled with dozens of twisted zombie silhouettes surrounding them. "Come on, I see something!" Roman yelled as the zombies shrieked again. Michael ran blindly towards Roman's voice, pulling Lucia behind him. The afterimage from the shotgun blast dominated his vision, making it difficult to see. He swung at a zombie he had seen in the flash of light and connected. Roman yelled something again and Michael headed towards the voice. He ran into something hard and cold and reached down, feeling that it was a metal rail.

"It's a bridge," Roman's voice came from close by.

"Great, so what do we do when we get to the other side?" Michael asked, shoving Lucia past him. Walking fast, he propelled the girl forward, and she went without complaint. Michael knew that as soon as the moon came out from hiding that a simple bridge would not stop the zombies.

"Won't know until we get there," Roman replied in a cheerful voice.

Michael fought a strong urge to throw his machete towards Roman's voice in the dark and let fate decide whether the fool died. He heard Lucia muttering under her breath in Spanish next to him. Apparently, he wasn't the only one not enjoying the boy's antics.

"There's a door here!" Roman called out from somewhere ahead. There was a brief screech of metal. "It's not locked."

"Wait!" Michael yelled. There was no point going into the building if something worse waited for them there. The bridge was narrow enough that there was a chance of holding it if they were lucky.

"You wait," Roman replied. The moon came out from the clouds just as Roman disappeared into the dark confines of what appeared to be a large utility building. Michael slowed down as he and Lucia approached the structure, expecting to hear Roman's agonized screaming.

Lucia's eyes widened as she looked behind them. "No time for sightseeing!" She said, pulling hard on his arm. Looking back, Michael saw hundreds of zombies pouring out of the woods, and a steady stream of the things was running down the narrow bridge towards them. Several were jostled over the handrail, screeching as they fell into the chasm below.

"Come on!" Roman yelled from the doorway. As they raced towards the door, Michael felt the bridge tremble beneath them. "Faster!" he urged. They flew through the entrance, and Roman quickly shut the door behind them. A split second later, they heard a crash and the door opened a few inches. A rotten arm snaked around its edge, angling towards Roman. "Help me!" He yelled, bracing the door with his arms.

Michael slammed his shoulder into the door and it crashed shut on the zombie's limb. Roman slid the lock bar into position and then stepped back. The zombie's arm quivered as it still strained to reach them. The pounding intensified and the door began to bend. "Not good," Roman said, backing away.

"We need to brace it somehow." Lucia spat out between ragged breaths. Michael could see her silhouette in the moonlight as it poured through a bank of windows near the sheet metal roof, illuminating the interior in soft light and sharp shadows. The girl was leaning against a stair rail and holding her large belly.

"Or find another way out," Roman added.

The door started bowing in its frame as the zombies piled up behind it. Michael pushed hard against it, hoping to buy them precious time. The zombie's arm bent towards him, its hand clenching and unclenching. "Start looking," Michael told them, his voice straining with effort. "And be alert. We may not be alone."

The twins split up. Lucia headed cautiously to the left, holding her pistol tight in trembling hands. Roman went right, brashly jogging into the dark with his shotgun. Michael soon lost them in the highly contrasted room.

The pressure was building on the door, accompanied by a strange vibration that was growing in strength. The lock began to buckle, and the metal around it began to tear. He wouldn't be able to hold it much longer. "Hurry!"

"I've got nothing," Lucia called out from the other side of the room.

"Same here," Roman said. "Nothing but machinery and it's all too big to move."

"Get over here then." Michael barked at Roman. "Lucia, keep looking and be careful!"

As Roman rushed over, Michael felt the sliding lock give and the door began to creep open. Michael's feet slid on the concrete floor as he scrambled to find purchase. Roman slammed up next to him, but his added weight only slowed the doors opening. The vibration had worsened to the point that Michael could feel it pulsating through the floor.

The vibration suddenly ended, followed by the horrible screaming of tortured metal. At the same time, the pressure on the door fell off completely, causing Michael and Roman to fall forward as it slammed shut. A few seconds later, they heard a series of loud crashes coming from far below.

They slowly backed away from the door. Beneath it, a large chunk of concrete was missing, with moonlight coming through the gap. The zombie's arm was only hanging by a few strands of tendon. An occasional tremor would run through it, making it dance and bounce around as it dangled.

"What... happened?" Michael asked as he tried to catch his breath.

"One way to find out," Roman said, yanking the door open. They caught a brief glimpse of a zombie before it fell into the empty abyss below, trailing its almost severed arm like a banner behind it.

As Michael had guessed, the bridge had collapsed under the weight of the zombies. He slowly approached the open door and saw gaping holes where the steel bolts had ripped from the concrete. Across the gap, the remaining zombies howled as soon as they saw Michael and began hurling themselves across the gap, falling just short of halfway.

"They do have a one-track mind, don't they?" Roman asked, laughing. They watched as zombie after zombie launched and then fell into the dark chasm. More came out of the woods, and the single-minded insanity continued.

Michael quickly grew bored of the spectacle and walked away, eager to learn more about the building. Roman remained at the edge, chortling with each zombie's suicide. For a moment, Michael was tempted to push the boy out the doorway. All it would take was one good kick, and Roman would be gone. No, he decided reluctantly after a moment's thought. He didn't know if he had it in him to do something so cold hearted. Plus, there was that gut feeling to help the siblings to worry about. Like it or not, he may still need the boy. Michael was also reluctant to admit that Roman had just saved their lives. Sure, he could have also led them to their deaths but Michael was just relieved to be alive at the moment.

"Michael!" Lucia said sharply, looking at him as if she knew exactly what he had been thinking. Michael was surprised to discover that he felt a little guilty. She stared hard at him for a few seconds and then said, "I've found a door."

Leaving Roman to his morbid entertainment, Michael followed Lucia through a moonlit maze of dark machinery to a ramp hidden at the back. Roman's laughter echoed eerily behind them. Lucia turned abruptly to face him. "I need to know if I can trust you."

"You can."

"Really? Then what was that back there?"

Michael looked back at Roman's direction and didn't say

anything.

"I see. I need to trust you, Michael, to protect all of us—even my brother. Otherwise, you can leave. Right now. I don't need a murderer around my baby. Understand?"

Michael flinched and looked down at Lucia. She stared up at him, her dark eyes black and angry in the moonlight. He finally nodded in agreement. "Good." She said, turning away as if everything had been resolved and headed towards the ramp. Michael watched her for a moment before following. *Okay,* Michael thought to himself as he followed her, *it won't be in cold blood.*

Lucia let out a hot hiss of pain and clutched at her belly. "No." She wailed, "Not now!"

"You okay?" Michael asked, rushing over to prop her up.

Lucia nodded; her jaw clenched tight.

"Contractions?" Michael asked, cursing inwardly at the timing.

Lucia let out a long breath, followed by a stream of what Michael assumed were Spanish profanities. "I don't think so. I think... Ah! I think my son is not happy about being jostled around." She let out a long groan and then slumped against him.

"You sure?"

"Sure, I'm sure." She replied with a wan smile. "I think his tantrum is over. Let's go." She said, grabbing his proffered arm for support. Together, they made their way up the ramp and deeper into the belly of the building.

At the top of the ramp was a short hallway that led to a metal door with a four-inch-square window covered with mesh. Peering through it, all Michael saw was black. There was no way to tell whether it was a room, hallway, or simply led back outside. It could be filled with quickened zombies or something worse. There was no choice but to check it out. The large space they were in now had too many unknowns for him to feel safe.

The moon disappeared again, entombing them in absolute darkness. He heard a sharp intake of breath from Lucia and a second later, felt her hand clutching his arm. "Where's Roman?" She asked in a hoarse whisper, and Michael realized he couldn't hear the boy's laughter anymore. "Roman!" Lucia called out before he could stop her. "Where are you?"

"Everywhere." A voice right next to them whispered

Lucia screamed, followed quickly by a bright flash and a loud concussion. In the brief moment of light, Michael saw Roman falling backward away from them.

Lucia screamed again. "Roman! Are you okay?"

"Yes," came a stunned voice from below them in the darkness.

"Good," Lucia said, her voice changing slightly, followed by a sharp slap.

"Ow! What the... why did you hit me?"

"Cause you scared me, you idiot. I almost killed your stupid ass."

"All I did was answer you!"

"Well, you scared me doing it."

"Enough!" Michael said. Couldn't they see that this wasn't the best time to argue?

There was silence for a moment, then the twins started up again, this time whispering furiously at each other.

"I can't believe you shot at me," Roman said.

"I didn't shoot at you. Besides, you scared me."

"I wasn't trying to scare you, sis!"

"Well you-"

A loud metallic clang echoed from the other side of the building, cutting off their argument.

"What was that?" Lucia whispered.

"Shh," Michael said. They listened silently for a few seconds, but the sound did not repeat. Michael did not trust that to mean that they were alone. Either they had knocked something loose on the way over, or a zombie or something worse was heading towards them in the dark.

"Watch the ramp," Michael told Roman and heard the boy's footsteps as he approached it. There were two soft clicks as he slowly pumped the shotgun. Michael then turned back to the door. Laying his ear against the glass, he listened for any sign that something was waiting for them on the other side.

"Hear anything?" Lucia whispered to him.

Michael started shaking his head and then realized the motion would be lost in the dark. "Nothing." He replied.

"Better make it quick," Roman whispered from the ramp. "I think I heard a scraping noise a few seconds... just heard it again. It's closer this time."

"Good enough for me," Michael replied, then turned to Lucia. "Give me your pistol. No wait, trade with your brother." The shotgun would be far more effective at clearing whatever was on the other side of the door. Or if things went south, hopefully give him time to back out quickly.

The moon broke free of the clouds as Lucia limped over to her brother and held out the pistol to him. Roman hesitated for a moment and then traded with her. Lucia shuffled back to Michael, handed him the shotgun, and said, "Be careful."

"Go wait by your brother," he said and waited until the

girl complied. Michael quickly checked the shotgun. It was a rare semi-automatic tactical model that was box magazine fed and most likely had been looted out of a private collection or police station. Pulling the clip, he saw five cartridges left, plus one in the chamber. Roman must have found more ammo on the biker's body.

Holding the shotgun ready, Michael tried the doorknob and found it unlocked. He closed his eyes and took a deep breath to steady his nerves. He opened his eyes, turned the knob fully, and pushed the door open. The moonlight cut a swath into what appeared to be a large room. Michael was grateful for the light, as he would have hated trying to clear the space in the dark.

He stepped into the room and paused, trying to make sense of the darkness beyond the moonlight as his eyes adjusted. There was only enough reflective light to give suggestions of things. It appeared to be a medium sized windowless room with several rows of desks with dead electronics on them, possibly a control room for the machinery below. There was a small break area next to the door comprised of an ancient stained sofa and a cheap wooden table with a stack of magazines on it. Another metal door with a small wire glass window was at the far wall. The room didn't feel wrong, so he took another step in and stopped again. Nothing responded. It was relatively safe if such a thing existed now.

"Hurry up!" Roman hissed. "It's getting closer."

Michael made his way to the far door and peered through the small window. All he saw behind the glass was pitch black. He would have seen the moonlight if it led outside, so it had to lead to another room or hallway. He locked and deadbolted the door, then went back out to the ramp.

"It's clear." He whispered as he exited the door to find Lucia and Roman nervously watching the massive workroom.

"Good cause we are definitely not alone," Lucia whispered back, relief stark on her moonlit face. "Roman, come on."

Michael watched the dark until the twins had gone through the door, then followed them in. He deadbolted this door too, and turned around to find the room in almost complete darkness. The twins were huddled together in a small pool of light coming from the door's tiny window. Lucia was looking around the dark room with wide, scared eyes. Roman, however, was looking at Michael, his expression unreadable.

"What now?" Lucia asked as she sat down on a chair.

Michael walked over to the break area and picked up one of the magazines. He ripped the cover off and then tore it into rough squares. He returned to the door and started sliding them between the thick glass and the window's metal frame. He didn't want to take any chances from leaving the window uncovered.

"Wait!" Lucia whispered desperately. "I'm afraid of the dark."

"Sorry," Michael said as he slid the last square of paper into place, cutting off the light and leaving them in absolute darkness.

# CHAPTER FOURTEEN

Lucia woke with a sharp pain in her stomach and a dull ache in her head. Her legs hurt too much to even think about, let alone move. Terrified and cold, she had laid awake on the uncomfortable couch for hours, listening to all the strange noises around her, real or imagined. Then suddenly, as if a switch had been flipped, it was morning. She must have fallen asleep, though she had no memory of it. Exhaustion would do that to a person, she guessed. She was surprised being pregnant that she didn't have to pee, but that just went to show how dehydrated she was. *Need to do something about that soon.*

She felt another sharp stab in her belly. Her son—he had to be a boy from all the pain he was causing her—was hungry and demanding his morning breakfast. "Shh," Lucia told him, rubbing her belly as she looked around at the unfamiliar surroundings. "We'll find food soon. I promise." She had no idea how she was going to keep that promise, but she would make it happen. She always did.

Pale sunlight leaked around the magazine pages stuffed into the window, giving the room a faded, antique look. Two curved rows of workstations formed a double horseshoe in the middle of the room with several office chairs scattered around them. Built in monitors and various knobs and buttons covered the stations. It reminded Lucia of NASA's control room that she had seen in a movie once a few years back, except this room was grungy and smelled faintly of chemicals, suggesting a more banal purpose than seeing people off into space.

She heard soft snoring and looked over to see Roman resting in a chair next to the couch, feet propped up in another chair and his shotgun cradled in his arms. Asleep, his face was serene and almost childlike, with none of the ugly surliness that was there when awake. Most likely her idiot brother had tried staying up all night to keep watch and protect her, and no doubt had fallen asleep before she had. Lucia rolled her eyes.

Across the room was the person Roman had no doubt been 'protecting' her from, peering through a gap in the covered window overlooking the ramp. Despite the distance, she could see that Michael looked exhausted, eyes bloodshot and his complexion pale. Obviously, he had been up all night keeping watch, which Lucia found far more reassuring than her slumbering so called protector next to her.

Lucia took the opportunity to study Michael since he was preoccupied with the window. She had always been good at reading people, but Michael was a complete mystery to her. All she could read was pain. A massive wall of it. It was not just his haunted eyes; his tortured soul seemed to radiate it too. She could feel its energy when he was nearby. Everyone had been through hell for the past several months but somehow Michael seemed to embody it.

Roman thought Michael was a threat, and maybe he was right, though she was reluctant to agree with her twin on anything. But she had seen madness in Michael's eyes last night after Roman had attacked him. She also knew that Michael had contemplated kicking Roman off the cliff after the bridge had fallen.

Lucia chewed her bottom lip as she considered this. Would Michael eventually snap and kill them all? Maybe the big guy was dangerous, but what other choice did she have? She was desperate to keep her baby safe, and so far Michael had proven himself to be a more capable protector than Roman ever had. Roman made problems. Michael seemed the sort to take care of them.

She let out a long sigh. So, all she could infer about Michael so far was that he was emotionally overwrought and maybe a little crazy. Who wasn't these days? Hell, she was beginning to question her own sanity after some of the things she had seen recently. Sometimes, a small part of her in the back of her mind wondered if the real Lucia was stuck in a padded cell in an asylum somewhere, screaming her head off, and all of this was a nightmare. No, this was reality, the *new* horrible reality and she needed to accept that. It was dangerous to think otherwise.

Another thing that bothered her was why Michael had changed his mind so quickly about staying with them. He had seemed so adamant about leaving them at first and then suddenly decided otherwise. Oddly, *after* Roman had attacked him. None of it made sense so she planned to get a straight answer out of him later.

Lucia winced as her son demanded his breakfast again. *Take it easy, little one. I'm hungry too.* But what to do about it? She slowly sat up and looked around the room, hoping to see a vending machine. Except for the lounge area, the room was sparsely utilitarian, with no vending machine in sight. She fell back on the couch, feeling an overwhelming urge to cry. *Not going to cry. Not going to cry. Nope, I'm not doing it.* She thought, fighting back the tears. *Stupid pregnancy, stupid hormones!*

She looked back at Michael and found him glaring at her with red eyes. She jumped a little before remembering they were just bloodshot from lack of sleep. *Yikes, those eyes could kill a person!* She only managed to hold his glower for a few seconds again before having to look away. *Dang it!*

"Hungry?" Michael asked in a soft voice.

"The baby is," She replied, forcing herself to look at Michael again. "Me too, I guess."

Michael nodded and walked over to Roman's chair. His head was flung back over the top of the chair, lolling back and forth with each laborious breath coming from his wide gaping mouth.

"Roman." Michael rumbled in a low voice. "Roman!" Her twin's only response was to start snoring loudly—an obnoxious grating noise that sounded like a weed whacker was tearing up his tonsils.

"Sorry," Lucia said, feeling embarrassed. "He's always been a deep sleeper."

Michael stared down at Roman for a long moment, then slowly slid the rifle off his shoulder. Lucia's heart suddenly lurched in her chest. Was Michael going to finish off Roman after all? Was she next? She fumbled at her coat, trying to pull the pistol free. Then, to her surprise, Michael simply sat the rifle gently against the wall next to Roman and then smoothly slid the shotgun out of his grasp. Lucia collapsed back against the couch, letting out a sigh of relief. Roman didn't stir, and Michael shook his head briefly before walking away.

He went over to the green door opposite the one to the ramp and peeled back a section of magazine covering the small window. He peered through the tiny opening for a long moment and then unlocked the door.

Lucia sat up straight. "Where are you going?"

"To look around, find food. Lock the deadbolt." Michael said and then slipped through the door, shutting it gently behind him. Lucia stared at the door, worrying if Michael had decided to take off after all. The thought froze her for a moment as she considered it. *No, he said he is getting food, so he is getting food. That's it. He'll come back. Nothing to worry about. Shut up, you stupid, pernicious thoughts!*

Lucia shook her head to break the trance and forced herself to her feet. Ignoring her stiff protesting leg muscles, she made her way over to the door and locked it. The deadbolt seemed to lock with the sound of finality, but she told herself that it was all in her mind. It is what it is and was what it was. She would know soon enough if Michael planned to come back. If not...

Lucia laid back down on the couch, and in a blink of an eye, the room was brighter. Disoriented, she sat up, trying to get a feel for how long she had slept. Thirty minutes? An hour? She looked around for Michael but he wasn't back yet. She felt a jolt of panic but fought to suppress it. *Use your logic*, she told herself. The building was probably huge, and of course it would take him a while to search it if that were the case. She refused to allow herself to get worked up. It wouldn't do her or the baby any good. Wasted emotions until she knew one way or another. Still, a little nagging voice was inside her head saying that Michael was long gone.

Irritated, Lucia wobbled to her feet. Last night's calisthenics had definitely taken a toll on her legs. Rubbing and stretching them didn't help much, so she limped around the room, hoping the movement would work out the kinks. Looking around the room, she wondered what the huge building's purpose was. Correction, she noted mentally, had been.

She hobbled over and sat down at one of the workstations. Many of the buttons and switches had acronyms and numbers above them. Lucia spent several minutes trying to decipher what they could mean. Eventually, she grew bored, flipped several random switches in frustration, and went over to the red door leading to the ramp.

Pulling back the torn magazine page, Lucia peered through the window and found a decayed face looking back at her. She slammed the page back into place and backed away from the door, her heart pounding hard. Had it seen her? "Roman!" She hissed under her breath as she fumbled the pistol out of her coat pocket. "Wake up!"

Roman groaned and mumbled something unintelligible, then rolled over on his side precariously in the chair and started to snore again.

"Roman!" Lucia hissed, but of course the worthless idiot didn't wake up. He was never there when she needed him, or if he was, then he only made things worse. She didn't dare say anything louder. Irritated, she picked up a pencil jar to chuck at him and stopped as a realization hit her. Why wasn't the zombie banging on the door? Curiosity getting the better of her, she gently sat the pencil jar down and crept back to the window. She hesitated, then pulled back the edge of the magazine page just enough to peek out.

The zombie was still there, swaying slightly from side to side. It seemed to be female, though that was more of a guess as its features had deteriorated greatly. Looking at its sad, soggy eyes, Lucia was surprised that a white film covered them. A blind zombie? Had she been blind before she turned? She lowered the flap of the torn magazine page to consider it. It did make some morbid sense that any defect of the living would carry over if they became a zombie. It would also explain why the zombie was not reacting to her presence. *How sad!*

Feeling emboldened behind a locked steel door and armed with a pistol, she removed the magazine page so she could study the zombie better. The miserable thing was about Lucia's height or a little shorter. Limp stringy hair fell from its torn scalp. It may have been red once, but it was so dirty that it was hard to tell. Sunken cheeks pinched around a pursed mouth, its grey lips thin and deflated. A metal ring rose from the torn, shriveled flesh of the zombie's nose, looking too much to Lucia like a black worm coming out of its nostril. Lucia's stomach rolled slightly at the imagery which, unfortunately, was accentuated by a sweet smell of decay coming through the door.

The zombie seemed so sad and pathetic that Lucia couldn't help but feel sorry for the poor thing, even though she knew it would rip her throat out if it could get at her. Slowly, she began to sway in tandem with the zombie. Back and forth they went, locked in perfect step like two metronomes in sync. Lucia felt a melancholy fall over her as she looked at the sad creature. A morbid thought occurred to her that this zombie was her mirror image, a harbinger of things to come.

"Who were you?" Lucia whispered. "Where did you come from?" The zombie groaned as if in response. It was a lonely, needful sound. Lucia felt tears come to her eyes. "I'm sorry you're lonely." She said, laying her hand on the glass as if touching its ruined face, continuing to sway with the zombie. "Did you have a baby?"

A quiet knock came from the other door behind her, and Lucia nearly jumped out of her skin. Another knock came, slightly louder. Lucia scrambled to cover the window and limped over to the other door as quickly as possible. She started to unlock it and then hesitated with her hand on the lock. "Who is it? She winced at the stupid question as soon as she said it.

"It's me," a muffled voice called through the door.

"Who's me?" She asked to make sure.

"Michael." He replied in his deep voice.

Feeling relieved, Lucia opened the door and smiled as Michael walked past her, arms full of junk food. "You found a vending machine!" She said, quickly locking the door, then followed behind Michael like an eager kid while trying to eye everything he was carrying.

She pulled up a chair as Michael emptied his load on one of the desks. Lucia quickly snagged a bag of miniature cupcakes. She tore it open with her teeth, tasting cellophane and a hint of tasty chocolate. *Oh, and that heavenly smell!*

"Didn't check the expiration dates," Michael warned.

Lucia ignored him and popped one of the cupcakes into her mouth. She did a sample chew and found it a little stale but still quite delicious. *Heavenly!* She thought, squinching her eyes shut in ecstasy. She stuffed three more cupcakes in with the other, not caring that her cheeks were puffing out like a chipmunk. She began to chew, and soon her mouth was filled with a thick slurry of dark, chocolaty goodness. Michael pulled a grape soda out of his jacket and sat it down in front of her. "Thank you!" She told him around a big wad of cupcake. She felt a gentle kick in her belly and added with a big smile, "My baby thanks you too."

Michael didn't reply. He picked up a bag of chips and walked over to Roman, quietly swapped the shotgun for the rifle, then went to the other side of the room and sat down. He pulled another grape soda from his jacket, popped the lid, took a sip, and then let the can dangle between his knees as he stared despondently at the floor.

Lucia wasn't sure whether to be irritated or hurt. She swallowed the last bite of cupcake and chased it down with a big swig of the soda. "Thanks again for the food." She prodded, curious to see how he would respond. Michael remained mute, his eyes far away and looking as though they didn't like what they were seeing.

"Did you figure out what this place is?" He still didn't answer. Lucia decided to go for shock value. "There's a zombie at the door."

"I know." Michael took another sip of the soda and then tore open the bag of chips.

"Are you worried about her?" She asked, with a nervous glance at the door.

"No."

"Good." Feeling like she had accomplished something with Michael finally responding and also feeling oddly protective of the zombie, Lucia snatched up her next sugary victim, a container of powdered donuts. She thought about asking Michael why he had decided to stay, but given his reticent mood, she saved the question for another time.

There was a loud yelp and crash as Roman tipped over his chair. Lucia shot a quick look at the door, expecting thumping to begin. No sounds came from it, so either the zombie had wandered on, or it hadn't heard the noise. A deaf, blind zombie? Naw.

Roman got to his feet and stretched, yawning something unintelligible. He stumbled over to Lucia and grinned when he saw the junk food. "What's for breakfast?" he asked, plopping down heavily in the chair beside her. *No how are you? How's the baby doing? Are you okay?* Lucia noted. Typical Roman.

Reaching out wide with both arms, Lucia hugged the food to her chest and told her brother in all seriousness, "Go find your own."

After breakfast, Lucia felt a sugar coma coming on, so she laid back down on the couch. Roman was still at the desk, noisily finishing a bag of chips and some cupcakes that she had finally relinquished. Michael still sat against the wall, using his knees to prop up his arms while he rested his head on them. Lucia watched him as she drifted off toward sleep, hoping it would prompt a dream about him. Maybe then she would know more about him. Dream reading apparently ran in the family, though she thought it was mostly bunk. She closed her eyes and drifted off.

Hours later, Lucia woke up disappointed from a dreamless sleep. She rubbed her eyes and then looked over at Michael's spot at the wall, wondering if he was still resting. He wasn't there! She sat up quickly and looked around the room. Michael was gone and so was his rifle. *Oh no, he took the rifle instead of the shotgun this time!* She got up as quickly as she could and limped over to Roman. He was sitting at a console flipping switches and pushing buttons, each one accompanied by simulated explosions and gunfire under his breath.

"Roman, where's Michael?"

He just shrugged and continued at his fantasy play.

"I'm serious. Where is he? When did he leave?"

"Big ugly left about an hour ago," He replied, shrugging again. "Good riddance."

"Why did he leave?" Lucia spun Roman's chair so that they were face to face. "What did you do?"

"Do?" Roman rolled his eyes. "Why am I always to blame for everything that goes wrong in your life, huh?" Digging his feet in, he forced the chair loose from Lucia's hand and spun back to the switches. "I knew he was going to do this. I knew he was going to abandon us the first chance he got. I tried to spare you this, but no, you didn't want to listen to me."

Lucia fought back a scream. Oh! Why did he have to be so irritating? He had to know that he was practically inviting her to smack the crap out the back of his head, and that fact only made her want to hit him that much harder.

Unable to resist the temptation, Lucia raised her fist, planning to lay her brother out. A soft knock came from the door. Lucia marched over to it, unlocked the deadbolt, and then yanked the door open to find Michael holding another armful of snacks.

"How dare you leave and not let anybody know where you're going or why!" Lucia snarled. "That was completely rude and inconsiderate of you. Don't you ever, ever, do it again."

Michael just stood in the doorway blinking, his expression never changing. That somehow made her even angrier. She was half-tempted to punch him in the face, scary man or not, to see if she could at least get blood from the damn rock. Instead, she started crying. She quickly turned away, not wanting him to see her like this, and found Roman staring at her in astonishment, mouth agape with a dumbfounded expression on his stupid face. Lucia abruptly spun and quickly walked away so that the only witness to her being a blubbering fool was a couple of cheap wall panels. No doubt they were exchanging looks and rolling their eyes behind her back. Oh, how she hated being pregnant!

"I've scouted the area around the building, and it appears to be free of zombies," Michael said in his soft rumble. "This is almost the last of the snacks." She heard crinkling noises as he deposited the food on the console. "I suggest you eat up and get some sleep because tomorrow we'll have to move on to find more supplies for you and your baby. Lock up after me."

Lucia suddenly felt horrible. The poor man had just been out making sure they were safe and had food to eat, and she just had to go and take his head off. Worse, there had been no anger, no reprobation to his tone, only the same sad, tired voice. She needed to apologize to him, she decided. Right away.

"Michael, wait!" She said, turning around, but he was already gone. Crap! She thought about chasing after him but stopped herself after taking a step. What could she say? *Sorry that I am a half-crazed pregnant woman?* Lucia sighed and made herself walk past the food. She deserved to go to bed hungry. No, wait, that wasn't fair to the baby. Crap again! She couldn't even punish herself right!

Lucia made herself pick up a container of cupcakes. She viciously ripped it open with her teeth and took a big bite, determined not to enjoy any part of the meal.

"Hey! There's a zombie out there!" Roman exclaimed from

beside the far door, shotgun cradled in his arms.

"Leave her alone," Lucia whispered.

Roman pulled back the magazine page and said, "Yep, she looks alone."

"Leave… her. Alone! " Lucia warned, standing up.

"No, I think I can get her," Roman replied, unlocking the deadbolt.

"Leave her alone!" Lucia shrieked, running over to her brother and shoving him away from the door. "Leave her alone!" Soft thumps started coming from the door. Lucia quickly locked the deadbolt then stuck her finger right in Roman's face and followed him as he backpedaled away from her.

"Leave her alone!" Lucia shrieked again as Roman fell back into a computer chair. She stood leaning over him, finger right in his face. "Leave her alone! You just leave her alone!"

Leaning back in the chair as far as he could, Roman swallowed hard and nodded emphatically, wide eyes never leaving her shaking finger. He finally threw his hands up and said, "Okay, okay, okay! I'll leave her alone. Look, I'm leaving her alone. Promise!"

Lucia glowered at her brother for a moment longer, then walked back to the door and gently pushed the magazine page back into place as the soft zombie thumps continued. She wasn't his weak, people pleasing sister any longer. That person had died yesterday when Roman had nearly gotten them killed by the bikers. Lucia had been reborn in flame and blood and would do whatever it took to keep her baby safe.

"Geez sis, I didn't…" Roman cut off as Lucia looked at him. When he wisely dropped his eyes, Lucia returned to the desk with the pile of food and sat down. Feeling surprisingly better, she took a big bite of a doughnut and savored it. Now, she could finally enjoy her meal.

# CHAPTER FIFTEEN

"It's a little off," Steph said, cocking her head to the side as she appraised the angel from below.

"Looks fine to me," Michael replied, shifting his weight carefully on the rickety old ladder. It creaked loudly, a reminder that even in its heyday it hadn't been built to support his weight.

"That's because you don't see things the way I do," Steph replied, smiling.

"What does that mean?" Michael asked distractedly as he studied the angel topping their humble Christmas tree. He would have preferred an artificial tree, but Steph had insisted on a real one. He didn't see why it mattered but if it made her happy, then he was happy. He just hoped she didn't ask where he had gotten it from, though there was a definite possibility that she would appreciate his back to nature solution.

"Just that we have different approaches to life, that's all," Steph said with a secretive smile.

"I see," Michael said, knowing he wouldn't get much more of an explanation out of her. Steph loved being mysterious.

Steph cocked her head to the right, humming under her breath. "A little more to the left."

Michael gently grabbed the pine frond under the angel and slowly bent it until Steph smacked her lips and proclaimed, "Perfect!"

He quickly climbed down the ladder before she changed her mind again and stepped back to get a better look at the angel. Yep, definitely crooked.

"Do you like it?" Stephanie asked, and Michael could tell she seriously wanted his opinion.

He looked at the ornaments decorating the tree, an eclectic combination of hand me downs and brand new, this being their first Christmas together after all. "It looks great," Michael said and then purposely began to frown, looking the tree up and down.

"What is it?" Steph asked, looking worried.

"It's not perfect, though. Seems to be missing something."

"What?" She asked with a catch in her voice.

Michael looked around the room, realizing he'd have to change his approach a little. The last thing he wanted to do was upset her. He needed to get her laughing. "I'm not sure. The tree is gorgeous, but…"

"It just seems to be missing something." Steph finished as if she could see it herself. She scowled, biting her lip as she studied the tree.

Michael tried hard to keep a straight face. He made a great show of looking around them and feigned a great sigh. "Maybe it's the room."

"The room?" She asked with a bigger frown.

"The, uh, ambiance."

Steph laughed. "Michael, how do you even know that word?"

"Must have heard it from one of your house improvement shows."

"Home improvement, huh? That's probably it. So, what's wrong with the *ambiance*? She asked with a giggle.

He looked around the room and focused on the Christmas tree again. "Maybe it's the tree after all." He said, stirring the pot to drive Steph a little crazier. He needed her off kilter if he was going to pull this off.

"Michael! You're just messing with me now, aren't you?" Steph asked. He turned away, nearly losing his composure. "Ha! I knew it." she squealed with delight. Steph picked up a throw pillow and mimed throwing it at him in disgust. "Brat."

"Beautiful." He replied and saw her melt a little.

"So, the tree really is perfect then?"

"Oh yeah, it's gorgeous."

"There you go, using fancy words again."

"Yeah, fancy that."

"A Christmas miracle."

Michael snorted. "I wouldn't call it that." *Not yet, anyway.*

"And the room's perfect too?"

He made an exaggerated display of studying the living room. "I guess."

"You guess!" She punched him softly on the arm and then danced away when he tried to hug her. She gave him a wistful look. "I wish other people could see you like this. Especially my family."

Michael shrugged and looked over at the tree. "How about we plug this thing in?"

Steph gave him a coy look that said; I know that you're changing the subject, but I will let you get away with it—this time. "Care to do the honors?"

He reached down behind the tree and switched on the power strip. The Christmas tree lit up, its lights slowly waxing and waning. He held his arm out to Steph, and she snuggled under it, wrapping her arms around his waist. They stood there, taking in the moment. "Perfect." Steph breathed.

"Well, almost," Michael said, deciding it was time.

Steph shoved herself away enough so that she could look up at him. "Oh, don't start that up again."

"No, I'm serious."

"Really." She said with a giggle, drawing out the word. "What is it this time? I swear if you use a phrase like feng shui, I will-"

"You."

"Me?"

"You're not perfect."

Steph started giggling again. "Yeah, well, you should have known that from the moment you met me."

"You're missing something."

"Missing something?" She did a cursory glance at herself. "Don't seem to be."

Michael went over to his coat hanging over a chair. He took a deep breath and then pulled out a small box hiding underneath it. He noticed his hand was shaking. He tried to regain his composure and then turned around to show it to Steph.

"What's this?" She gasped, her eyes widening in surprise.

"Something to commemorate our first Christmas together. He wanted their first Christmas together to be special, especially since Steph loved the holidays so much.

"Commemorate, huh?" She said as he handed her the intricately wrapped box. "There you go with those words again."

"Fancy." He agreed.

She started to open the lid and then gave him a suspicious look. "My mom helped you, didn't she?"

"Maybe." The idea had been his, but Steph's mother had helped fill in the details. The next part was all him, however. "Open it."

Steph carefully pried the lid off and gave a small gasp as she pulled out a small porcelain teapot.

"You like it?"

"Love it!" She said, setting it down on her coffee table carefully. "My mom definitely helped you. No way you picked this out on your own."

"Think you know me, do you?" He replied, grinning.

"Yeah, you're pretty predictable." She replied as she picked up the teapot again. A soft rattle came from it. "Oh no! I hope it's not broken." She gave him a worried look. Michael struggled not to smile, knowing what was coming next. Steph lifted the lid to look inside and gasped very loudly. She slowly pulled out a silver chain with a gold ring attached to the end of it. "Oh, Michael." She said in a stunned voice.

Michael got down on one knee and then clasped her tiny hand with both of his. Stephanie giggled and then suddenly burst into tears. She looked so sad that he hesitated before rushing into the next part.

"Will you marry me?"

"Yes! Oh yes!" She said with a huge smile and jumped into his arms. She gave him a quick, hard kiss on the lips and then hugged him fiercely to her. Kissing the top of his head, she said in her sweet, angelic voice, "I love you."

"Love you too," Michael replied, and Steph's hug tightened in response. Then, unable to resist, he asked, "Still think you know me?"

Laughing, she tried to wiggle out of his arms, but he pulled her to him and stole a kiss. Steph resisted only for a moment and then returned the kiss with enthusiasm. She hugged him again and whispered in his ear, "Brat."

# CHAPTER SIXTEEN

"Brat." The whispered word echoed as Michael woke. Groaning softly, he opened his eyes and let the cold reality of his surroundings chase away the unwanted warm memories of the fading dream. Best not to think about her, the past, or any of it. These dreams of the past were worse than any nightmare he had ever experienced. He preferred the nightmares to the dreams; at least they reflected reality.

Michael stood up and stretched, wincing at the stiffness in his back. After Lucia had yelled at him, he had decided it best to give her some time to calm down. He had spent the remaining daylight yesterday exploring the building, a utility station of some sort. Later, he spent the night sleeping in the hall with his back propped against the control room door.

Michael picked up his rifle and machete and made his way down the hall, quickly removing the makeshift tripwires he'd set the night before with some string he had found in a drawer. He passed several small box-like offices he had searched the day before. He didn't know how anyone could work in such a small, windowless space with barely enough room for a desk, let alone a person sitting behind it. It hadn't made sense to him before the world had gone to pot, and he still didn't understand it.

He walked up some stairs and opened another door, then took a right into a room almost twice the size of the offices. In it sat a lone small table with several worn chairs around it and two vending machines. Across the room, uncomfortably close to the table, was a cheap wooden door that led to a bathroom. Michael wondered how the workers could stand to have toilets so close to where they ate.

The water had long ago evaporated in the pipes and now noxious sewer gas emanated from the sink and toilet. Holding his shirt over his nose and mouth, Michael took a deep breath and held it, then quickly walked to the two vending machines. The first one was half full with sugary beverages, and while the other held snacks, it must have been due for a restock because it was practically empty. They would need to leave the building soon to find something more sustainable.

Michael unlocked the door to the snacks with a key he'd found while searching the desks and picked up the four remaining packages of cupcakes. He grabbed four bottles of soda from the other and quickly exited the room, then dropped the shirt from his face. Michael exhaled explosively and then took in a deep breath of clean air.

He made his way back to the control door and was raising his free hand to knock when he stopped to reconsider. If yesterday was anything to go by, Lucia was primed to give him another earful about being out all night this morning. No doubt explaining to her that he'd been safe, that sleeping in one dark room was the same as another, would be ignored.

For a brief moment, Michael was tempted to prolong the inevitable by scouting the building and the surrounding woods again but dismissed the thought with a sigh. He couldn't risk Lucia opening the door to find him gone. She might go looking for him, which could end poorly for both of them. Or, worse— because there always seemed to be a worse to consider these days —he could come back and find that something had killed Lucia and her baby. Oh, and hopefully Roman too, if that was the case.

Maybe they weren't awake yet. He put his ear against the metal door and soon heard a scraping sound followed by a squeak. There was definitely someone awake. Michael braced himself and then knocked softly on the door.

Several seconds passed, and Michael heard a surly whisper, "Who's there?" Roman's voice.

"Michael."

Roman grumbled something in response, then the dead bolt was unlocked after a long pause. The door opened a crack and a shotgun was shoved in Michael's face. He didn't dare move as the door inched wider, revealing Roman. The boy glared at him with bleary red eyes, then looked back at his sister sleeping on the couch.

Michael contemplated knocking the shotgun away while the boy was distracted, but Roman sighed, lowering the gun. "Be very quiet," he said in a hushed voice, motioning to Lucia. "Believe me, you don't want to wake her."

Apparently, Michael hadn't been the only one to get an earful last night. He nodded and slipped past Roman, resisting the urge to plant a fist into the boy's ribs. Stepping softly, he dropped off the food at the desk and silently made his way to his usual spot at the far side of the room. He propped the rifle and machete in the corner, then slid down the wall until he was sitting on the ground.

Roman plopped down in one of the chairs by the desk and winced as the chair creaked loudly. He shot an alarmed look at his sister and let out an exaggerated sigh of relief when she didn't move. He picked up a cupcake and tried to slowly open the package, causing the cellophane to crinkle loudly. The boy seemed incapable of being quiet.

"Probably best to let her have those." Michael said in a low voice.

Roman's head shot up. "What, why? There isn't anymore?" He whispered loudly.

Michael shook his head. "Have some soda instead."

"Great," Roman said glumly, picking up a bottle.

Michael settled back against the wall and began ruminating about what their little group needed to do next. Obviously, they needed to leave soon to find more food. He could try hunting with the rifle, but Lucia required more than a simple protein diet. A gunshot could also bring a zombie swarm down on them. That reminded Michael that they had a handful of bullets, cartridges, and shells between the three of them. They needed to find more.

They also needed to rebuild their supplies and find a more secure location. A lone house would be relatively safe but the chances of finding ammo and camping equipment would be slim. They could try searching several houses but that increased the odds of encountering something nasty and lethal. No, Michael decided reluctantly, a town was the best place to find everything they needed. Zombies would be worse, but he was confident he could get in and out without issue if it were just him. Lucia would probably insist on coming along, but after what had happened in Bethsdale, he wasn't going to back down.

He would leave her tied up in a house with Roman if he had to.

Where should they go after that? The past several months had only been about surviving day to day. What was the big picture? Find a safe house and hunker down for the winter, hoping that nothing came knocking and that the three of them didn't freeze to death? Should they head south out of the mountains, avoiding the winter storms but increasing their exposure to zombies or worse? Michael had a feeling in his gut that South was the answer, but it was hardly tangible enough to be trusted. Could he trust it after what happened to Rachel?

Michael thrust that line of thinking far away and looked at Lucia slumbering on the couch. She was the unknown factor in all of this. Regardless of the outcome, her pregnancy would affect every decision he made. Would she be able to keep up if they chose to go south? More importantly, when was she due? It would be very bad if Lucia suddenly went into labor in a field somewhere, especially if there were zombies nearby.

A rustle came from the couch and Lucia sat up, rubbing at her eyes with her hands. Roman turned slowly in his chair and gave his sister a cautious look. Lucia dropped her hands and quickly peered around the room as if looking for something. When she saw Michael, her face lit up with a big smile. "You came back!"

Michael was so surprised by the girl's reaction that he could only nod.

"Big ugly came back a few minutes after you fell asleep last night," Roman said, spinning an empty pencil jar in his hands.

Michael viewed the boy askance. *Why is he covering for me?*

"Oh good, 'cause I was worried," Lucia said. Then her smile faded. "Michael... I'm... I'm sorry about what I said last night. I...

overreacted."

There was a loud rattle as Roman nearly dropped the pencil jar. The boy was staring open mouthed at his sister but quickly shut it when Lucia glanced at him.

Michael watched all of this with fascination. What had happened after he had left? Lucia turned back, giving him a tentative smile. Sibling dynamics aside, it was probably best to make peace and reciprocate. "I... was the one that was out of line." He offered. "I should have let you know what my plans were. I'm just... not used to having others around."

Lucia nodded slightly with every word Michael said, giving him the distinct impression that she was he was counting his words. Michael dismissed the thought as ridiculous. Why would she do something as silly as that?

"Forgiven!" Lucia exclaimed, favoring him with another smile. Roman cleared his throat loudly, and she turned to her brother with a grimace and snapped. "What?" Yesterday's Lucia was still in there, at least where her brother was concerned. What had happened between the two of them? As far as he could tell, her intentions towards him were real and not a mask, but as soon as her attention was directed towards Roman, they switched instantly to barely contained contempt and anger.

Roman hesitated, then said, "Just thought if you were handing out apologies, sis that..."

"Yes?" There were ominous implications when she spoke with that word.

Roman cleared his throat again, quickly glancing between his sister and Michael. "Never mind." He mumbled under his breath. He stared at the door to the ramp for a moment, looking lost. He grimaced, shook his head, and started spinning the pencil jar again.

Lucia turned back to Michael and asked, "So, what do we do now?"

"You get to eat," Michael said, standing up. "There are some cupcakes on the desk."

"Yay!" Lucia said with a tinny enthusiasm. She pushed herself to her feet with some effort, then waddled over to the desk. "Aren't you guys going to eat too?" She asked, surveying the cupcakes with a predatory gleam in her eyes.

"Already ate," Michael said.

"Yup." Roman quickly added. "Sure did."

"Goody, more for me and the baby," Lucia said, tearing open one of the packages. She took a large bite and then asked thickly around a mouthful of pastry, "So, we're leaving today?"

"As soon as you're done."

"No more food?"

"Nope."

Lucia's eyes bounced between them and then narrowed. "Then you guys didn't eat anything this morning?" She asked with a slight edge to her voice. Roman cleared his throat and started intently studying the pencil jar. Lucia's eyes flicked over to Michael, expecting an answer.

Michael didn't answer, but he didn't look away either.

"I see," Lucia said, placing the half-eaten cupcake on its cellophane.

"Does that mean I can have one?" Roman asked hopefully.

"No!" Lucia and Michael said at the same time.

Roman threw his arms up in abject defeat. "You two are driving me nuts."

Lucia spared a frown for her brother and then turned back

to Michael. "I don't like being lied to."

"Then don't be difficult."

Roman whistled and dramatically rolled his chair a few feet away from his sister.

"I'm difficult," Lucia stated, the words clipped.

"Right now, you are. You and your baby need the food more than we do."

"And you don't?" Lucia asked, looking down at the cupcake in her hands. Tearing off a piece, she said, "Can't have my mighty 'protectors' fainting from starvation during a zombie attack." She gave Michael a hurt look. "You could have just told me the truth. I just may have agreed with you."

"I wasn't willing to take that chance. You need to eat, and you haven't always been rational."

"So, I am irrational too?

"At times, yes."

Roman, who had been miming eating a bag of popcorn as he watched them, let out another low whistle.

"Shut up!" Lucia screamed at her brother, slamming both palms on the table. Roman abruptly reclined back in his chair and became very interested in the ceiling. Lucia took another bite of her cupcake and then asked quietly with her eyes downcast, "Anything else that I'm doing wrong?"

"Just that you need to listen to me. Otherwise, I'm gone."

Lucia put the last piece of cupcake on the desk. "Not very subtle, are you?"

Michael didn't say anything; this was far from the first time he'd been accused of being blunt. Steph had actually liked that quality in him for some reason.

"Okay, how about this," Lucia said firmly, "I'll promise to

listen to you...more, if you promise me one thing in return."

"And that is?"

Lucia gave him a very direct look. "That you stop threatening to leave every two minutes."

"Twice. It's only been twice."

"Promise." Lucia insisted.

"Fine." Michael acquiesced. He would simply stop threatening to leave and wouldn't give Lucia any warning if he did.

"And I can't be held accountable if I'm 'irrational.'" She said with finger quotes. "I'm pregnant, dammit."

"Fine, then I can't be held accountable when you're irrational either. I will do what I have to do to keep you and the baby alive."

Lucia suddenly surprised him with another brilliant smile. "Deal!"

Roman let out a long, exasperated breath. "Finally."

"Oh, and I am not responsible for my brother," Lucia added.

"Neither am I."

"Hey, I am responsible for myself." Roman protested.

"Deal." Michael and Lucia said at the same time and Lucia grinned at him. Roman gave them both a look like they were crazy and rolled his eyes.

"Okay," Lucia said, "What's the plan? I mean, I get that we have to leave, so where are we going to go?"

"That's what I want to discuss with you," Michael said. "When are you due?"

"In a couple of months, Mr. Blunt."

"Good," Michael said, ignoring the girl's levity. "We may

have to walk for a while to find another place to stay. Do you think you can keep up?"

Lucia ate the last little bit of cupcake and then sucked the crumbs from her fingers. "I'm going to have to, aren't I?" She looked down at her pregnant stomach, and her face became determined. "I will keep up."

"Good, then let's go," Michael said, walking over to the corner to pick up his things.

"Now?" Lucia asked, her eyes widening.

"Best not to waste daylight."

"I guess I'm ready then," Lucia said, pushing herself off the chair with some effort. "Need to find a restroom first."

"The bathroom here is pretty bad. You may want to use a bush outside instead," Michael said as he unlocked and opened the door. Lucia started to follow him through and then stopped as if she'd forgotten something. She turned and looked back at the door to the ramp with a sad expression.

"Lucia?" Michael prompted

"What?" Lucia asked, distracted. "Wait, oh no. No bush— not going to happen." She said, giving Michael her full attention. "You guys can go find a tree if you want to. There is no way this pregnant body is squatting behind another bush if I can help it. I need a toilet."

Michael led them down the hall past the small offices. Roman stuck his head in one, and his eyes crinkled in abhorrent distaste. "People worked like this? Really? Definitely not for me!" He declared loudly, backing out as if the career choice was somehow contagious.

*Great.* Michael thought acerbically. *We finally have something in common.*

They continued up the stairs and Lucia slowed down as they approached the break room. "Ugh! What's that smell?" She looked up at Michael, her eyes watering. "Did someone make a mess in the bathroom or something?"

He shook his head. "Nothing like that. The water's evaporated in the pipes."

"Oh, and that makes it smell this bad?"

"Yes."

When they entered the break room, Lucia quickly covered her nose and mouth with her hand. "Horrible! Disgusting!" She exclaimed. "Smells like someone murdered a toilet. Gag a muffin!"

"Gag a maggot." Roman corrected quietly under his breath.

As Lucia approached the bathroom door, her steps became tremulous. Grasping the handle, she looked back at Michael and then forlornly at the hallway behind them as if second-guessing using a bush for a privy. She took a deep breath and, gagging a little, opened the bathroom door. "Oh! That made it worse. A lot worse! I don't know if I can do this here."

"Try covering your mouth and nose with your shirt," Michael suggested, doing the same with his shirt. Lucia quickly followed his example.

"Any better?" Roman asked, holding his coat over his nose.

Lucia shook her head. Her eyes were watering a little. "No, not really."

"You could always use one of those offices or something."

Lucia lowered her shirt enough to give her brother a scathing look, then quickly covered up again. "No, I'm going to use the toilet." Rounding her shoulders, she took a step towards the bathroom and then stopped. "You guys need to leave 'cause there is no way I'm shutting this door."

"Gotcha," Roman said, heading towards the hallway.

"Wait, load up on fluids first," Michael said, walking over to the vending machines.

"Hurry." Lucia urged.

Michael and Roman quickly unloaded the machine, stuffing various beverages in their coat pockets. Between the two of them, they had enough soda for a few days if they were careful.

Michael left the room, and behind him heard Roman call out to his sister, "All yours. Enjoy!"

"Gee, thanks."

"Light a match," Roman suggested.

"I wish. Probably blow the building up."

The two of them made their way back to the stairs to wait. Michael walked around the corner to give Lucia more privacy, and Roman lounged against the wall, lost in thought.

"The smell is making my nose burn," Lucia's muffled voice came down the hall.

"Try breathing through your mouth," Roman suggested.

"Aw, yuck!" Lucia shrieked. "Now I can taste it!" A few seconds later, there was a retching sound. "I think I'm going to throw up."

"Well, you're in the right place." Roman snickered.

"Shut it! Ugh, you're not helping." Lucia yelled. Then, in a lower voice as if to herself, she began chanting, "Wish I was a guy, wish I was a guy." The chanting went on for a few seconds, and then hearing a squeal, Michael looked around the corner to see Lucia barreling down the hall, moving faster than he'd ever seen her.

"Hey, you forgot to flush," Roman said with a big grin to his sister when she came to a stop in front of them.

"I hate you." Lucia told her brother, "Deeply, truly hate you. Just so you know."

"Love you too sis," Roman said, grinning.

Lucia punched her brother hard on the arm and quickly walked past the two of them. "Let's get out of here."

Several hours later, their small group was only about a mile or so from the factory. Despite following a relatively level dirt maintenance road, Lucia's pace was agonizingly slow, and she had to rest frequently. She was obviously getting frustrated with herself, but aside from an occasional emphasized grunt, she didn't complain.

Roman, on the other hand, seemed unable to stop. He complained about being hungry, cold, the weather, and his feet. Each topic segued into another in an endless loop. He finally crossed the line when he began to gripe about his sister stopping for another break. Lucia's response was simple and direct. She picked up a larger stone from the road and chucked it at her brother's head, narrowly missing it. Roman cut off mid-sentence with a yelp, then seeing his sister's stormy face, decided to silently stand far off to the side. When they began walking again, Roman took point several dozen feet ahead of them. He started complaining again immediately but was far enough away that only an occasional word could be made out.

Michael kept a close watch on the woods around them as they walked down the dirt road. Something felt wrong, and the sensation had been building since they had left the factory. There was an energy to the air that seemed oddly familiar, yet he couldn't place it. Michael looked up at the sky, feeling like he was missing something obvious.

"I need another break." Lucia gasped, limping towards a fallen tree lying next to the road.

"Roman!" Michael called out.

Roman looked back in disbelief. "Again?" He asked in a pique of fit. "Of course again!" He answered himself. Crossing his arms tightly across his chest until they bent his slight frame, he glared off into the woods, continuing the conversation with himself, occasionally emphasizing a choice profane word.

"Doesn't seem to understand, does he?" Michael said, sitting down on the far end of the log. He pulled a soda from a pocket and gave it to a grateful Lucia.

"Oh, he does. Believe me, he does, yet he always thinks I can do better for some reason." She paused and took a long pull from the bottle. "Like, I am slowing him down on purpose or something. I'm sure in his rabid mind that it's my fault for putting him out because I am pregnant. Never mind that a few months ago, before all this, well, crap happened, he was over the moon with the news that he was going to be an uncle."

"Want me to shut him up?"

"Tempting. Very tempting," Lucia said with a wan smile. "But then he'd be the one slowing us down. He's just hungry, that's all. Makes him insufferable."

"He must be hungry all the time."

"True."

They sat silently for a while. Michael listened as Lucia's breathing slowly evened out. She appeared to be on the verge of exhaustion, and he doubted that they would get another mile out of her today. He looked up at the sun overhead and frowned.

They were losing time. The wrong feeling was stronger now, and the air seemed to have a strange electricity that innervated his arms and legs, making them tingle. Michael's intuition was hitting him over the head like a frying pan, telling him that something was wrong. Very wrong.

"Do you feel that?" Lucia asked, rubbing her arms briskly and shivering.

"Do you?" Michael replied, surprised.

"Yeah, for like the last hour or so. I wrote it off as having a pregnant moment, a weird one. Maybe a bad case of the heebie jeebies, you know? But it seems to be getting worse."

"Any idea what it could be?"

She started to shrug, then stopped and squinted up at the clear blue sky. "Strange. It kind of reminds me of how it sometimes gets before a bad storm but times ten."

Michael's eyes went wide. *That's exactly what it is!* He jumped to his feet and whipped his head back and forth, scanning for clouds.

"What's wrong?" Lucia asked worriedly, looking up at him with concern.

"You're right, a storm is coming."

"You sure?" Lucia studied the sky. "I don't see any clouds."

"I'm sure," Michael growled, pulling the girl to her feet.

"How do you know?" She leaned heavily on him, teetering.

"I just do."

"Okay, so what should we do? Head back to the factory?" Lucia asked glumly, looking at the road behind them.

"We don't have any choice. There may not be anything else out here for miles."

"Okay, then let's get Roman and…" Lucia's words fell away

as she looked at the road ahead. "He's gone!"

# CHAPTER SEVENTEEN

"Stay here!" Michael growled, pulling the rifle free from his shoulder. He cursed as he took off towards where they had seen Roman last, doubting something had gotten the boy in broad daylight. More likely Roman had simply wandered off, forcing Michael to find the idiot instead of shelter from the approaching storm.

"Roman!" Michael heard Lucia scream behind him. Glancing back as he ran, Michael wasn't surprised to see Lucia hobbling after him. Any thought of stopping her was muted by the angry look of determination on her face.

Up ahead, Roman stepped out of the woods and gave them a lazy beckoning wave, then headed back into the trees. Well, at least he wasn't dead, though that could change when Lucia caught up to him. "Wait!" Lucia screamed, but Roman ignored her.

*Must run in the family,* Michael thought wryly as he reached the spot where Roman had been seconds before. He discovered a well-used dirt path snaking off into the woods. Roman was already out of sight. He started to follow, then turned to see Lucia limping up behind him, red-faced and puffing hard, looking as though she was about to collapse.

Switching his rifle off to his dominant hand, Michael met her and offered his arm for support. She clamped down on it with angry, claw-like hands and said, panting, "I'm going to kill him."

Michael was more curious than angry at this point. The dirt path had to lead somewhere and if it was some kind of shelter, then it didn't matter how it'd been found. The storm was coming and there wasn't enough time to return to the utility building. They started down the trail, making slow progress despite Michael feeling the need to hurry. Lucia grew weaker and heavier as she relied on him more for support. Finally, they came around a bend and found Roman standing at the crest of a hill. He saw them and excitedly urged them to move faster with his arm.

"Oh, you better believe I'm coming," Lucia hissed. Letting go of Michael's arm, she stomped towards her brother, her small hands clenched into tight fists. "Roman!" She shrieked. "I'm going to ki...oh wow!" Lucia gasped. Only steps behind, Michael was also stunned at what he saw below.

At the bottom of the hill, nestled by a half ring of trees, was some kind of camping resort backed by a massive lake that mirrored the sky, mountains, and trees around it in crystal clear definition. A large two-story building, probably a hunting lodge, was built into a small hill at the lake's edge. Trails led like the spokes of a wheel from the main building past cabins and other small buildings into the woods beyond.

"I'm thinking it's some kind of summer camp, maybe a scout camp or hunters lodge," Roman offered, pointing down at the buildings.

"Roman, if you ever wander off again, I will kill you," Lucia said in a distracted voice as she studied the buildings below.

"Um… okay?" Roman replied, giving his sister a nervous look and edging away slightly. Clearing his throat, he quickly added, "I think there has to be food down there, maybe in the main building."

"Oh, I hope so," Lucia said, rubbing her stomach. "Think anybody is down there?"

"Haven't seen any movement down there so far," Roman replied with a grin. "Looks safe to me."

"Uh-huh. Sure." Lucia said flatly and promptly asked Michael. "What do *you* think?"

Roman gave his sister an angry, hurt look and started to say something but choked on the words when Lucia, still keeping her eyes on Michael, reached out and made an odd twisting motion with her hand. Roman quickly backpedaled out of range of his sister's arm, cupping his left ear protectively. Lucia gave her brother a knowing look. "That's what you get for blatantly trying to distract me with the possibility there may be food. Don't think I didn't catch that. I'm still angry with you for wandering off… Don't test me!" She snapped and turned back to Michael. "Well?"

Michael quickly pulled his rifle free and glassed the buildings below. He didn't see any sign that anyone or anything occupied the camp. Promising, but that didn't mean that there weren't zombies or worse hiding in the buildings. "Looks safe on the surface level."

He would've preferred to watch the camp for a while just to be safe, but they didn't have the luxury of being patient or careful. He could feel the storm growing like an angry mass behind them. There was a faint odor of burnt umber in the air, ozone saturated with frozen water molecules. Michael hoped they wouldn't be snowed in, though down looking at the main lodge, he had to admit there were worse places to wait out a storm—if they had enough supplies. At this altitude, they could be snowed in for weeks. Hopefully, Roman was right and they would find food and lots of it.

"Guess we'll find out," Michael said, checking the rifle. Five rounds left. Lucia and Roman had about the same. "I'm going to head down… alone." He decided as he said it.

"Not happening." Lucia quickly interjected.

Michael turned to face her directly. "You promised to follow my directions, remember? You two will stay up here just in case things go bad down there."

"I thought you said it was safe."

"No, I said we'll find out, and this is how we'll find out. By my going alone."

"Okay!" Lucia snapped, throwing her hands up in the air. She looked back down at the buildings below. "Salvation or damnation." She said in a soft, wistful voice. "Why does it always have to be that way, now?" Her eyes fluttered closed, and she let out a frustrated sigh as her shoulders dropped in defeat. "Do what you want." Then she gave Michael a tight-lipped smile. "But if things go south down there, you best believe we are coming to help."

Behind Lucia, Roman shook his head slightly and made a small indication with his finger that they would remain on the hill. *Good.* Michael thought though he had to wonder if Roman could actually stop his capricious sister from trying to save him. "I'll signal when it's safe to come down."

"Um," Lucia said, still looking unhappy about him going alone. Her eyes oscillated between the two of them. "Um. Um.

Ugh!"

"Just spit it out, sis," Roman said.

"No," Lucia said as if answering an annoying question. "Um, just had a thought... I hate pregnancy brain so much... but no, that's not the thought... oh!" Her eyes lit up. "Michael, what if you traded your rifle with Roman so he can cover you?"

Roman's head popped up, and he looked at Michael in amusement. Michael could tell by the knowing look in the boy's eyes that he'd already guessed the answer.

"Not happening," Michael said.

"Nope. Never." Roman added, shaking his head solemnly. "No bueno."

"Oh, you two frustrate me so much!" Lucia said, her face reddening with anger. "You guys need to work things out."

"Not happening," Michael repeated.

"Nope. Never." Roman said. "No bueno."

Lucia let out a scream of pure frustration.

"Welp," Roman said, looking down at the buildings below. "If there is anything down there, they now know we're coming."

"Oh no!" Lucia cried, slapping her hands over her mouth. She looked at Michael with dawning horror. "I am so, so, sorry."

Michael carefully watched the camp below. Nothing had stirred as far as he could tell. Shrugging, he said, "It is what it is." Not much he could do about it now.

"Sorry," Lucia repeated, her face red again but this time for a different reason. "Maybe you could give me the rifle, and I could cover...," she offered weakly, trailing off at the end without conviction in her voice.

Michael shook his head.

"Nope. Never." Roman said. "No buen--."

Lucia cut her brother off with a hard backhanded fist to the chest. It connected with a loud, hollow thump that caused Roman to grunt in pain. "Shut it." She hissed.

"Gotcha." Roman wheezed, rubbing his chest. "Ow."

Michael quickly glassed the camp again. He wished again that there was more time to watch, maybe even approach it from a different angle, but his gut was telling him that they needed to find shelter fast. If something was down there waiting for him, then so be it. "I'll wave if it's clear."

"Be careful," Lucia said in a soft, urgent voice.

"I will."

"Good," Lucia said, rubbing her arms. "The storm must be coming fast 'cause I just got a chill."

"Storm?" Roman asked, eyeing his sister askance, then looked up at the cloudless sky. "What storm?"

"Stay here and stay out of sight," Michael told them. With that, he started down the hill. Behind him, he heard the twins bickering in hushed tones, but their voices were soon lost in the rising blustery ambiance.

His approach to the camp was fast yet studious. The hill afforded little cover, so Michael wanted to get downhill to the buildings as fast as he could. Halfway down, he thought about stopping to scope out the camp again. *If I do, I may miss something in the peripheral.*

At the bottom of the hill, Michael stepped onto one of the trails leading to the main lodge and started to follow it. Up ahead, two clusters of cabins were split by the trail and Michael slowed to a stop as he approached them. With only a few rounds left, he was in bad shape if he encountered anything. He had the machete as a backup but preferred to keep anything at range if possible. The cabins were small and likely only had several sets of cots inside them. There probably wasn't anything waiting in them. If there were zombies or humans, the tall weeds would have been trampled. The camp looked untouched, but he wasn't going to let his guard down.

He continued past the cabins, following the winding trail until he reached the main lodge. The building was huge, probably between fifteen and twenty-thousand square feet. It towered over the camp two stories high, looking more like a small hotel than a lodge. Several large windows with thick winter blinds sat on either side of the main doors, looking out over the West side of the camp. A long stack of wood nestled up to the windows and ran the long length of the wall. Three large brick chimneys poked out of the roof. No smoke, he noted, though that didn't necessarily mean that the massive building was uninhabited.

Michael reached the foot of the stairs and turned back to the camp to reassess it. The wind was picking up, causing the tall weeds and trees to undulate back and forth. Seeing nothing of note, he glanced up the hill at where the twins were hiding and was relieved to see they were out of sight. They were actually following his instructions for once, a minor miracle, that.

Michael turned back to the lodge and cautiously made his way up the wood stairs, keeping an eye on the dark windows for any sign of movement. He stopped on the large deck at the top and studied the large double doors a few feet before him. *Well, intuition, is it safe or not?* He thought as he tried to peer through the dark-tinted glass without success. Safe or not safe? Nothing. He felt nothing. The building was likely safe, but he couldn't be sure until he went in. Schrödinger's building, he thought dryly. It was both safe and unsafe until he went inside.

He swapped the rifle for the machete and then hesitated. There was a feeling of...

A hand clamped down on his shoulder, and Michael's muscle memory instantly took over. He pivoted hard, knocking the hand away, and had the machete up to strike before the initial shock had even registered.

"Michael!" Lucia screamed.

Looking down, he discovered that the body that he was about to hack into was Roman. The boy had fallen down and had his arms up in front of him for protection, a look of horror on his face. "Get away from me, you psycho!" He yelled, kicking at him. Michael quickly backed off, lowering the machete. How the hell had they made it down the hill so quickly?

Roman scrambled for his shotgun that he had dropped on the deck. As he picked it up, Lucia stepped between them, raising her arms up. "No fighting!"

"What is wrong with you, freak?" Roman shouted as he scrambled to his feet.

"I told you to stay on the hill!" Michael yelled back. "Can't you two follow simple instructions?"

"We did!" Roman yelled before Lucia cut him off with a hand gesture.

"We did." She said calmly, though her eyes were frightened. Frightened of what, him?

"No, you didn't," Michael replied before Lucia cut him off as well with her hand.

"Listen. We *did*. We watched you make your way through the camp, and then when you got in front of the lodge here, you just froze."

That didn't make any sense. "I... froze?"

Lucia nodded, fear in her eyes. "You just stood, staring at the building. Not moving. It was... weird."

"Creepy." Roman insisted. "Just call it what it is."

"Creepy." Lucia agreed apologetically.

"Sorry," Michael said, baffled. He turned to look at the lodge. "I was just... just trying to tell if the building is safe."

Roman snorted and said, "By staring at it for ten minutes?"

"What?" *Ten minutes? Had it been that long?* Roman had to be exaggerating. Michael could swear he had only been looking at the building for only a few seconds. He looked at Lucia for confirmation.

Lucia nodded again. She reached out to put a hand on him and then dropped it as if she thought better of it. "You okay?"

Michael rubbed his head in confusion. "Yeah, I was... lost in thought, I guess."

"I called out your name. Several times." It sounded like an accusation.

Had she? Michael wondered. He felt very confused. He hadn't heard a thing. "Maybe... maybe your voice was lost in the wind."

"From five feet away?" Roman snorted. "You don't happen to have narcolepsy, do yah?" He gave his sister a sardonic grin. "Imagine that, you having a narcoleptic protector. For some reason that strikes my funny bone just right." He gave an ugly chuckle.

"I don't have narcolepsy," Michael growled distractedly. *What the hell had happened then?*

"I don't find that funny at all, Roman." Lucia admonished

at the same time, her eyes never leaving Michael. "Are you sure you're okay?"

"I'm fine." Michael insisted, turning back to study the building. Had it done something to him?

"Do you think it's safe?" Lucia asked.

Michael heard the underlying question all too clearly. *Are you safe to be around?*

*Am I?* People tended to die around him, after all.

He was torn. If the building had affected him somehow, then they needed to leave as quickly as possible. A geist or some other unknown horror could be waiting inside. But the storm was approaching fast, and they needed shelter. Even if they stayed in one of the outlying cabins, they wouldn't last long in a blizzard, snowed in without any food or heat. Their best hope lay in front of them, but there was a good chance it might also kill them. Lucia had been right about their choices. Salvation or damnation, with only a slim difference between them. One extreme or the other, that's all that remained for them.

"Enough waiting, I'm starving," Roman said, shoving roughly past them.

"Wait!" Lucia called out. "Stop!"

Roman ran up the stairs, kicked one of the doors in, and stepped inside before they could stop him.

# CHAPTER EIGHTEEN

"Roman!" Lucia cried, taking a step towards the open door. Michael barred her way with his arm. "Wait." Lucia glared at him and pushed against his arm but he held firm. She finally gave up and instead held onto his arm for support, anxiously chewing on her lower lip. They both waited impatiently, Michael half expecting to see Roman's blood spray against the windows. The seconds ticked on onerously, and no sounds came from the lodge. Michael took a moment to look at the grounds. Usually, a place like this would be thick with hunters this time of year.

Lucia suddenly let go of his arm and put a hand to her mouth, retching a little. "Um," she said, swallowing hard. "I don't know how much more of this waiting I can take. It's making me nauseous."

Michael quickly directed Lucia to one of the stumps outlining the main path. "Stay here. I'll check on him." He told her and waited until she gave a curt nod. Rifle in hand, he cautiously made his way up to one of the big windows. The interior was dark and cavernous, with several rows of wooden tables surrounded by chairs.

Roman stepped into view; his movements were cautious,

not showing any of the bravado he had displayed only minutes before. That the boy hadn't been immediately torn apart was a good sign, though as far as Michael knew, he hadn't stepped into the deeper shadows yet. "He's alive."

Behind him, Lucia let out an explosive exhalation and started muttering under her breath in Spanish. It was so fervent that Michael wondered if it was prayer, swearing, or a mixture of both. Roman began to clear the large room in an oddly familiar manner with his shotgun.

"Your brother served in the military?" Michael asked, looking back at Lucia in surprise.

"The Army," Lucia replied. She snorted and added, "Before he went AWOL." She then grimaced and rubbed her belly as if it hurt her.

"Why?"

"Because he's Roman!" Lucia snapped. "Sorry, I'm—no! I am not sorry. I can't stand this. I need to come closer."

Michael considered for a moment before waving her forward. If nothing had torn Roman apart, they should be relatively safe on the deck. *Hopefully.*

Lucia settled in next to him, holding his arm again as she peered through the dark glass. Roman was following the edge of sunlight projected through the windows and stopped by a shadow covered doorway. He considered it for only a second before stepping over the line and disappearing from sight. Michael shook his head in disbelief. The boy either had guts or was a complete and utter imbecile. Michael was more inclined to believe the latter.

Several long minutes passed, and Lucia started muttering again. Michael didn't know much Spanish, but he was certain she was swearing this time. Finally, she broke off and asked harshly in English, "Where is he?"

"Here." A voice whispered loudly beside them.

They both jumped and turned to find Roman standing beside them with a huge grin on his face. Michael had his machete half drawn, ready to strike. He eased his grip on the handle but didn't let go.

"Don't you dare do that again!" Lucia yelled, trying to slap her brother. Roman laughed as he fended her off.

"What?" Roman asked, laughing. "Sneaking up on you?"

"Yes—no. I mean no. Breaking into the lodge without knowing if it was safe first."

"How else are we supposed to discover whether it's safe, huh?" Roman said, looking over at Michael. "Stare at the door for another ten minutes?" He added with a smirk,

"So, you're sure it's safe then?" Lucia asked in a voice that plainly said she didn't trust the answer.

Roman gave his sister an irritated look and then pointed at himself with both thumbs. "I'm still alive, aren't I?"

Lucia gave him a flat stare.

Roman snickered and continued on in a droning tone as if reciting from a list, "No sign of cannibal bikers, zombies, poltergeists, wolves, or anything else that goes bump in the night." Then his face and tone brightened. "Oh, and by the way, I was right about the food. I found a kitchen—a big one—with a fully stocked pantry."

"Wait," Michael interjected. "You searched this building, top to bottom, in five minutes?"

Roman shrugged, "I searched the first floor, more or less. Basement doors are locked."

"More or less," Michael repeated flatly. "What about the second one?"

Roman's expression became confused. "Second what?"

"Floor, you idiot!" Lucia snapped. "The second floor."

"Oh… there isn't one."

"What does that even mean?" Lucia demanded as Michael looked in disbelief at the building towering over them.

Roman grinned his joker grin. "You'll see. Come on. Easier to show than to tell." He started moving towards the front door.

"Michael?" Lucia asked. Roman first looked confused then hurt as he realized what his sister was asking. He flashed angry eyes at Michael.

Michael sighed. "He survived walking around in there, so the lobby is most likely safe-"

"Good enough for me," Lucia said, roughly shoving past her brother before Michael could stop her.

"Wait!" he yelled, but she ignored him. The fool girl was just as crazy as her brother. "Stay in the lobby. I need to check the rest of the building." He said awkwardly to her back. So much for listening. *Damn it!*

"Roman, you better not be lying about that food," Lucia called over her shoulder as she went in.

"I'm not," Roman said, giving his sister a big grin. He then turned to Michael. The grin became commiserative as if to say he knew how Michael felt, but then the humor faded from his eyes. *We have unfinished business,* those eyes promised. "After you." The boy gestured towards the open doorway.

Michael tightened his grip on the machete and walked past Roman, never breaking eye contact with the boy. Roman's grin widened as he followed him in.

"This place is wonderful!" Lucia exclaimed, doing a slow pirouette as she took it all in. "Well, except for all of the dead animals."

The room was huge, with vaulted ceilings and enough seating for dozens of people. Roman had been right, Michael admitted reluctantly. There wasn't a second floor. Hunting trophies adorned the walls amid antique camping and hunting gear, and various mounted animals stared down at them with uncaring glass eyes. Above their heads was a massive chandelier made out of various animal horns.

A massive two-story stone fireplace dominated the far end of the hall, with an enormous moose head hanging above the hearth as the room's crowning glory. Below it was a wide stone shelf covered with a collection of trophies and a mixture of well-used oil and hurricane lanterns. Within the hearth, a large bundle of logs and crumpled newspaper was already prepared on the iron rack, covered with a faint layer of dust and cobwebs. Along the wall next to the fireplace was a long bench against the glass windows. Along another, a large firewood holder with enough wood for a few days. Above the firewood were faint irregular circles on the wall where something had been removed.

"Barricade the doors," Michael said to Roman.

"Why me?"

"You broke them."

Roman looked at the door and lapsed into his usual apathetic shrug. "I don't know how."

Michael scoffed and grabbed a thick branch from the log pile, then shoved it violently through the two door handles.

"Ohhhh." Roman drew out, eyes wide with feigned

amazement. "That'll do it."

"Did your dumb ass break anything else around here?"

"No, but I'm about to break your-"

"Sure would be nice to be warm." Lucia interrupted, easing herself down on one of the three dark leather couches that formed a large U facing the fireplace. She pulled a crocheted blanket off its back, shook the dust off, and wrapped it around her shoulders.

Michael glared at Roman a moment longer, then turned to assess the wood pile. They would need a fire if the storm were as bad as he felt it would be. Typically, snowstorms this high in the Appalachians sometimes brought temperatures far south of zero, but the coming storm felt like it would be anything but ordinary. There should be enough wood outside on the deck and in the log holder to last a week or so. The storm wouldn't last that long, would it? Nothing was normal post apocalypse, so it was best to be prepared. He picked up a box of long matches from the hearth and removed a match.

Lucia abruptly sat up with a concerned look on her face. "Are you sure that's safe? I wasn't suggesting…"

"We'll find out." Kneeling, Michael struck the match on the side of the box and let out a relieved breath when it didn't blow up in his face. He let the small flame lick the various edges of the newspaper.

"Wait, won't that draw unwanted attention?" Lucia asked, though she sounded more worried that she was right and Michael would kill the flames. "I mean, someone might see it."

"Doubt it. Storms coming, remember?" Michael replied, watching the flames begin to stretch and grow as they consumed the paper. Some of the twigs caught, filling the air with the satisfactory sound of crackling as they burned. Normal flames, Michael noted with relief. No raging inferno to consume them.

"Know that for a fact?" Roman asked as he joined them.

"Yes." Michael and Lucia said at the same time.

Roman snorted and jabbed a thumb at the windows. "You sure about that Big Ugly? You don't need to stare at that clear blue sky for another ten minutes just to be certain?"

"Enough!" Lucia said, bringing her palms together with a loud crack. She looked up at the cavernous ceiling as if appealing to God. "There *is* a storm coming, Roman. I. Can. Feel. It." She accentuated each word with a clap of her hands.

Roman chortled, then quickly threw his hands up in mock defense when Lucia glared at him. "Hey, I'm hoping Big Ugly is right too, sis." When Lucia gave him a look of disbelief, Roman added, "No, seriously. He'd better be, 'cause if he ain't then most likely something nasty is coming through those doors tonight. Zombies being attracted to wood smoke and light and whatnot."

Lucia gave the lodge doors an uneasy look and then turned to Michael for reassurance.

"I'm right," Michael said, pulling a burning twig from the newborn fire and lighting one of the lanterns. "Stay here. And I mean it." He told the twins as he adjusted the flame. "I'm going to check the rest of the building."

Roman snorted, crossing his arms. "I'm telling you; this place is safe."

"We'll see," Michael said. *Hopefully, I won't find out the hard way if it isn't.*

"I could go with you…" Lucia offered, but Michael shook his head. "Okay, be careful then. I-we need you." She added.

"We? We need him, sis? We?" Roman asked, sounding profoundly offended.

# CHAPTER NINETEEN

Michael left the bickering twins and approached a closed door off of the main room. After pressing an ear to it for a moment—and trying to tune out the bickering—he opened it slowly to discover a relatively lavish set of bathrooms, each with enough stalls for five people. He quickly checked each stall and then left the room. Luckily, there wasn't any buildup of nasty-smelling gas like the utility building.

Lucia broke off from arguing with Roman and asked, "Everything okay?"

"So far," Michael replied.

"Told you," Roman said.

"Bathroom's over there," Michael said with a hike of thumb.

"Oh, goody!" Lucia exclaimed, immediately making a beeline waddle towards the bathroom.

"Light a match," Roman called after her.

"Ha, ha."

Michael walked over to the banister and peered over the rail. Pots and pans lay haphazardly on the steps as if someone had tossed them down. "Did you check the basement?" He asked Roman.

"I'm not suicidal."

"Well, did you lock the door?"

Roman nodded in an exaggerated manner.

"What's with the pots and pans then?"

Roman shrugged. "I don't like basements."

Michael had to agree, looking down at the basement door shrouded in darkness. Better to check it out during the day. Better to never check it out at all, if possible. He moved on, and through another door was an office with two desks back-to-back. A large map of the camp and outlying buildings was on one of the walls. Michael studied it for a moment and saw there was a shooting range a half mile west of the camp. That could mean an armory with guns, ammo, and possibly archery equipment. That also meant that the armory would be locked to keep thieves out.

Michael looked around the office, seeing nothing but an empty peg where a set of keys could hang. He checked all the desk drawers and came up empty. Worst-case scenario, he could attempt to break into the armory. Michael looked out the window and sighed. It was getting dark. The armory would have to wait until morning. Hopefully, the storm would keep the zombies and their ilk away. He did not like relying on hope, especially as short on ammo as they were, but there wasn't much he could do about the situation.

Behind the office was a small room filled with various equipment and supplies. He found enough lamp oil stacked on two shelves to keep them in light for months if they were careful, plus a few small boxes of candles and matches. He quickly searched for ammo and didn't find any. Michael moved on, adding a mental note to come back later and inventory the supplies.

Following a narrow, cramped hallway leading from the office, Michael discovered a door leading outside. Looking through the small glass pane, he saw more cabins and what appeared to be an outdoor amphitheater with a raised podium. After checking the door locks, he continued down the hallway into the kitchen.

The kitchen was easily as large as those found in a fine dining restaurant. Polished stainless steel was everywhere, reflecting the lamp light like dozens of small candles. A set of long, thin windows ran along the ceiling on the outside wall, bringing in meager light. Another banister and stairs were set against the same wall with a small silver chain across the stairway that blocked access.

Michael walked over to the banister and peered down into the stairway. Pots and pans littered this stairway, too. Roman's poor but effective attempt at an early warning system. The bottom of the stairs ending in darkness, making it hard to see if there was another door he could lock. He thought for a moment about navigating down the pot strewn stairs to see, then instead unplugged a large ice maker from the wall and rolled it over to block the stairs. That, plus the chain and Roman's "warning system" should give them enough of a heads up if something came up the stairs. He made another mental note to check both basement doors, this one and the one in the main room. He could ask Roman if he locked this one, but Michael did not trust the kid.

On the other side of the room was a large entryway, through which he could faintly hear that Lucia and Roman were still arguing. Michael walked up to a pair of commercial size refrigerators, sniffed, and decided to leave the rotting innards alone. Seeing a door marked pantry, he opened it and whistled in appreciation. It was a large rectangular room with row after row of shelves filled with bulk goods, from condiments to canned dinners. There were dozens of tubs full of dehydrated rations and sacks of powdered eggs and milk under the shelves. Several others had dry cereal and rolled oats. Barrels of water lined the wall on one side of the room. It was a treasure trove of food storage, easily enough to last them through winter and beyond.

*Would it be so bad to winter in this remote place?* Michael wondered. So what if they were snowed in? They would be perfectly isolated for the next six months, and the world could pass them by. Maybe the nightmare would be over by then. He could even hunt and supplement their supplies with fresh meat. They could... a familiar feeling came over him, and Michael sighed bitterly. They would need to leave soon, a few days at the most. He should have known better than to think that they would have a reprieve from the horrors of the world. For whatever reason, they needed to move on. He did not always understand these feelings, but they had saved him enough that he couldn't ignore them. The twins, especially Roman, would undoubtedly have other thoughts on the matter, and he was not looking forward to that conversation.

Michael picked up a large can of the ravioli and another can of fruit cocktail and took them over to the commercial can opener. He slammed the opener into each can and spun the handle slowly while thinking of and discarding several different approaches to telling the twins the bad news. No way around it. He would just tell them straight out. Michael picked up the cans, grabbed some plastic bowls and spoons, and then brought everything to a table by the fireplace.

Roman was staring out the window at the lake and Lucia was sleepily watching the fire. She perked up from her stupor as he approached and sniffed the air. "Food!" she purred, limping over to the table. She grabbed a spoon and started eating directly from the can of fruit cocktail. She paused after the first bite and a shiver seemed to go through her. Hugging the can to herself, Lucia took it over to the fireplace and sat down on the couch. She began to stuff large mouthfuls of the fruit cocktail into her mouth, barely pausing for air. It was a messy and noisy spectacle. Roman looked at his sister with disgust as he scooped ravioli into his bowl before walking away to sit at one of the other tables.

Michael filled his bowl with ravioli and sat on a rocking chair beside the couch. The fire was fully engaged now, providing a warmth that he may have found pleasant at another time. Might as well get it over with. "We can't stay here long." He said, watching the flames dance.

Lucia paused, a heaping spoon an inch from her juice-smeared face. "What?"

"We need to leave."

"Now?" Lucia asked, sitting up and looking around the room with panic in her eyes.

"No-" Michael started to say but was interrupted by Roman slamming his spoon down on the table.

"Leave?" The boy demanded. "What do you mean, leave?" Lucia made a shushing gesture at him which Roman promptly ignored. "No, I won't be quiet." He turned to confront Michael. "I saw the pantry, man. We are out in the middle of nowhere, have plenty of food to eat, a roof over our head, plus a fireplace, and I will say it again, *foods* to eat! Why the hell are you thinking about leaving when we can winter in this place?"

Michael braced himself. "I get—I have a feeling, in my gut, that we should leave."

"Oh, *a feeling*," Roman said in a voice dripping with sarcasm. "In your gut. Well then, that's every reason in the world to leave a safe place stocked with food. 'Cause your gut had a feeling!" He shouted loud enough to have it echo off of the rafters.

"Roman," Lucia said sharply. "Shut it!" She paused to make sure he listened, but Roman only spluttered. Lucia gave Michael a direct look. "Tell me more about this feeling. Do you mean like intuition or something?"

Michael nodded. "Something like that." He shifted in his chair, feeling uncomfortable discussing the subject with Lucia or anyone else.

"I see. Have you had them before?"

Michael nodded mutely.

"Do you trust these feelings?" Lucia asked, eyes searching his face.

"Yes." Could he really trust them after what happened to Rachel? *Do I have a choice?*

"Are they always right?"

"Kept me alive so far." *And killed Steph and Rachel and...*

Roman barked an ugly laugh. "Yeah sure, just like you have a feeling that a storm is coming." He said, pointing to the cloudless, darkening sky that backdropped the expansive windows.

"It is coming," Lucia said, turning to look at her brother. "You seriously can't feel that?"

Roman licked his finger and held it up as if trying to check for wind direction. "I don't feel anything."

"Funny. Very funny. I can't help it if you have the sensitivity of a rock."

"Nice, sis. Funny."

"Wait!" Lucia said, throwing up a hand to silence her brother. Her eyes widened, and she said, "You had one of these before, didn't you? After you saved Roman from being barbecued alive by those bikers."

Roman scoffed at that, and Lucia snapped her fingers twice and held her hand up to him again without looking away, eyes intent on Michael.

Michael nodded.

"So that's why you stayed." Lucia nodded as well. "I've been wondering about that."

"Bottom line," Michael interrupted, "is that I always follow these feelings." He said this to Lucia as she was the one he needed to convince. "You can stay if you want, but I'm leaving after the storm."

"Do you know why? Why we need to leave, I mean?

Michael shook his head.

"I can't change your mind?"

"No. my gu—" He shot Roman a look then continued, "My intuition says to go, so I'll go."

"So go. Goodbye and good riddance." Roman said, gesturing with his hand impatiently as if telling him to be off already.

"No, remember he said that *we* need to leave," Lucia reminded him.

"We," Roman put a strong emphasis on the word, "don't

need to go nowhere."

"You can stay if you want," Michael told him.

"Oh, I'll do whatever I want." Roman blustered. "I go where I want, how I want, when I want." He jabbed his spoon at Michael. "You go ahead and leave. I'm pretty sure that your scary, imaginary storm ain't coming to get yah. A zombie might bite your ass, 'cause they're *real*, but not some ridiculous figment of your imagination." He looked at his sister. "With Big Ugly gone, we'll have food for a year. More than a year!" Roman looked at Michael defiantly. "I'm not leaving, and neither is Lucia. Right sis?"

"Okay," Lucia said softly, closing her eyes.

"See?" Roman said. "In fact, why don't you leave n—"

"Okay," Lucia said again, turning to Michael. "I will go with you."

"What!" Roman exclaimed, jumping to his feet. "Don't tell me you are believing all this happy crappy."

Lucia nodded. "I've made up my mind. But can we leave after the storm?"

"Yes," Michael said, surprised. He had expected Lucia to put up a bigger fight. Even tell him he was crazy and to get the hell out.

"Storm?" Roman said in a strangled tone. "I'm sick to death of hearing of some stupid storm. There is no storm, and there is no danger here!" Roman's voice dropped as he pleaded, "Listen to me, sis! Michael's just some nut job stranger we met only a few days ago-"

"Who saved your life!" Lucia interjected.

"-and your brain isn't working right 'cause you're pregnant and that's why you are making these crazy decisions.

You need to trust me right now, your twin brother, your only living relative. We need to stay here."

Lucia shook her head. "No Roman, the truth is that I'd rather leave with Michael than be holed up with you all winter."

"See, now you're really talking crazy. It isn't logical to—"

"I don't care about logic. I care about keeping my baby safe!"

"Yeah, sure sis." Roman sneered. "Ignore logic, ignore reason, and just listen to Michael's gut. You know what my gut is telling me? I'm hungry!"

"Then you better eat up because we are leaving as soon as this storm is done." Lucia jabbed a finger at her brother. "Because you go where I want, how I want, when I want," Lucia said, mimicking Roman's speech from earlier. "Remember, you owe me."

"I owe you nothing." Roman spat. "I'm my own man."

"You owe Dom then," Lucia said, and Michael was surprised by how quickly that shut Roman down. The boy clamped his mouth shut, and his head fell forward as if in defeat. He shook it as if trying to wake from a bad dream.

Lucia nodded as if she expected this reaction. "We leave after the storm." She said firmly, turning back to the fire.

Roman walked over to his sister and put a hand on her shoulder. She glared at him until he dropped it. Looking her straight in the eyes, he pleaded, "But sis, we are *safe* here. We are out in the middle of nowhere and nothing will find us. I'm telling you, it just isn't logical—" He took a deep breath. "It's-Like I said it isn't logical to leave just as it isn't logical to believe some crazy *stranger* who claims to feel a storm is coming when it is obvious there isn't."

"Enough of this." Lucia snapped, clapping her hands together with each word. "You're talking in circles. I trust his *feelings* more than I trust your so-called logic. We will leave when the storm's over. I've made my decision. No more discussion."

Roman's face turned an ugly red. "That's just stupid crazy, the both of you, crazy." He sputtered. "This place is a good place. I know it, I can *feel* it!"

"Roman, I trust your feelings even less than your logic," Lucia said calmly. "This conversation is over. Now go away and let me enjoy my meal." Lucia turned away from her brother and picked up her spoon.

Roman hesitated and then put a hand back on his sister's shoulder. "Sis," he pleaded, "Think of your baby. It just isn't safe."

There was a loud crack as Lucia's hand connected with his cheek. "Don't you dare try using my baby against me like that!"

Roman's face went red, then white with Lucia's purple handprint contrasting sharply on his cheek. Without another word, he walked over to the front door, yanked the branch violently out of the handles, and left, slamming it shut behind him with a loud crash.

"He'll be back," Lucia said and went back to eating. "When he gets cold."

"Um." Michael started.

Lucia's hand shot up. "Don't want to hear it."

Michael nodded and took a bite of cold ravioli.

After a moment, Lucia turned to him with a rueful laugh. "Sorry, hormones." Looking at the door, she let out a long, irritated groan. "Oh, he doesn't help either. Not at all."

When Michael didn't say anything, she continued

speaking but almost as if to herself. "Think I was too hard on him?" Lucia thought about it for a moment. "I don't know. He got my husband killed." That hit a little too close to home than Michael expected. He could only stare at Lucia. She finally nodded and turned back to the fire.

"I wish it were as simple as saying it was a mistake in judgment, but it was Roman's arrogance that killed my Dominic. He's so impatient and impulsive. Always been." She shook her head and took another bite of the fruit cocktail. "Won't ever apologize. Hell, he would have to admit he is wrong first and Roman thinks he never does anything wrong! He..." She paused and took a deep breath to calm herself. "But he is my little brother, you know?" She said as if reminding herself. "I hate him but still love him too. I have to. Only family can make you feel that way. Most days I can't stand to be around him but it would break my heart if he left." Lucia shrugged. "It is what it is. He's my baby brother." She repeated as if reassuring herself then gave him a direct look. "You better be right about leaving."

"I am."

"You better be, or both of us are wrong."

Michael looked at the girl in confusion.

Lucia shrugged as if embarrassed. "I also have a feeling we should leave." She held up a hand and went on quickly, "Not that I get feelings like you do, you know, in your, uh, gut. My... woman's intuition, we will call it, agrees with you. I knew it as soon as you said it. Could be the storm I'm feeling, but I'm pretty sure that it is something else. Somethings..."

"Coming." Michael finished for her. A wolf.

Lucia gave him an odd look, and he realized that he had said the word aloud.

Michael sighed and gave Lucia a quick rundown on wolves. "Like wolves in-"

"Sheep's clothing. I get the reference." Lucia shivered. "Like we ain't got enough to worry about."

They both looked at the broken front door as the wind caused it to creak and move. "Lock it," Lucia told him after a long moment, her voice cold and decisive.

Michael got to his feet. "You sure? Roman won't be able to get back inside tonight."

Lucia turned to look at the fireplace. "Do it. I'm not taking any chances."

Michael walked over to the door and peered out the window but didn't see a sign of Roman.

"My brother will be fine," Lucia said, her voice clipped, then forced a laugh. "He will knock if he wants in."

Michael caught her wiping her face out of the corner of his eye but didn't see tears when he turned to look at the girl.

"You sure?" He asked again, picking up the thick branch.

"I am. My baby is the most important thing to me, and I can't afford to worry about Roman anymore. He will have to take care of himself and frankly, I'm not going to let his decisions put my baby in danger anymore. Do it."

Michael shoved the piece of wood back through the door handle. After one more look outside and seeing nothing, he returned and sat at the table. They sat quietly for a while, not talking, not eating.

"Do-did you have kids?" Lucia asked awkwardly after a few minutes.

"No."

"I'm sorry." Lucia said. Michael couldn't tell if she meant

asking the question or that he never had kids. He shrugged. It didn't matter.

They sat quietly in a long silence, watching the fire. Lucia finally put down the half-empty can of fruit cocktail and sighed again, closing her eyes. "This fire is making me sleepy. You think I wouldn't be able to with Roman out there and wolves and things but I am exhausted. That isn't even the word for it. Anyway, I think I will sleep by the hearth tonight, just lay here in the warmth. Help me up."

Michael stood and helped Lucia to her feet and accompanied her as she limped to the couch. She pulled the afghan down from the back of the couch and wrapped herself in it. Easing her head down on her arm, she made a content sound, then half rose and looked at Michael with worried eyes.

"You're not going to leave, are you?"

"I won't."

"Promise?"

"Yes."

Lucia settled back with a relieved sigh, gently rubbing her large belly under the blanket. The motion slowed and stopped as she drifted off into sleep.

Michael sat watching the flames for a long time. They were hypnotic, inviting him to fall under their spell as well. He forced himself to his feet and threw another log on the fire. He stood before the hearth, numbly watching the flames as they hissed and popped.

Lucia suddenly cried out in her sleep, her hand slipping from the blanket to reach toward Michael. A whimpering sound escaped her lips. Just like Rachel had, what? Only a few days ago? Michael was surprised by that, it seemed like weeks—months even since the girl had died. He promised himself he would not let the same thing happen to Lucia. He stared at the hand for a long moment, then gently picked it up and slid it back under the blanket. Lucia's whimpering smiled briefly and whispered, "My sweet Dom."

Michael settled on the floor with his back against the couch so he could watch the entrance. Cradling the rifle in his hands, he let out a long sigh and wondered when Roman would try to kill him.

# CHAPTER TWENTY

Michael woke with a start, shivering despite the roaring fire next to him. Gasping for air, he sat up and fumbled for his rifle. The phantom nightmares chasing him faded away, resolving into Lucia standing over him with a worried look on her face. She withdrew her extended hand as if yanking it from a flame and then tried to cover it with an overly cheerful smile. "Was just about to wake you for breakfast." She frowned and gave him a searching look. "Dreaming?"

Michael shook his head. "Nightmare." He replied in a gravely parched voice. Movement caught his eye and looking over at the large rectangular windows on the other side of the room, he saw a blanket of white flurries swirling around the glass. A low wind whined as if eager to extinguish the warmth and life inside. The lake and surrounding area were now more of a suggestion than anything cohesive.

"It's really coming down out there, isn't it." Lucia continued, carefully easing herself down in a chair at the closest table. Laid out on it were several small cans of fruit and a box of animal crackers. "Looks like you were right about the storm after all." She said, plopping a cracker in her mouth.

"Still think it's a good idea to leave?" Roman's sullen voice came from the direction of the kitchen. The boy was leaning against the doorframe, his head bent down towards the open can of peaches in his hand. He looked at Michael askance, the angle giving his eyes a sinister look. Roman made an encompassing wave with his free arm, fork in hand. "So, great prognosticator of storms, when does your gut say that this one's going to end."

"Don't know," Michael said thickly as he slowly got to his feet. He was surprised to see Roman already inside the lodge. *Must have been sleeping pretty hard if his knocking on the door in the middle of the night didn't wake me up.* Michael stretched and winced, body stiff from sleeping on the floor. Still beats sleeping in a tree, he reminded himself. He hobbled over and sat down across from Lucia.

"Not exactly to the point, are they?" Roman asked, scowling. "These *feelings* of yours, I mean." He dropped the fork into the can with a loud clank and disappeared into the dark kitchen.

Lucia patted the table near Michael's hand. "Ignore him. You were right about the storm. I'm sure you're right about leaving."

"Still," Roman continued as he returned to the kitchen door with another small can in hand. He stabbed a piece of pear and glowered at it. "I have to go where she goes. She's my sister." He gave a helpless shrug. "Family, you know." Lucia's eyebrow shot up at Roman echoing her sentiment from the night before.

"And she goes where you go." Roman pointed his fork at Michael accusingly. "And you lead us to our deaths. That's what my gut tells me. Fine. Whatever. I've resigned myself to the fact that you're going to get all of us dead." He looked down at the can of peaches and stabbed one with his fork. "I'm good," he grumbled, falling back against the doorframe. "Whatever."

"Anyway," Lucia said brightly as she shot her brother a look that was anything but. "Get some food in you. Not that we're going to do much with the storm and all," Roman snorted but Lucia continued unperturbed, "No offense, but you are starting to look skeletal and need to make up for some lost calories. We all do."

Now that she mentioned it, Michael noticed that Lucia's haggard face was looking thin too. Hollow dark rimmed eyes looked out from concave cheeks. He could even see the faint general shape of her teeth and gums through the skin around her mouth. Only her large belly belied the near anorexic frame the girl had. Eating for two when one was eating you. "You eat," Michael replied. "You need it more than I do."

"I'll have you know that I'm on my third can," Lucia said proudly, dancing her shoulders proudly with each word. "Oh, and I'm not stopping there. It feels like," She took a bite and then noisily spoke around it, "It feels like my baby is absorbing it as soon as I eat it." She laughed as she swallowed. "I'm not even close to stuffed. I swear it feels like my stomach is still gnawing at me. Anyway, eat." Lucia insisted as she took another bite. She pushed a small open can of carrots at him. "Eat."

Michael took the can, and after a brief moment of scrutinizing the orange-colored slices inside, he took a small sip and shuddered at the taste. He set the can down, and his eyes turned to the large bank of windows framing the lake in the background. Snow was accumulating quickly on the window panes. He wondered how the storm would affect the zombies and their ilk. Would they freeze? What about a wolf?

"What are you thinking about?" Lucia asked curiously, around another bite. Juice dripped down unnoticed her chin.

"Nothing."

"Well, then eat. Come on, you are making me sound like a broken record. Get some food in you."

Michael reflexively took another sip from the can without thinking and gagged.

"Sorry," Lucia said, taking the can from him. "Hmm, maybe carrots are a little strong first thing in the morning." She looked at the cans scattered on the table before her, "Um, what about—"

"Eggs."

"What?" Lucia gave him a confused look.

"I'm going to make some eggs," Michael said.

Lucia's face lit up like the sun. "Oh, we have that?"

Michael nodded as he stood up and pushed the bench back.

Lucia pushed all of the cans away from her and turned to confront her brother, "Why didn't you tell me we had eggs?"

Roman shrugged and took another bite from his can. He pointed his fork at her. "You didn't ask, and you weren't complaining."

Lucia rolled her eyes. "Well, that's because I didn't know we had eggs." She turned back to Michael, her eyes bright. "I'd like some, please."

"They're powdered," Michael warned and heard Roman say the same thing in parallel. The boy gave him a suspicious look as if Michael had done it on purpose.

"They sound... marvelous!" Lucia breathed the last word

as if she could already taste them. "Make a lot."

Michael first went over to the fire to stoke it and add a few logs. He could probably rig the stove in the kitchen with a propane tank if he found one but this would do for now.

He walked over to the kitchen door. Roman refused to move and only gave way, reluctantly at that, when Lucia exclaimed, "Roman seriously?" Michael's eyes never left Roman as he slipped past him in the frame, and the boy reciprocated. It felt like sparks would start glinting off their eyes if they held much longer. The only good thing he could say about Roman was that the boy was consistent. A consistent pain in the ass, that is.

Roman watched him suspiciously as he gathered items to cook breakfast. Michael ignored the unfriendly eyes and picked up a large iron skillet instead. It would do. Lucia, after all, had told him to make lots. He grabbed a jug of distilled water, a can of powdered eggs, a few seasonings, and a silicone spatula. On his way back to the door, he heard Lucia preemptively tell her brother, "Move."

Roman looked down at the can in his hand and then at the cans on the table in front of his sister. He made a sour face, mumbled something unintelligible, and then went to sit in a wooden rocker that faced the bay windows that overlooked the snowy lake. He started shaking his head and muttering. Michael wasn't sure if he was upset at him or the weather. His guess was both.

Michael carefully set the items he had gathered on the floor by the fireplace and placed the iron skillet directly on the hearthstone. Indirect heat was the secret to not burning eggs, especially powdered ones in an iron skillet. He measured the powdered eggs and water by eye in the skillet and began stirring.

After a moment, he added black pepper to the mix and picked up the container of onion powder.

"What's that?" Lucia asked curiously.

"Onion powder," Michael replied.

She made a sour face just like her brother had moments before. "Oh, I don't like onions."

"It's needed to make the eggs taste good."

"But…"

"Nonnegotiable."

"Nonnegotiable?" Lucia's voice went up an octave.

"Yes. You trusted me about the storm and leaving the camp in a few days, correct? I think you can trust me about making eggs."

Roman gave a shrill whistle, followed by "Shots fired."

Lucia stared at Michael blankly for a moment, then settled back in her chair in what could only be considered a pout. "Fine, do… whatever you feel is best."

"You're wasting your time, bro." Roman warned as he came over to the table and sat in a chair next to his sister at the head of the table. "She's not going to like them."

"Shut it." Lucia snapped irritably.

That set the twins off into another round of bickering. Still, Michael was able to nearly tune it out to a low, droning buzz as he focused on adding a little of the onion powder and slowly agitated the eggs with the spatula. They quickly came together, and soon he had a large pan of steaming rehydrated eggs. Michael picked up the pan with a panhandler and set it down on a trivet in front of Lucia.

Lucia hesitated only a moment before reaching out with two fingers and plucked a morsel of scrambled eggs and plopped it into her mouth. Her eyes went wide. "Yum!" She said, blowing on her fingers. "Oh, hot too, but I don't taste the onion at all." She gave him a big smile.

"Of course you would like it," Roman muttered darkly.

Lucia gave her brother a pugnacious look. "Are you telling me you'd rather my breakfast taste bad than you be wrong?"

Roman opened his mouth to respond and then shut it promptly.

"Realized that you weren't going to win that one, huh?" Lucia asked smugly, plopping another glob of eggs in her mouth. "Good call."

"Whatever," Roman grumbled.

Lucia giggled, then covered her mouth with a shocked look. "Wow. Honestly, I never thought I'd do that again. And all it took was some eggs."

"Powdered eggs." Roman corrected.

"Whatever." Lucia mimicked her brother from moments before. "Tell you what. I'm in such a good mood now, I'll let you have some. Oh, and you too, Michael, obviously."

Roman stared at the eggs, then shrugged and put a heaping ladleful of eggs in a bowl.

"Some! Not all." Lucia admonished, snatching the ladle away from Roman.

Roman made an inarticulate grunt, gesturing to the relatively small bowl of eggs in front of him, but only when compared to the large skillet of eggs. He swallowed noisily, saying, "I left you plenty."

Lucia smiled smugly at Michael. "Guess that means he likes your eggs too."

Roman scowled. "I never said that." But Michael noted that

217

the boy hadn't said he hated them either, but maybe that was only because he was too busy stuffing his face.

Michael settled on the bench and didn't object when Lucia insisted on loading his bowl with eggs. As he took a bite from the virtual mound of eggs in front of him, his mind settled into figuring out what he needed to do next, torn between checking out and securing the basement or heading to the shooting range.

"I think I may check out the shooting range in a few hours," Roman said around a large wag of eggs as if reading his thoughts. "See if I can find some ammo for our guns."

That clinched it. Michael dropped his fork back into his bowl. "I'll go." If there was really something bad coming their way, then they needed more ammo.

Roman opened his mouth to object, but Lucia quickly interrupted, "Shut it, Roman." She said, raising her palm to block his face.

Roman pushed his sister's hand away with a grimace. "Fine."

"Um," Lucia asked Michael. "Are you having one of your... feelings?" The last word came out in a whisper as if she was embarrassed to ask or worried that it may embarrass him.

"Yes." Michael lied. He hadn't felt anything beyond a proactive need to find more ammo. If lying shortened the argument, so be it.

Roman scoffed and said, "Really?" The word had an odd nuance as if he knew Michael was lying. They locked eyes for a long moment. Did Roman know he was lying? If so, how?

"Enough, you two." Lucia eyed both of them and quickly added, "Roman, you can stay here and protect and keep me and my baby company instead." She looked around the large room.

"Maybe we can find some good board games around here or something."

Roman's suspicious eyes calmed as he looked at his sister. "If we find a game, I go first."

"Deal."

Michael studied the twins. Something felt off in that interaction. Roman usually put up more of an argument. Maybe he had imagined it. Michael looked out at the falling snow and sighed. Might as well get it over and done with. If he waited, then that would mean more snow to trudge through. Wearily, he stood up from the table, pushing back the bench with a squeak.

"You heading out already?" Lucia asked in surprise.

"Yes," Michael answered.

"Sure you don't want to finish your eggs first?"

"No, I'll finish them when I get back." Michael walked over to his pile by the fire and began dressing for the weather.

Roman shot a hand up, index finger extended towards the ceiling as if making a point. "If you come back!" Again, there was that faint odd note as if Roman knew something.

Lucia stuck a finger in Roman's face. "Stop being morbid. Of course he's coming back." There was, however, a slight tremor in her voice with the last word, making it unclear if it was a statement or a question.

"I will," Michael replied, mildly surprised that he meant it this time.

"Promise?"

"I just did."

Lucia let out a long sigh and turned to look worriedly out the windows that framed the snowy lake. The snow-covered rowboat rocked gently, tugging at its line. "Okay. Be careful out there. Just... just get the ammo and get back here." She told him awkwardly.

"Yeah, don't trip, chocolate chip," Roman called out, mouth full of eggs again.

Lucia gave Michael an embarrassed smile, and then her face turned serious. "And keep an eye out for Wolves."

Roman paused long enough in his masticating to give his sister an odd look, then shook his head and went back to eating.

Michael shouldered his rifle and brushed his hand across the coat pocket, feeling the hard cylinder that was the road flair. He tied the machete to his belt and decided he was ready to go. He made his way to the door without any preamble or pretense.

"Lock up," Michael told the twins as he pulled the small branch out of the door handles. He stepped out quickly before they could respond and let out a sigh of relief as soon as the door shut behind him. He needed some time alone, and the long walk to the shooting range should provide it. Adjusting the rifle strap, he quickly scanned the surrounding area. Nothing but unbroken snow around the lodge and cabins as far as he could see. That was a good sign. Michael looked up briefly at the thick snowflakes falling from the gray sky, then shifting the pack on his shoulders, he started towards the shooting range.

# CHAPTER
# TWENTY-ONE

Lucia watched the broken doors close behind Michael. *Please keep your promise. Please come back.* She pleaded in her head, then turned to find Roman watching her with a speculative look as he picked at his eggs. "What?" She demanded, placing her hands on her hips.

Roman looked at the eggs on his fork, then shook his head and sat them on his plate. "Nothing." He got up, walked over to the door, and picked up the branch Michael had discarded. He studied it briefly, then shoved it through the two door handles.

"Come on, I know when you have something on your mind. There is something that you want to say. So say it."

Roman grimaced, then shrugged as if to say, you asked for it. "Do you seriously mean to go follow him"—his hand flicked disdainfully at the door- "instead of staying here?"

Lucia felt an instant spike of irritation. "We went over that yesterday. Why are you bringing it up now, especially when things are going so well this morning?"

Roman quickly threw his hands up defensively. "Hey, you

asked, sis." He pointed at her with one finger. "Insisted is more like it, right? So you can't get mad at me for speaking my mind."

Lucia took a deep breath and let it out slowly. That was true, she admitted to herself reluctantly. "I did and... I can't."

"So?" Roman prodded, his eyes searching hers.

"So what?" She asked, pushing down another spike of irritation.

"Do you plan to follow his gastric poo doo voodoo?"

Lucia couldn't help but laugh. It did sound absurd when put that way. "Seriously?"

"Super." He said with a wry grin.

"Yes." She said slowly after a moment of consideration. "I believe him."

Roman's smile turned sad, and he nodded as if that finalized something. "Okay then."

"Okay? "Lucia asked suspiciously. "Okay, what?"

Roman held his hands imploringly. "I'm not going to argue."

Lucia cocked her head to the side. "Now that's a surprise. Why not?"

Roman sighed as he sat back down in his chair. "Look, I'm tired, weary, and hey I can tell your mind is made up. I also know I'm not going to change it. A huge waste of time and energy if I tried."

"Seriously?" She asked again, surprised.

Roman shrugged. "Super." He repeated, this time without the humor. "You will do whatever you want no matter what I say. Plus..." He trailed off awkwardly.

"Plus?" Lucia prodded. "Come on, It's like pulling teeth with you today. Out with it!"

Roman picked up the fork and scooped up another large bite of eggs. "Well, it's like you said. It's a good morning. Probably the first since everything went to hell, and I don't want to ruin it. We're inside, safe and sound, and actually warm for once, with some good food, too." He shoveled the eggs into his mouth and began chewing noisily.

Lucia was shocked. Maybe all it took for Roman to grow up was the end of the world. She remembered telling her friends that hell would freeze over before Roman grew up. She looked out the window at the snow. That apparently had already happened. "Thanks, that's very... magnanimous of you."

Roman made a face. "Magna what?"

"Nice. Very nice of you. Generous."

"Well, why didn't you just say that?"

Lucia only sighed in reply, feeling anything else would lead down the path of them arguing, and that would ruin the morning. She looked out the large windows instead, watching the snow. Hopefully, Michael was alright, and hopefully, hopefully, he would return.

Roman shrugged and shoveled another bite of eggs into his mouth. "Yah know, I'd never tell Big Ugly this, but these are some damn good eggs."

"Huh?" Lucia said, blinking rapidly at Roman as his words caught up to her. "Oh." she smiled and took another bite, too. "They are, aren't they?"

"The secrets in the onion powder." They both said at the same time and laughed.

Roman gestured to the half-filled pan. "Do you mind?"

"Not at all." Apparently, she was feeling magnanimous, too.

Roman was silent as he shoveled more eggs onto his plate. He took a big bite and chewed noisily for a moment, then swallowed hard and asked, "Hey, do you remember that time when we were kids and we woke up early? Mom and Dad weren't up yet, and we were hungry so we decided to make breakfast?"

Lucia couldn't help but laugh. "Remember? It's one of my favorite memories from when we were kids." They had been around four or five and despite never cooking before, they managed to cook a large breakfast.

"I'm surprised we didn't burn the house down," Roman said, chuckling at the memory.

"True, but we ate good!" Lucia replied, and they both laughed. She couldn't help but smile. Moments like this, when Roman wasn't being a complete a-hole, were far and in between. This was a good morning.

Roman shoveled more eggs into his mouth and then continued. "Mom and Dad tried to act upset when they woke up, but I think they were more surprised than anything at the amount of food we cooked. But hey, we were hungry."

"Not after we were done cooking." She reminded him.

Roman let out a loud whoop. "Oh yeah, we did so much taste testing that we were stuffed by the time the food was done."

"Stuffed? We both ended up puking everywhere."

"You puked on Mom." Roman accused, pointing a lazy finger at her.

"I did not," Lucia said indignantly,

"Yeah, you did," Roman said with a big grin. "Right after she picked you up and gave you a hug because your tum tum was hurting."

"Oh yeah," Lucia said slowly. "Guess I must have blocked that memory—Oh! Now I remember. You puked on the dog!"

"Sure did!" Roman said proudly.

"Oh, and then he puked too!"

"Several times." Roman agreed proudly.

"Poor little guy. Guess he did too much tasting, too. What was his name?"

Roman shrugged. "Dunno. I forgot." Lucia was not surprised. Roman had a tendency not to remember anyone's name except for really close friends and family. That's why he made up nicknames for everyone he met. He remembered those for some reason. "I want to say his name was Billy or something like that. Anyway, Mom and Dad were so pissed."

Roman laughed, saying, "I think they were more upset that time we woke up early and played car wash."

"Wow," Lucia said, taking a slow bite. "I think I remember that too." Her wall was fast approaching. Finally full, what a fantastic feeling. One that she had honestly never thought she would feel again.

"We took all of the chairs from the dining room and lined them up in the kitchen." Roman prompted.

"Yes!" Lucia remembered. "Then put all of our dolls on them and sprayed them all down with the sprayer from the sink."

"A lot of spraying," Roman added.

"Everything was soaked!"

"Well, we tried to account for that by tearing up all of Dad's newspapers and magazines and covering the floor with them."

"Yeah, cause paper is so absorbent," Lucia said. "Those

toilet paper commercials lied to us."

"They definitely did. Kid logic. What a mess." Roman shook his head ruefully amidst an amused chuckle.

"We were grounded for what, two weeks?" Lucia asked.

"Three, and they started setting their alarm early on the weekend after that."

"That's why they did that! I always wondered why they never slept in and hadn't made the connection."

"Fun times," Roman said, stirring the egg remnants on his plate.

"Bad memories."

"Yeah."

"I miss them. Mom and Dad, I mean."

"I do too."

"They are in a better place now," Lucia added sadly.

"Anything is better than here." Roman agreed, finally pushing the plate away from him.

That was too close to discussing their current situation. Lucia felt sadness return as the good feelings from nostalgia faded. She looked out the window at the snow for a long moment, then turned to find Roman watching her.

"What?"

"You're worried about him. Big ugly, I mean. No, it's okay." He added the last when she shrugged uncomfortably.

"A little, I guess."

"I'm sure he will come back, maybe a little worse for wear from the weather. But he will be back."

She didn't answer but instead went back to looking out the window. Hopefully, he would come back. Hopefully. Roman's chair squeaked across the floor, and she turned to find him looking at her mischievously.

"What?"

"I found some cocoa," He cocked his head towards the kitchen, "back there. Want some?"

This day was getting better by the moment! "You've been holding out on me? Some hot cocoa would be delightful."

"I'll get it going. You better eat some more eggs. They are getting cold."

"Okay," Lucia said, taking another bite automatically. The eggs were near room temp now, but she didn't mind, and her baby didn't either. She could swear she felt contentment radiating from her womb. She took a few more bites as she waited for Roman and realized she was full. Finally. A miracle in itself. She sat, relishing the feeling and watching the snow fall outside the windows, listening as the flames popped and crackled in the fireplace. She didn't have to worry about Michael. He would come back. He promised he would.

Roman soon reappeared humming and carrying a metal teapot, two oversized coffee cups, and a large commercial tin container of hot cocoa mix. He set the teapot in the bank of hot coals and then put the cups and the cocoa on the table. "This is going to be good!" He exclaimed, rubbing his hands together.

Already feeling a food coma coming on, Lucia waddled her way to the couch and wrapped a blanket around her. She fought back sleep as Roman tended the fire, both waiting quietly until the teapot began to whistle. Roman took the teapot off the fire and poured hot steaming water into the mugs. He added two heaping spoonfuls of cocoa, looked at her then winked and added another two heaping spoonfuls. He stirred them and then brought the mugs over to the couch. "Careful, hot." He told her as she took one of them, and then Roman sat quietly in the chair next to the couch. Lucia blew on the hot cocoa for a few minutes, then took a sip and sighed. Hot chocolate heaven.

"Hey, I'm curious. What was that about, warning Big Ugly to look out for wolves?" Roman asked.

"Oh, nothing really. Michael thought he saw a pack of wolves on his way into the camp." Lucia had decided against sharing Michael's concerns about a wolf showing up. Roman wouldn't believe her, and the last thing she wanted was to start another argument with him. Especially now that they were finally getting along.

"Oh. Cool."

They both sipped silently for a while and by the time Lucia finally threw the cup back and drank the dregs, a nice warmth emanated from her stomach like a small radiant bonfire. She exhaled happily, sleepily smacking her lips. Now, all she needed was a big fat nap. She fumbled with the cup, and it fell to the floor and shattered.

"Oh no!" Lucia said, her eyes popping open. They felt so heavy. She fought to keep them open, but the pull of sleep was so strong.

Roman laughed and said, "Don't worry, sis I've got you." He knelt down and started picking up the pieces.

"Very nice..." She told him with a yawn, settling into the couch. "...of you. Very nice." Her voice slurred a little, but she didn't mind. It was more of a purr than a slur.

Roman beamed at her. "Get some sleep."

"Okay." She said breathily as she passed the point where reality and unreality met. His voice followed her into sleep. "I got you, sis. I will always protect you."

"Mmm hmm." She breathed, snuggling into the warm cocoa bliss as it surrounded her.

# CHAPTER TWENTY-TWO

Michael slowed to a stop as he approached a bend in the trail. Past a few young cedar trees, he could see the shooting range or at least the hint of it through the thick falling snow. He quickly hid behind one of the trees, unlimbered the rifle, and glassed the range. It was a long half-building facing a long field with three simple ranges dug into a low, wide hill. At one end of the building was a shack with a padlocked door. The armory. It had to be. Ammo would be there if there were any.

Michael shivered and adjusted his coat against the wind as it howled in his ears but otherwise paid the cold weather no mind. He watched the surrounding area for a long moment, but the snow obscured his vision, and the wind dampened any sound. He very much doubted that anyone was out here. Anything, on the other hand...

Michael checked his gut and sighed bitterly. Nothing. No precognition gas or whatever the hell Roman had called it. No answers and no choice, as always. The worst-case scenario always seemed the most likely now after the world ended, so he always prepared for the worst. Still, he scoffed against the notion that someone would be this far out in the mountains and stupid enough to be out in bad weather. *I am.* He reminded himself, deciding to be more cautious. No excuse for getting sloppy just because he was cold.

He watched the range for a few more minutes and then snorted softly. Rifle at the ready, Michael started slowly towards the range, rifle at the ready. He hugged the tree line, scanning everything around him as he went.

A root or fallen branch caught his foot, and Michael nearly tripped on the uneven ground hidden by the snow. He slowed down even more, not wanting to chance a fall. Most people didn't realize how badly a fall, even a short one, could screw a person up. These days, it would likely be fatal. He was forced to focus more on the ground before him than on what could be lurking in the woods. Not good.

Finally, his foot crunched on gravel, the sound muffled through a thick layer of snow. Michael slowed even more as he neared the armory's door and stopped as he suddenly felt eyes on him. He looked discreetly around in front of him, but all he saw were snow flurries and the hint of woods in the distance. Casually, he checked his back trail and put a hand up to his mouth as if holding back a yawn. The feeling faded as quickly as it appeared. Weird. Could there be a geist in the shack? No, the feeling had come from behind him, his back trail, not the armory. Maybe his mind was playing tricks on him. There was a latent paranoia that was always there when one was out in the woods. Maybe, but the worst-case scenario rule of Murphy's thumb told him he wasn't alone out here. He needed to grab the ammo and get back to the lodge as quickly as possible.

Michael stepped towards the shack's door and abruptly stumbled forward as his foot sunk deeper into the snow than expected. There was a simultaneous metallic sound and a nearly instant feeling of something biting painfully into his right ankle. He fell forward, slamming his head hard against the metal door. Blinding pain and bright lights simultaneously exploded in his head, but that was nothing compared to the instant agony he felt in his ankle. It felt like something was trying to bite through it. Instinctively, he tried yanking his foot away and nearly blacked out as the pain grew infinitely worse.

Michael bit off a strangled scream and contorted his body to see what thing from hell was consuming his foot. Twin metal bands with large teeth held his mangled ankle in a vise. Bear trap, the thought floated up numbly through pain and fear. Someone had set a trap. Someone—they could be coming. Watching eyes...

Michael painfully looked around and saw his rifle a few feet away. He lunged for his rifle and then screamed again as the bear trap held his foot, the teeth biting deeper, tearing the injured flesh. Looking back, he saw a thick chain running from the trap to a thick metal stake hammered almost entirely into the ground. He quickly sat up, then put a shaking hand to his head as the world swam violently. He felt something warm was running down his face.

Michael pulled his hand away and noted that it was red with blood. Head wound. Scalp laceration. Quick blood loss. The disjointed thoughts swam up through the pain onslaught, years of training and conditioning providing automatic answers. He lifted the scarf from his neck with badly shaking hands and wrapped it loosely around his head. That would have to do. No way he could tie it.

Next, he had to get the bear trap off his ankle somehow. The eyes could return any moment.

Michael tried to carefully slide his hand towards the bear trap, but his fine motor skills seemed to be missing. Either he was injured more than initially thought, or his fingers were numb with the cold. Or both. He forced the pain away and assessed the bear trap. He wasn't familiar with them outside of movies or secondhand accounts. Michael gingerly reached down again and felt around where the teeth bit deep into his skin for a moment, then felt along the trap itself. There wasn't a release mechanism that he could tell. He tried prying the jaws apart and managed an inch before his numb hands slipped on the blood slick jaws, and they snapped back down on his ankle. Ice cold metal burned hot as it bit deeper into his flesh. Sharp teeth grinding on bone.

Michael screamed out loud this time and fell back against the frozen ground. The gray snowy sky and tree topped horizon started to spiral, resetting every time he blinked in a nauseating manner. Whether it came from blood loss or hitting his head, it didn't matter. There was no coming back from this. He was done. He didn't fight the blackness but embraced it. "Finally." Michael choked out as the world fell away.

# CHAPTER TWENTY-THREE

Lucia floated gently in a warm golden abyss, contentment radiating from within. Distantly, she heard muffled noises but paid them no mind. Everything was perfect. A warm sun shined on her face, and she could hear a bird trilling. A cool breeze wafted from an open window, contrasting deliciously with the sun's warmth. There was an odd thumping in the distance. Dom must be up early, making breakfast. More likely, he had let her sleep in late and was cleaning the house. She smiled as she drifted on white clouds of bliss. Nice, sweet, thoughtful. Those words embodied her husband. This had the beginnings of a perfect morning.

A sharp crash of glass breaking thrust Lucia out of her sleepy bliss. She quickly sat up, looking around their tiny bedroom in confusion. The sun glowed in from the window, the cool breeze danced lightly on her skin. Everything seemed as it was, perfect. Had she dreamt the glass breaking? "Dom?"

A bright, tinkling sound of broken glass being swept up came from below. Lucia let out a frustrated sigh. So much for perfection. She swung her legs out of the warm bed and shivered as the gentle cool breeze hit them, now feeling a little on the cold side. She grabbed her light robe from the nightstand and slipped it over her shoulders.

The sun dimmed slightly as she made her way down the stairs. Abruptly, there was a low growl. Lucia paused at the foot of the stairs, confused as to where the sound came from. She turned towards the family room and jumped as a loud but flat crash came from behind her. She spun and somehow found herself in the kitchen. Dom was shaking a dustpan over the garbage.

"Sorry, didn't mean to scare you," Dom said, flashing his bright, wide smile that was so endearing. Lucia looked around, confused about how she had gotten so quickly to the kitchen. Dom gave her a slightly comically concerned look. "You okay there, sleepy head? You look lost. Must have been in some deep sleep."

"I-I guess," Lucia said, confused. She realized that her head felt a little foggy now, as if she had awakened straight from a dream. "I may go sleep some more." Dom shook the garbage can, and Lucia caught a waft of rancid meat, her stomach rolling with revulsion. Covering her nose and mouth, she asked, "Mind taking that out? It smells horrible."

A baby cooed behind her, and Lucia turned around to find a baby with really big, really cute pinchable cheeks sitting in a high chair, eating—no more like playing with pureed carrots. He, including the high chair and even the floor, were covered in them.

"You should have seen little Dom when I broke the glass," Dom said proudly with a chuckle. "His face went from absolute shock to '*what did you do*' in a split second." Dom made an exaggerated expression, eyes wide and mouth agape. "Then the poor kid had a giggling fit." Little Dom drooled and nodded his head as if agreeing.

"I bet!" Lucia said, her heart melting. She took a step towards him and tripped. Confused, she looked down. It felt like her foot had caught on something, but there wasn't anything on the floor. Weird.

"Cute little guy, isn't he?" Dom asked.

"Huh?" Lucia asked and looked up in surprise to find Dom cradling Little Dom in his arms, looking down at his son proudly.

"I said," Dom said distractedly, making exaggerated faces at his son. "That our son is absolutely adorable. And you know it, don't you, little guy." Little Dom cooed in response. Dom beamed at Lucia and said, "He looks like you."

Lucia smiled, and the confusion melted away. "Nuh-uh, He looks like both of us."

"True." Dom agreed. "Though he gets his best features from you."

Lucia smiled and reached out with both of her hands. Dom held little Dom out to her, and as Lucia reached out to grab her son, she felt another odd pull on her foot, like someone had grabbed her toes and pulled on them.

"Everything okay there, kiddo?" Dom asked, a concerned look on his face.

"Huh? What?" Lucia looked back up, and her smile returned. She couldn't help but smile at her husband holding her son. She should get the camera and—Another tug, stronger this time, and she almost fell. "Dom!" Lucia cried out, panic edging her voice. The rancid rotten meat smell was back and much worse now. The cold draft returned, giving her chills. Lucia frowned, looking around for the source.

"It'll be okay," Dom said, and Lucia looked up in confusion. Little Dom was swaddled now, and Dom was standing by the open front door, dressed as if going on a long trip. "You don't need to worry anymore. Our son is with me now." He said with a gentle smile.

"What?" Lucia asked, feeling panic rising. Another tug, more insistent. She looked quickly down. Nothing. She looked back up. "Dom?" She asked, her voice frightened.

"Don't worry, love bug. We will be seeing you soon." Pure light poured in the door, obscuring her husband like a luminous inverted shadow as he turned to go into the light.

"Dom!" Lucia screamed. Another hard yank, and the dream blew apart like smoke.

Lucia's eyes popped open, and discovered, to her horror, that the world spun, and her vision swam. Oh, she felt wrong. Very, very wrong! "Dom?" She cried out, her voice sounding wrong to her ears. No, that wasn't right. Dom was dead. Wasn't he? Her thoughts seemed muddled, like her head stuffed with sleep-infused psychedelic cotton. She shook her head to clear it and immediately regretted it as the world lurched.

"Michael?" She called out, tongue thick and mouth dry. "Roman?" The bright light blinded her as she looked for them. Then, the light became muted as if clouds had passed before the sun. "Hello?" A slight breeze stirred—where had it come from?— caressed her face. Just like her dream. Had it been a dream? Her thoughts were confusing, jumbled, and ill formed.

The breeze wafted again, colder now, and the air smelled rotten. Lucia gagged as her stomach boiled and the room spun.

Something scratched at her foot and then yanked hard, pulling Lucia off the couch. She landed with a painful thud. "Ouch!" She said and then felt something large clawing its way up her legs. She looked down as the sunlight brightened, craning her head around her protruding belly to find the top half of a zombie making its way up her legs.

Stunned, she could only take in details. The zombie's body was rotten past gender, with a masticated face framed by greasy black hair. One arm ended in a stump, with strips of flesh that looked like old torn leather. It used its other hand—despite missing several fingers, Lucia noted —to pull itself up towards her pregnant belly. Behind it, she could see a trail of brown red gore leading back to the two front doors. The glass in one door was half broken, and a smear ran down the front of it. The lower bisected half of the zombie lay behind the door, legs still twitching. It reached towards her belly and her beautiful baby in utero.

"Roman! Michael!" Lucia screamed, kicking the thing off her and away from her baby. "Help me!" Where were they? She tried to sit up and was nearly overcome as the room spun violently. She fought back the urge to vomit as she felt the zombie grab her foot again, interminable as death. Lucia kicked repeatedly at the thing's mangled face, its jaws seemingly the only thing untouched and working too well. She could hear the sharp click-click-click as the rotted teeth snapped together. "Help!" She screamed again. Where were they? Michael... was gone... left good? Panic spiked through the confusion, providing clarity like a lightning strike, and just as quickly faded away. Michael was gone. No, shooting range. Promised to be back. Roman, where was her brother? "Roman!" She cried out. "Wake up!"

It grew darker as a cloud passed in front of the sun, and the zombie growled as it quickened. Stronger now, it began tearing at her legs and feet as she fended it off, trying to get one of them into its jagged, broken mouth. One strong bite was all it would take. Lucia kept kicking until her leg muscles felt limp and weak and burned with fatigue. She didn't know how much longer she could fight the thing off.

"Roman!" She called out again. Wait, he had eaten the same things as her. Was he sick too? Passed out somewhere? She looked around the room, at the couches, at the chairs, at the empty kitchen door. "Roman, wake up!"

Abruptly, the sun returned in all of its brilliance, cutting a bright swath across the room that included Lucia and the zombie. The undead corpse groaned as it slowed, movements becoming weak and futile. Lucia pulled her knees in and then kicked the thing off her. It landed on its back a few feet away with a wet thump. It immediately began to turtle, slowly rocking back and forth, twisting and contorting its arms and torso to right itself.

Lucia tried to sit up, but the room swam so much that she almost passed out. She fell back, tears streaking her face. "What's wrong with me!" She sobbed. Was she sick? Was she drugged? Adrenaline and fear fought against something heavy in her body. Her thoughts were cloudy, it was hard to focus. Thoughts kept sliding away.

Had the eggs been bad? The cocoa? Oh no, her baby! The thought hit her like a lightning strike. Some things didn't go past the umbilical cord. Please God, whatever it was, let it be one of those things. It had to be one of those things. She took her eyes off the zombie, focused on the life force in her womb, and felt... nothing. "OH NO!" She wailed. Dom's words haunted her from the dream. "Our son is with me now."

The zombie groaned again as it heaved itself right side and started clawing towards her, bloodshot eyes lit with a dark light. Exhausted, Lucia kicked at it futilely, but the thing kept coming. She struggled to pull her pistol from the pocket, but the coat was wrapped underneath her body. She reached out instead, and setting her feet and palms of her hands on the wood floor, she scootched herself a few inches away from the zombie. The thing clawed towards her with its one arm, more than making up the distance she had moved. It reached out and grasped at her right foot, fingers looking like pale jerky that ended in bone nubs. Sobbing, Lucia slid back again, trying to move further this time. The room swam again. "Roman!" She cried out, voice slurring as if she was half asleep. "Wake up!" Nothing. "Roman!"

The zombie clawed at her feet again, forcing her to pull away. She kicked at the zombie and again pulled herself in the opposite direction. "Please. Wake up. Please, my baby, my heart, my everything, wake up!" She wailed. Only the zombie answered with its corrupted utterances. It was only a dream. She kept telling herself. It had to be. Not a nightmare manifest.

Lucia prayed desperately in Spanish that the sun would stay out of the clouds. Each time they passed through a section of shadow, the zombie became more animated, quicker, and stronger. Alternately, in direct sunlight, the creature visibly lagged, and Lucia was able to put more distance between them. Only to lose more than that in the next section of shadow. Sun or shade, regardless, the thing never lost focus on her, fueled by whatever evil compelled it.

On the other hand, Lucia knew she was running out of energy, adrenaline losing its battle against whatever was in her system. Exhausted, she pulled herself away again and sensed she was going into deeper shadows. At the same time, her hand found nothing when she reached back behind her, and she nearly fell back. Lucia looked and saw that she was at the edge of the stairs, could see the pots and pans, see the dark abyss down past them.

Just then, the sun slid behind another cloud. The quickened zombie snarled and launched itself at her with one quick pull of its arm. It landed on her chest, maw snapping at her face, hands, whatever fleshy part of her presented itself. Lucia screamed wordlessly as she fought back. The zombie bit the thick sleeve of her coat, rotten teeth chomping hard repeatedly as if trying to gnaw through. Lucia cried out in pain as the blunt teeth bruised her skin through the fabric. More glass shattered in the distance, but she could only focus on the nightmare before her.

The efforts to fight the zombie pushed her back until, suddenly, they were tumbling down the stairs. Lucia cried out in pain and fear as they landed, pots and pans crashing around them. Enlivened by the darkness at the bottom of the stairs, the zombie gave her no quarter, its ferocity unrelenting.

Lucia had no room to think, desperately fighting back but was quickly losing the battle. Her strength flagged, and her arms and legs heavy. Her hand abruptly brushed against the pistol in her pocket. She fought to get it out, fending off the thing with one forearm while trying to pull the pistol free with the other, but it was still caught in the folds of the pocket. The zombie ravened her arm through the coat sleeve, and Lucia screamed as pain ripped through her wrist, then was forced to flinch back as it began to snap at her face as if trying to eat her screams. Shards of broken teeth rained down on her face.

Lucia felt her energy fading quickly. No! She refused to die this way. Refused to let her baby die. Little Dom had to be alive. He had to be! Lucia twisted the pistol in her pocket and fired. A bullet ripped through the zombie's throat, knocking its head back, but to no apparent detrimental effect that she could see. Lucia tugged harder on the pistol, and it finally came free with a tearing sound. Lucia grabbed the zombie by its greasy, matted hair and screamed defiantly in its face. The zombie hissed in return. She slammed the barrel against the thing's head and rapidly pulled the trigger, screaming with each pull. Three blinding flashes paralleled by thunderous booms resounded in the small space, and cones of gore exited the opposite side of the zombie's head. It collapsed on top of her, weakly twitching, the dark, malevolent light fading in its mad eyes. Lucia collapsed too, falling back against the mangle of pots and pans, too weak to push the foul thing off her. Her vision swam violently, and everything became distorted as she teetered on the edge of passing out.

Another groan came from up above, followed by others. More than one. She had to get out of the stairwell, out of the building. Dazed from the fall and whatever it was that was making her sick, there was no way she'd make it up the stairs in her current condition. She would not, could not, focus on that right now. Roman would have to fend for himself. She had to get her baby to safety. That was the only thing that mattered.

Lucia kicked weakly at the rotting corpse until its torso slid off her. Painfully, she pulled her legs out from under the zombie and slowly got to her knees. She wobbled as the world spun violently, then turned her head and noisily vomited. Rehydrated eggs dyed a sickly yellowish brown by hot chocolate splattered on the steps and the zombie. The revolting sight, fueled by the zombie's rancid smell, made her vomit again. She heaved until her stomach was empty and still had to fight against the urge to be sick again. More glass broke above, followed by dull thumps.

Wiping her mouth with her uninjured forearm, Lucia tried the basement door and found it unlocked. She opened it quickly and was greeted with a wall of gloomy shadows that faded into pitch black. She paused, fearful of the dark, praying that there wasn't anything waiting for her in there. A guttural gasp came from above. Lucia looked up to see a female zombie looming over the banister, its awful gaze locked on her. No choice, as always. Lucia slipped into the black, quietly closing the door behind her.

# CHAPTER TWENTY-FOUR

Slow, muffled footsteps approaching on the snowy gravel woke Michael from his cold grave. He didn't recognize the sound at first, as it seemed oddly close and far away at the same time. Shivering, he opened his eyes to find himself blinded by a bright sun that peeked out of broken clouds. Michael weakly held a hand up to block the glare and turned his head to see a blurry shape approaching him.

The slow steps and ill formed shape triggered something in the befuddled recesses of his mind. Zombie. The word was like a bucket of ice-cold water had been dumped on him.

Michael fumbled towards the rifle, fingers painfully digging in the icy snow mere inches from it. The footsteps stopped. Michael cried out as the pain in his ankle renewed but continued to struggle for the rifle. His fingers barely brushed the stock, and then the zombie abruptly moved forward and kicked it away. Michael fell back, freezing and exhausted, looking up at the snow falling in his face from the gray sky. "Go on," he whispered bitterly. "Bite me. Kill me."

"Oh, I plan to kill you. Biting is not my thing, though."

Michael's eyes popped open, and discovered Roman sitting on a nearby stump, cradling his shotgun in his hands. He looked down at Michael's trapped foot and whistled shrilly. "Hope you had your tetanus shot."

"Help me." Michael gasped. His thinking still felt cloudy. Something was wrong.

Roman laughed, "After all the trouble I went to put you there?"

The confession cut through the confusion like a hot knife. "Y-you did this?" Michael gasped, his words sounding oddly disembodied to him.

Roman put a hand to his chest and bowed from the stump. "Of course I did." He said, matter of fact. "Wasn't about to let you get me and my sis killed. So-called gaseous clairvoyance aside, it was pretty stupid for you to think we would follow you to our deaths." He looked around and made an encompassing motion with his hands. "I mean, look at yourself. Take a good, hard look. The whole universe has decided to prove you wrong, and there you lay with the proof of it."

"I'm not wrong," Michael said, then lunged for the rifle again. His fingertips brushed it momentarily, then he screamed as the bear trap cut him short again. Excruciating pain lanced up from his ankle as the metal teeth tore through his flesh.

"Nuh-uh," Roman said, quickly jumping up from the stump and aiming the shotgun at Michael. "We'll have none of that." He danced around Michael's outstretched hand and picked up the rifle. "See!" He chortled, presenting the rifle as evidence. "Here's more proof! The universe, it doesn't want you alive. I don't want you alive. No one does."

"Lucia does." The words were barely out of his mouth before Roman kicked him across his face. Michael's head exploded with new pain.

"No," Roman continued angrily. "She doesn't. In fact, this whole plan was her idea."

"Liar," Michael said through thick, swollen lips. "I always knew you'd try to kill me."

"Woo, can't get anything past you. Well, except for the good ol' jaws of death gnawing on your foot." Haloed by the brilliant sun, Roman grinned down at him and then suddenly stomped hard on Michael's gut. He doubled over in pain, gasping for breath that wouldn't come. The motion caused tension on the bear trap and his ankle, and Michael spasmed between involuntarily trying to curl from the pain in his gut while simultaneously trying to release the unbearable tension on his ankle.

"Didn't see that coming, did you?" Roman asked gleefully and then kicked Michael hard in the side. "Gut didn't warn about that one either, did it?" Then he stomped down on Michael's trapped ankle. Michael screamed, nearly blacking out from the agony.

Roman crouched down next to Michael as he writhed in pain. "I've thought hard and long on how to kill you. It's been my sole focus since the moment we met. I usually prefer a simple approach, to be honest. But I can be a man of schemes when needs be." He turned to look behind him, towards the direction of the hunting lodge. "Speaking of which, I was planning on simply blasting you with my shotgun, but, you know, I think we are just too close to the lodge, and the sound may wake her up so…"

Roman shouldered his shotgun and picked up the rifle from the ground. He gently brushed snow from it, then suddenly brought the rifle stock crashing down on Michael's forehead. Brilliant epileptic stars burst before Michael's eyes as his head rebounded from the ground. His entire skull rang, resounding like a death knell. It reverberated throughout his body. Wherever it went, he no longer felt pain. Darkness crept in at the edge of his vision.

"No one wants you here, so die already." He slammed the rifle's stock down on Michael's head again, and all Michael saw and felt for a moment was blinding pain. The shadow people snapped into view as Roman drew the rifle up for another strike. They surrounded Roman and Michael, not moving. All their countenances were facing Michael. Michael reached out to them with a bloody shaking hand, but they remained still, watching impassively.

Breathing hard, Roman examined the rifle. The barrel was now bent, useless. "Best that you accept that you are already dead. Better for everyone, especially my sister. Hell, even for you. You want to die, don't you? You're like all of those zombies. A walking corpse that doesn't have the grace to die." He lifted the rifle high above his head. "Just another zombie that needs to be put down."

Michael closed his eyes. This was the end. There was no more fight left in him. Roman was right, damn him. "Do it."

A sudden muted shot came from the direction of the lodge.

"What the hell?" Roman said, eyes going wide as he looked up in surprise. Three more shots followed a moment later. "No, no, no, no, no." Roman exclaimed in a rapid, frantic voice. "Why do these *things* always happen to me?" The question was angry and pleading. With one regretful glance towards Michael, he took off towards the lodge at a dead run.

Michael watched him go—a dark, blurry form moving in the white. The shadow people suddenly moved; they all seemed to tip forward and fall on him, and then he was consumed by shadows.

# CHAPTER

# TWENTY-FIVE

Lucia turned slowly from the door to find the darkness nearly absolute. *Please, God,* she thought shakily as her eyes slipped across the eigengrau. *Please let there be no zombies, no ghosts, no nothing.* She listened intently for any sounds of danger, but all she heard were loud, hollow bangs and scrapes from above. More glass breaking. How many zombies were already inside the building upstairs? Five perhaps? It sounded like twenty. The sounds reverberated and echoed, making it impossible to tell if any originated from the basement.

Lucia looked down at her belly in the dark for all the good that did. Always before, she could feel her baby's life force, whether he was asleep or awake. Sometimes, she could swear she even felt Little Dom's emotions bubbling inside her. Now, there was nothing! A lifeless void that annihilated her. "My baby's dead." She whispered as tears flooded down her cheeks. "My baby's dead!" She shrieked into the black, not caring if she awakened something. She wanted nothing more than to collapse on the spot and die from her broken heart.

Thought became action, and Lucia fell hard to her knees. She didn't feel the pain of them hitting the hard concrete floor and no longer felt the injuries sustained from fighting the zombie. Her only reason for living was now gone. There was nothing left to live for. Had there ever been, or had she fooled herself into believing what? That she would find a safe place for her baby to grow up? She couldn't keep him safe in the safest place, her womb! Lucia screamed out again in anguish and pain. Sniffling, she started to wipe the tears from her cheeks, then wearily let her arms fall. Let the tears be her mourning veil, her death shroud.

A loud crash came from the door behind her. Lucia gasped and quickly looked back into the darkness. She could only make out a dim outline where the light bled through the crack. What had caused it? Had another zombie fallen down the stairs and hit the door?

The sound did not repeat, and Lucia quickly looked around at the encroaching black for signs of life or death. Seeing nothing, she slowly and painfully got to her feet and started creeping slowly forward. There was an odd, faint, coppery smell to the air that she could not place, that overrode the underlying yet expected dank, musty smell.

Lucia swayed as another wave of dizziness hit her again. Abruptly, she turned her head and threw up. This time, she stopped trying to fight the reflex and instead just puked her guts out. It felt horrible every time she threw up, but she did seem to come out of the other side feeling a little better. Inspired, she stuck a finger down her throat and triggered her gag reflex. *I will never eat eggs again.* Lucia vowed as she threw up again. Or drink chocolate. Or anything. Finally, she was left breathless, exhausted, and fighting against dry heaves that wracked and twisted her abdomen. So much for the food. So much for everything.

The food had been poisoned. That was the only thing that made sense. But that frustratingly didn't make sense! Why would anyone poison food? Wait—Roman! He had also eaten the eggs and far more of it than she had. If he was still alive, then he was in rougher shape than she was. Sadly, she doubted it. Roman being alive, that is. If the poison hadn't got him, the zombies surely had.

Tears started anew as she mourned the loss of her twin. She didn't like him much in the end, but she still loved him. He was her family. The last, and now she was the only one left. She felt an overwhelming sense of loneliness and loss. Everything had been taken from her in a shockingly short amount of time.

Had Michael poisoned the food? Lucia stopped moving at the malignant thought. He had been so quick to leave after he had made breakfast. And had taken all of his gear. That was more than a little suspicious. But why? Why would he poison them? Why not just simply leave? She shook her head. That made as much sense as Roman poisoning her. Absurd.

Wait, Michael had eaten some of the eggs. Was he sick, too? She pictured him doubled up on the snowy ground, surrounded by zombies. But maybe he was okay 'cause perhaps it had been the cocoa that was poisoned, not the eggs, and Michael hadn't had any of that. He could still be out there, alive. He could even be on his way back from the shooting range. Didn't matter, now that little Dom was dead. Michael, if he were still alive, would only come back to find walking corpses.

Who had done the poisoning then, if it wasn't Roman

or Michael? Lucia numbly put a hand on her temple. Errant thoughts flooded her head like a broken sluice gate, each fast and slippery, rebounding off the other without cohesion. There were too many questions that her heavy feeling brain frantically tried to understand.

Abruptly, two words sprung up out of the spinning abyss of her mind. Poisoned bait. Lucia remembered her uncle Jay talking with her dad about leaving poisoned food for critters, as he called them. Raccoons, opossums, and even field mice would eat the tainted bait and then go off and die, leaving the rest of the unspoiled food alone. Had the hunters or somebody else poisoned some of the food to protect their food storage? If so, then they deserved a special room in hell. At the rate things were going, they were probably already there. "Good." She snarled quietly into the black.

After a moment, Lucia pushed all of that side. Anger and rage would not help her now. Her eyes must have adjusted to the dark as she suddenly realized she could make out a small faint light far in the distance in an oddly straight line. A curtained window or another door?

Lucia took a slow sliding step forward, then another. After a few steps, she bumped into something hard with her left hip and gasped at the sudden, sharp pain. Tentatively, she reached out with her hands and felt smooth, cold metal. Just a table set against the wall. Her hand errantly brushed something that crashed to the floor.

Abruptly, the dark writhed before her eyes. Lucia recoiled and backed away. Was it her eyes playing tricks on her, or was something there? Was that a whisper? Did something just touch her, pull her hair?

Loud banging came from somewhere behind her. She turned away, and her cheek brushed against something cold and metallic in the dark. Lucia flinched back and heard a rattle as she hit something there, too. Tentatively, she reached out and felt hard metal loops—chains.

Sniffling and confused, Lucia looked around and still saw nothing in the dark. She reached out with a tentative arm and felt around her, finding more chains. They surrounded her. Why were there chains in the basement? The coppery smell was strong now. She could almost taste it.

Lucia knelt and brushed her hand around the floor to see if the chains were connected to something. She felt only damp concrete, but then her fingertips scraped against a small metal disc perforated with tiny holes. A floor drain. Chains. Lucia's confused mind insisted there was a connection here, but what?

She reached out to one of the chains again and traced along it with her fingers until she found a hook at the end. A hook? Why would there be a hook? She wondered as a chill slipped down her spine. Chains and hooks under a *hunter's* lodge? "Oh no!" She gasped as a horrible realization hit her. This was where they slaughtered the animals they brought back from the hunt! Lucia yanked her hands back from the cold chain as if she had touched a hot stove.

Hunters chained up their kill and drained their blood. Dressed them. Funny, it was called that when it really meant cutting their fur off. A hysterical giggle bubbled up in her, and she squelched it by pressing her hands tightly to her lips, realizing too late that they smelled and tasted strongly of blood. Revulsion made her stomach threaten to bloom with nausea again, but she fought it off and spat repeatedly, trying to clear the awful taste from her mouth.

Lucia struggled to stand up, her hands first brushing and pushing away the chains, then grasping them to help pull herself up. She felt a panic attack coming and fought against it, though a small discordant part of her wanted to let it reign free. She stood, holding onto the chains, swaying for a moment.

Banging came from the door behind her, stronger, more demanding. Absently, she thought the sun must have gone dim again, hiding behind clouds. Lucia forced herself to let go of the chains. There was a decision to be made here. It wasn't to live— no, that had been taken from her the moment her baby had died. The only choice left to her now was where she was going to die. And she did not want to die in some nasty basement that reeked of old blood where animals had been slaughtered!

Little Dom deserved a better resting place. He deserved to be in the sun. He deserved to be alive! Lucia started sobbing again. She couldn't give him the gift of life, so the least she could do was give him a good place to die. She looked around for an exit, a way out, and was surprised to see a faint line of light in the distance.

There was a faint rustle in the chains behind her, and she shivered as a cold wind came out of nowhere. Lucia gasped and spun quickly, accidentally knocking the chains around her and causing them to rattle against each other. She searched the dark, her breathing fast and too loud in her ears.

Then it was gone. Had she imagined it? As the chains settled around her, she heard nothing and then heard the chains rustle around her, the sound circling her without a breeze to convey it. A sudden coldness came over her, and a profound sense of dread followed it. The blood smell became stronger.

Lucia felt like she was falling down inside.

The sounds above became muted, replaced by an oppressive silence that pushed at her from all directions. Suddenly, rapid, unintelligible whispers assaulted her ears, and what she could make out of the torrent forced her to cover them. Madness, hatred, malice, menace. Something terrible had happened down in this cellar. "Leave me alone!" Lucia shrieked at the onslaught, covering her ears. She had to get out!

She only took one step forward and then screamed as several chains snapped towards her and wrapped tightly around her forearms, biting painfully into her skin. The chains slowly lifted Lucia from the ground, and it felt like her arms were going to be ripped from their sockets. She flung her head back to scream, but an external force clamped down on her mouth. Instead, she screamed in her head as silent tears poured from her eyes.

The unseen force squeezed and constricted her. Disjointed amorphous images assaulted her, too fast to make sense of. The icy cold dread intensified until she thought she would pass out. Lucia fought against it, refusing to die in this basement. She was filled with a visceral urgency to say something, to scream, that kept building until she felt like she would burst.

"Leave me alone!" she somehow managed to scream.

Abruptly, as suddenly as the onslaught had begun, the poltergeist let her go. Lucia felt its presence withdraw as it fled impossibly fast, wailing in an otherworldly voice. The chains wrapped around her arms went slack and then caught her as she fell. She swung and slammed hard against the wall before hitting the floor. Lucia lay gasping for breath, dazed and brutalized. The horrible images and feelings melted away, and now she only smelled a musty basement instead of a slaughterhouse.

Why had the geist run away?

Lucia was not waiting to find out. She shook the chains from her arms and felt deep welts and scratches along them where the hard metal had bit deep into her skin. It didn't matter. Nothing mattered but getting out of this hellish basement. She suddenly had a sad vision of her skeleton with her baby's skeleton lying together on the cold concrete floor in the dark. She wanted better for him, to die somewhere where sunlight could shine on him. Her baby had been in the darkness all of his life. He deserved to rest where he could feel the sun. Part of her knew something was wrong with that thought, but she was past caring. She needed to get out before the geist came back. The banging behind her had grown even harder and faster. She could not go that way. There had to be another way out.

Lucia looked around, but all she saw was black. Vertigo threatened to overwhelm her as the black started to spin. Closing her eyes did not help. She opened them and saw a faint line of light in the distance. The sun was back out!

Lucia forced herself to her feet, carefully ensuring not to touch the chains. They could be a trigger to bring back the geist for all she knew. She made her way towards the light, feeling the dreadful menace begin to build again behind her.

The sun went out again, and with it, the light. "No, no, no, no, no." Lucia whispered frantically. She kept moving forward in the dark, hoping she was heading towards the door, that it was a door and not a window. The horrible feeling continued to build. It felt as though, at any second, something would snatch her up and annihilate her.

She stumbled a few more steps and almost sobbed as her outstretched hands hit wood. A door! It had to be. A quick swipe of her hands confirmed it. The oppressive feeling behind her was almost a physical force. A heavy pressure began to bear down on her.      "GET OUT!"

Lucia couldn't tell if the voice was in her head or if she had heard it. Or both. It reverberated through her as if slow, icy, cold ripples on a pond.

"I'm trying!" She screamed back at the force, scrambling to find the doorknob. She heard the chains rattling behind her again. They began thrumming as if something was spinning them at a high speed. Her fingernails scored the wood as she looked for the knob. Sobbing, she finally found it, fumbled with the lock for a terrifying moment, then opened it.

Bright sunlight painfully blinded Lucia, but she didn't stop. She went through the doorway in a flash, then turned and slammed the door behind her. She collapsed against the door, too weak, too overwhelmed to go on. Maybe this was as good a place to—.

Something struck the door violently behind her, causing it to jump in its frame. Panting, Lucia backed away slowly, but it did not occur again. After a long moment, she released an explosive breath of relief, and as she inhaled deeply, she noticed a strong, familiar charnel smell of decay.

She turned and found herself surrounded by zombies.

# CHAPTER
# TWENTY-SIX

**M**ichael floated on warm eddies; his body curled up around itself. He didn't know how long he had been floating or how he'd gotten there. Wherever here was. Curious, he opened his eyes and realized he wasn't floating on water but in the air, hovering above snowy treetops.

He looked down and saw a broken, mangled body lying in the fresh snow. He floated closer and realized that it was his body. *I look dead*, he thought matter of factly, feeling no emotions other than curiosity as he floated above it. *Am I dead?*

A movement off to the side drew his attention. A young man running along a trail, racing towards the hunting lodge in the distance. Roman. Michael recognized and simultaneously dismissed the realization that Roman had done this to him. That was of earthly matters, and they no longer concerned him.

Michael ascended into the sky, finally free from the shackles of mortality. He rose, disregarding what was going on below or what had been. He was too caught up in the feelings of pure love and warmth to care. He was finally home.

On a whim, Michael started exploring the frozen forest, floating high above the trees. The bright sun suddenly pierced through the large fluffy clouds, and Michael basked in it. He looked up and didn't see the sun. It must be hidden by clouds, he thought. His eyes were drawn to a bright, glowing light on a cloud, almost as if it were reflecting the sun's light. No, he realized with a start that someone, a *personage*, was on the cloud, and *they* were radiating the ethereal light. Curious, Michael floated up, drawn as a moth to flame. The light grew brighter as he approached until he could not make out any details of the person, only an outline. Oddly, the intense light did not hurt his eyes.

Suddenly, the light flashed once and then went soft, and Michael saw a woman perfected, sitting on the edge of the florescent cloud with a radiant smile almost as bright as the sun behind her. She wore white, flowing robes that appeared to be made of shimmering light.

"Hello, Michael." She said in a sweet, familiar voice.

"Is it really you?" Michael asked, stunned.

"Of course I'm me, silly," Steph said, and her smile widened. "Who else would I be?"

Michael couldn't help but return his wife's smile. It felt good. It had been far too long since he had a reason to smile. His eyes hungrily took in everything about Steph. She was flawless now; even the small scar on her chin from a fall on ice when she was a teenager was gone. He looked down at his hands and frowned at seeing small scars on his knuckles.

"Where are we?" he asked, looking up at the soft blue sky and exquisite scalloped clouds surrounding them. Indescribable beauty, but his eyes quickly drew back to Steph.

"Where do you think?" Steph asked with her bright laugh. Michael found himself smiling again. Oh, how he had missed that laugh. It was something that he had never thought he would hear again. "Is this... is this heaven?" he asked in a hushed tone, worried that speaking louder would disrupt everything.

Steph gave him a coy look. "Let's just keep things simple and call it that."

Michael looked around quickly and then whispered, "Does this mean I'm dead?"

Steph shook her head. "Not yet, but we have a few things to discuss before you return."

"Return?" Michael felt cold for the first time. He looked down and saw that he was again floating over his injured body. It was lying in broken sunlight, surrounded by a circle of red splattered snow. "You mean I have to go back?" He pointed down at the body. "To that?"

"Yes," Steph said patiently, ignoring the body below. "You must go back."

"But why?" Michael suddenly felt like a condemned prisoner who had his execution stayed, only to be told it was still moving forward. "I don't want to go back! Back to that miserable place. Back to that broken, disgusting body. I'm here now. Can't I stay here with you?"

Steph shook her head solemnly. "No. Not yet."

"Um, can't you put in a word with the big guy?" Michael looked up at the sky above them as if he thought he would see God's face towering over them.

Steph laughed as she shook her head. "It wouldn't do any good."

Michael's face fell. "Am I... am I meant for the other place then?" He asked in a quiet voice.

"Hell?" Steph asked in surprise. "No, my love, not that place either."

"But, why bring me here only to send me back?" Michael asked, perplexed.

Steph leaned towards him. "Because you and I need to talk about a few things before you are sent back to your task below."

"Task? What task?"

Steph shook her head. "We will discuss that in a moment, but first, you need to forgive yourself."

That came as a sucker punch to Michael. "I-I can't. There are so many things I've done wrong."

Steph shook her head and held up a hand to stop him. "No, one. There is only one thing you need to forgive."

"What?" He asked, perplexed.

"Surviving."

"What? Sorry, I'm not following," Michael said, confused.

The clouds above them changed, and Michael looked up to see two babies in utero hugging each other. Somehow, Michael found he could feel the love and warmth the two shared in their bond, which was also shared by the love of their mother in her womb. Then, abruptly, one suddenly slipped away, and the other's light dimmed and went out.

"You survived being born, but your twin did not," Steph said.

Michael frowned and thought about that for a moment. His life would have been very different with a sibling, a twin, no less. He'd come out first and survived. Maybe if his brother had come out first, he would have lived instead. Michael had always felt guilty about that, irrational as he knew it was. There were also feelings of loss and loneliness of not only being an only child but also twinless.

"You survived the car crash that killed your parents." Steph continued, interrupting that train of thought. Another gut punch. Harder this time because, unlike his twin, whom he had never known outside of utero, he had vague memories of his parents, especially his mother. The clouds changed, showing a young boy with curly black hair sitting in the back of a station wagon. He was humming contently to himself as he played with a toy spaceship. Michael heard voices and looked to the front of the car. Mom and Dad. Talking in the front seat. Michael found tears in his eyes as he saw his parents for the first time in decades. Just as he remembered. Before...

"I'm hungry." Michael heard his younger self say.

He heard his mom laugh, sweet and fond. "Of course you are, my little, growing boy." Then his dad's gruff but warm voice followed. "We'll be at the diner in a few minutes. Think you can hold out?"

There was a loud pop as a tire blew.

Abruptly, his parents were screaming and yelling. His father was frantically driving, swerving. The car hit a cement barrier with a crash, flipped in the air, hit the ground, and rolled several more times. Michael's perspective changed, and he was his young self again. He could hear his mom weeping. He looked up to see her by herself, hanging in the air from her seatbelt in the upside down car. Later, he would learn that his father had been thrown from the vehicle and had died instantly.

Ignoring his injuries, Michael crawled on the ceiling of the flipped car to his mother. There was blood everywhere. She stopped crying when she saw him and gave him a sad, reassuring smile. She reached out to cup his face with a bloody hand. "I love you." She whispered hoarsely. "Remember to be happy. Promise me that you will." Then her light, too, went out.

Michael found himself back in front of Steph. She wasn't watching the images, only his tear-stricken face with eyes were full of love and compassion.

His grandparents had taken him in after the fatal crash, and while they had loved him fiercely, it had been a long time before he had fulfilled his promise and felt happiness again. It was short lived, however. His grandparents were elderly, and both had passed away in the few short years ahead. While these weren't sudden deaths, they still hurt him as they had been his only remaining family. With them gone, he'd moved in with a high school friend. Then he joined the army as soon as he had graduated to find himself and...

"You survived the ambush that killed your squad while on patrol." The clouds changed, showing the faces of his squad. They were so young looking now.

Another hard punch. His squad had been his second family, his brothers, but in truth his family when he was younger. All of them had been surrogates for his lost family.

The clouds changed yet again. His squad had been en route to a remote village on a humanitarian mission, bringing medical supplies, food, and water. An IED exploded and wrecked their Humvee. Michael, stricken and unable to move, remembered hearing bullets pinging off metal and the cries of his squad, his friends. He had listened as, one by one, those cries faded until there was silence. He should have died with them, should have—.

"You could not save me." The words hit Michael like a tidal

wave. This one would have brought him to his knees if he hadn't been floating. The clouds changed again and he saw himself leading a group of survivors through a darkened, burning city. Steph was limping at his side. Suddenly, as the sky began to lighten, one of the survivors started attacking the others. Michael watched helplessly as the man hit his wife so hard she landed twenty feet away. The man ran off, chasing after a few of the survivors. Then he saw his former self cradling his dying wife.

Michael turned from the vision in the clouds to look at Steph. She continued to watch him with a mixture of impartial compassion. The image of her dying did not seem to affect her at all. Michael wished he could say the same. It was as if he was still there, raw, and feeling it again for the first time. Steph's voice from the cloud vision drew his attention back to it.

"I'm dying."

"No, no, no, no!" Michael cried but was pulled into the clouds again, and he was there, crying and cradling his dying wife.

Steph shook her head slightly, and then when she spoke, it was with the muted timber of someone slipping between life and death. "Beware the wolves in sheep's clothing."

Michael saw confusion and indescribable pain in his other countenance. "Shh, don't speak."

Steph's past self suddenly spoke loudly and clearly. "Beware the wolf!"

"Okay, okay, I will." Michael saw his other self promise in a broken voice. He looked down and closed his eyes, not wanting to witness his wife's death a second time.

"Beware." Steph's voice was barely audible now, as if what

she had previously said had taken all of her energy. "Beware, for they hate you most of all. Shepard those in need."

"I tried so hard." Michael cried as the vision faded. "I couldn't...I can't protect. You're dead. I failed you."

"You need to let that go," Steph's angel told him. "There wasn't anything you could have done to help. You're not responsible for my death. It was my time." The clouds changed to show visions of his parents, his squad, and Steph. "You could not save any of them. You must forgive yourself so you can be here with me."

Michael shook his head.

"Look at the clouds again." Steph insisted. "Look at the lives that you touched, blessed by being with you."

Michael did and saw his parents, his squad, and Steph. "All I see is my failures." He lowered his head and saw his ruined form below. "That's where I deserved to be." Or worse, he thought bitterly.

"Or worse?" Steph said sternly.

Michael looked up, surprised that she had read his mind, but she quickly continued. "Michael, you need to let this go. None of this was your fault. This misplaced guilt you carry keeps you from my side. You are worthy of heaven."

"I'm not," Michael insisted through gritted teeth. "Rachel."

Steph shook her head solemnly. "Rachel was always on a path to self-destruction. She was simply a tool to put you on your path so that you could be where you were needed most. You don't need to carry that burden."

"It isn't that easy."

Steph made a very unladylike, let alone un-heaven-like snort. "Forgive yourself, maybe give yourself a break for things outside of your control, and you can be with me forever? I'd say that is pretty easy."

He stared at the broken body, which represented his failure. "It was my responsibility to protect you, my squad, and everyone. I should have done better. I need to be able to save at least somebody."

"You wouldn't be a shepherd if you thought otherwise." Steph said with a gentle smile.

"Shepherd?" Michael looked up from his bloody body in surprise.

Steph nodded. "A special soul. One that guides and protects his flock."

"Flock? What flock?"

Steph laughed. "Okay, one that protects people, then." She cocked her head to the side for a moment, then continued, "Maybe you need to see yourself through my eyes. The way I see you."

The clouds changed again, and Michael noticed a subtle hue change to red and pink. The images resolved to show Steph broken down on a dark dirt road in the middle of the night. Michael watched as his former self pulled up behind her in his decrepit pickup truck. Steph saw him approaching and locked the door.

Michael could tell as he watched the images that Steph was scared at first, but then the Michael in the clouds didn't speak to her. Instead, he motioned for her to open the trunk. Steph complied, and Michael quietly replaced the tire. After he was done, he put the tools away, closed the trunk, tapped it a few times with his hand, and started walking to his truck without another word.

The vision panned to show Steph arguing with herself in the car. "I just knew I had to tell you thanks, for some reason unknown to me at that time." Steph explained. "It's funny how God works sometimes." Michael was already in his truck, however, and started to drive around her. Steph, in a panic, starts her car and pulls out sharply in front of Michael, and he nearly hits her.

"Are you crazy? What are you doing?" Michael roared as he got out of his vehicle. Steph stepped out of her car as well and surprised him by walking right up to him in the middle of the night on a deserted road. Michael sees fear in her eyes for a moment as he towers over her, glowering, but then her eyes narrow in surprise for a second, and then she lit up the night with one of her trademark smiles. "Wait, sorry! I just wanted to thank you..." He heard Steph say without missing a beat in front of his glowering past self.

"You saw something back then, didn't you, that made you not afraid," Michael asked, voice hushed again.

"I saw you," Steph told him. The real you—the one that you try so hard to keep hidden from the world—the best part of you. I had a sudden insight into who you were, and I fell in love with you at that moment. I knew then I was going to marry you. Plus, I prayed later, and God confirmed to me that I would."

Michael was stunned. "I didn't know that." He watched as the Steph in the clouds smiled and hesitantly reached out to touch his arm. Seeing this as an observer, Michael realized something for the first time. "Hey, you were flirting with me!"

Steph nodded, and Michael was surprised to see her blushing. The clouds around them changed to match her hue. "I was trying, lamely, I admit. Not normally my forte. But I wasn't about to let you go."

"Why?" Michael asked.

Steph shook her head. "You still don't see yourself as I do. Let's continue."

The scene on the clouds changed again. Michael and a nervous Steph stood on her father's porch. Michael watched as his past self put a hand on Steph's shoulder reassuringly. "It will be okay," he told her, and he saw Steph visibly relax.

"You had a way back then that made me trust and believe you." Steph said, watching, "You spoke with such quiet conviction. I knew we were going to be okay with my father, no matter what."

The door opened, and Steph's father stood at the threshold, his blunt face a thundercloud. "Hey Daddy," Steph in the vision said, nonplussed, and a miraculous change came of her father. He thawed out and smiled and swept his daughter up in a big hug. Then his eyes fell on Michael again, and his eyes became cold, challenging. Michael returned the look, then grunted as Steph elbowed him hard in the gut. Michael watched his former self extend a hand and watched as Steph's father looked down at the hand for a moment before turning and walking back into the house.

"Oh, he really didn't like you," Steph laughed.

"I know," Michael replied.

"You two were too much alike."

Michael looked over at his wife in surprise. "What does that mean?"

Steph gave him another coy look. "Temperament wise, you two were like two peas in a pod. Outwardly, you were large, scary, and imposing. Inwardly, you were both good people with big hearts, and you both loved me fiercely."

"He never forgave me for marrying you."

"Well, you did take the light of his life away from him," Steph said fondly, then giggled. "I also don't think he liked the fact you were closer to his age than mine,"

"Only by a year," Michael grunted. "Did he know that you chose me?"

"Um, I like to think we chose each other," Steph said with a prim look.

"We did," Michael quickly agreed. "Though apparently I didn't really have a choice in the matter."

"Exactly. Do you remember when you fell in love with me?"

"I thought you were, um, very cute that night., uh, with your car, but it wasn't then."

"Go on."

Michael thought about it for a moment. "It wasn't a moment. Like you felt with me, I mean."

"What was it then?" Steph prodded.

Michael thought about it for a long moment, and then the words came out quickly, "It was a million little things. It took a while, too long, for me to let my guard down. But you never gave up on me. I realized it one day."

"And?" Steph nudged again.

"And... I realized that you never would."

Steph was glowing again. "A girl likes to hear these things. Too bad it took dying and being in heaven to hear it."

"Um, sorry," Michael said, taken aback.

"Too soon?" Steph asked with an half apologetic smile.

"A little." Michael said, wincing.

"Ah, well. It was still nice to hear." She cocked her head to the side for a moment, and her eyes widened. "You need a win." She whispered excitedly.

"What?"

"You need a win!" Steph repeated. "Perfect. Then you can be with me."

"Wait, you are going a little fast for me."

"Go back. Be the hero I always knew you to be. Finish this one last task." The clouds changed, and Michael saw Lucia in jeopardy. "Save them so you can forgive yourself."

"Then we will be together?" Michael asked, feeling his very soul trembling as he waited for her response.

"Forever," Steph promised and leaned forward to kiss him gently.

The clouds changed again, and Michael saw perfect beauty surrounding them again. "Does everyone get this treatment?"

Steph's smile became secretive. "Even one soul saved is cause for celebration here." Her face became solemn again. "Are you ready to return?" She held up a finger. "I warn you that it will be difficult. Very difficult."

"No, I—." This could be the last time he saw her if he failed. No, he would do whatever it took to come back to Steph. He closed his eyes and said, "Yes. I am ready."

Michael started to feel a pull from behind and quickly reached out and gently ran his fingers through Steph's hair.

"Brat," Steph breathed, looking up at him with a fond smile.

Then, suddenly, he was flung back out of the warm light. He closed his eyes as he fell to the earth below, to his cold, broken body. The impact of his soul caused his body to jerk awake.

Michael screamed as all the pain in the world crashed down on him.

# CHAPTER TWENTY-SEVEN

**A** bright, uncaring sun mocked from a now cloudless sky. The storm had blown itself out, but a new one was brewing for Lucia. Stark in the brilliant sunlight, hundreds of zombies shuffled around the lodge grounds, their movement slow and clumsy. Oddly, they had not taken notice of her yet.

"From the pan into the fire..." Lucia whispered under her breath. She closed her eyes, fresh tears streaking her cheeks as she fell to her knees in the gravel, barely feeling it bite into her flesh. That pain was nothing next to what she felt in her heart and soul. She was utterly spent. She could not go on. Did not care to go on. Lucia heard guttural gasps as the nearest zombies finally took notice and looked up to see them start their slow shuffle toward her. She closed her eyes again, wishing it was already over with. She had broken her maternal promise to her baby. Lucia wanted to laugh at herself. What had she expected in such a miserable world? How had she ever been so delusional that she thought she could keep her baby alive?

She thought she heard a voice shouting her name in the distance. She refused to open her eyes. It was just her strained mind playing tricks on her. "Lucia!" Louder this time, more insistent. Lucia shook her head and looked up but couldn't see anything through the dozens of zombies approaching her. Had she imagined it? She shook her head. It didn't matter. Soon, nothing would matter. She lowered her head, numb to all.

She pulled the pistol out and placed it against her head. *Sorry, little one.* Tears flooded her vision, blinding her. Lucia pulled the trigger and heard nothing but a dry click. Had she pulled it? The world spun in its inanity. She repeatedly pulled the trigger, but the clicks did not lie. There was nothing left. She had nothing left. Lucia let the gun fall to the ground and impatiently waited for death to find her. She saw their feet shuffle closer and closer. Finally, stiff fingers wound themselves in her hair. Lucia helplessly watched as a corpulent corpse leaned down, its gaping maw growing inhumanly wide, skin and flesh tearing at the edges of its mouth.

A shotgun blast wiped the thing's face away, and it fell behind her with a loud thud. Lucia turned numbly to find an angry and bloody Roman fighting to get past the zombies. He laid into the zombies with the shotgun, alternatively blasting or swinging it like a club.

"Get up!" Roman cried out as he came closer. "Come on, what's wrong with you? Get up!" he demanded as he reached her side.

Dazed, Lucia could only stare up at her twin. She opened her mouth to explain why all of his efforts were for naught, why he should have just stayed away and left her, but the words escaped her. Now her twin would die too. Everyone in this world, this hell would die. It was so apparent to her now. Lucia didn't get up. She started crying instead.

"Why aren't you moving?" Roman snapped as he dragged her to her feet. "Are you injured? Are you bit?" He ran his hands quickly over her neck, checking for bites. Lucia shook her head, not at Roman's questions but sad that he had prolonged her death by a few seconds.

"I'm going to get you out of here," Roman promised, but his voice lacked conviction. Rotten death closed in on them from all directions now, and they had only seconds left. Roman released her, and she fell back down to her knees. Screaming in rage, Roman blasted his shotgun until it clicked empty, but the zombies didn't stop coming. Wouldn't be long now, Lucia noted distantly. A zombie grabbed her hair and pulled hard on it, causing her to scream in pain. Of course, her last moments wouldn't be painless; nothing in this world was.

Roman grasped his gun by the barrel and swung it like a bat at the zombie holding her. It went down in a spray of ichor. A zombie grabbed Roman, and another one tripped and fell against him. Roman floundered and then shoved them away, knocking down other zombies. More closed in, and he desperately fought back, breathing hard from exertion.

Lucia felt a hard nudge against her back that nearly knocked her over. A zombie reached down, exposed phalanges like white, dull claws. It grabbed her roughly by the throat, and Lucia closed her eyes as it leaned in for the kill. A horrible pain was coming. Yet that would have nothing on the pain of losing her baby. *Sorry, my little one.* Lucia had hoped—a ridiculous feeling that now realized—that she could have at least found a good resting place for the both of them. She should have known there were no mercies left in this unkind world. *I will see you soon in heaven.*

Then everything stopped. Everything went quiet. The shuffling of feet, the groans, even the creaking tension of sinew, the cracking of joints. An unsettling quiet overcame the area, only broken by a light wind that seemed to emphasize the absence of sound.

Lucia opened her eyes and looked up in surprise. A forest of zombies surrounded her. Standing still. Not moving, not shuffling. Frozen as if someone had hit the pause button.

"What's this happy crappy?" Roman asked, eyes wild. He tore free of the zombies holding him and shoved them away. They fell down like mannequins. Roman backed away and ran into one behind him. With a yelp, he spun around, ready to swing. But that zombie fell to the ground, too. "What the hell?"

Lucia gasped and looked around in shock. All of the zombies were still as statues, absolutely still. She felt overwhelmed. This was all too much. Was this all a delusion, a side effect of the poison? Lucia slowly and carefully stood up, worried that making the wrong move might trigger the zombies to attack again.

The horde did not react.

Emboldened, Lucia grew closer to one of the undead. She braced herself and then looked directly into its dead, bloodshot eyes and instantly felt the familiar jolt of pain directly to her soul, but at the same time, it seemed to stare through her.

"Come on, sis. Let's get out of here," Roman said, beckoning to her with his free hand.

Then she heard footsteps approaching, soft in the snow-covered gravel. Clear, sure steps. Strides of a human. Not the ungainly gait of a zombie. Was it Michael? No, somehow, Lucia knew it wasn't him. She backed away from the sound and began looking for a way out, but the zombies were too thick around her.

The footsteps grew closer, and a wave of zombies reacted as something moved through them, parting them like a shark swimming through a school of fish. No, it definitely wasn't Michael. Roman stepped protectively in front of her and gave her a fearful backward glance.

Lucia backed away until she brushed a zombie behind her. She spun, ready to fend off an attack, but it stayed inanimate, its bloodshot eyes seeing through her, too.

She turned and watched as the dead sea parted in front of her. The zombies came to life for a moment, their movement unnaturally fluid and synced, stepping back, then becoming statues again.

A man stood in the space between. Normal for all appearances except for the fact that he was far too immaculately groomed and dressed for the apocalypse. A perfectly groomed beard and an expensive suit with no wear.

Lucia giggled at the absurdity of it all. She couldn't help it.

The man looked at her, and Lucia shivered. It felt like she'd just been splashed with ice-cold water. Blue cobalt eyes stared at her. Michael's eyes.

No, it wasn't Michael, and those weren't his eyes. They were a similar color but weren't tortured like Michael's. An electric light seemed to emanate from them. It could have been a trick of the sunlight, but Lucia knew it wasn't. Everything about the man screamed wrong to her.

"Who the hell are you?" Roman asked, holding the

shotgun ready. "You are all kinds of wrong, man."

The man grinned in response, and Lucia then knew. A wolf. That was what Michael called them. Was it controlling the zombies somehow? Yes, that made mad sense in this insane world.

The man—no, the wolf—looked at her sharply, and she realized she had spoken aloud.

"Wolf." It said, then smiled as if flipping a switch. Humor crinkled the eyes, but none was found in them. "How do you know that... word?" It asked in a voice throaty but smooth like velvet. His movements were twitchy and weird, as if trying to contain something wild and fey inside.

Roman looked over his shoulder at her. "Run." He told her under his breath.

Run? Run where? Hundreds of zombies surrounded them, and she could barely walk, let alone run. There was no hope. Roman didn't realize it yet. She said nothing and just stared at the man—no, the wolf. She absently corrected herself again. Oddly, she still wanted to only think of it as a man even then.

The grinning mask dropped, and irritation replaced it. He made no motion, but something grabbed her arms. A zombie. "No!" She wailed, fighting against its iron grip.

"Get away from her!" Roman yelled, turning. Three nearby zombies quickly jumped on him. Moving fast in bright sunlight as if it were dark! Now they were well and truly screwed. The tight jumble that was Roman and the zombies suddenly froze. She could see him, caged in by the arms and legs of the now frozen zombies. She heard muffled cursing.

"Stop!" Lucia screamed, fighting against its grip. "Leave him alone!"

"Never you mind." The wolf told her. "They won't hurt him." A silent 'yet' seemed to follow, like an unspoken promise. "As long as you answer my questions." It grinned again, showing too many teeth.

Lucia looked at the wolf in surprise. Questions? What questions?

The wolf nodded as if she had spoken those words aloud. "Where is he?"

"He?" She looked at Roman, confused. Did he mean Michael? She turned back to the wolf. "I don't—"

Anger flashed in those hard cobalt eyes, and the zombie's hand tightened hard enough to make Lucia cry out.

"The shepherd." It drew the word out in the hiss of a snake. "We've been looking for him for a long time."

A shepherd? What the hell? "I-I have absolutely no idea what you are talking about," Lucia said honestly.

"Ah." The wolf replied, implying that it was sad that she could not answer and would not be saved from her fate. The zombie holding her bent its head towards her neck, stopping at the last second. Her skin writhed as its bloated worm like lips brushed her skin.

"Stop!" Roman cried out.

"I don't know where he is!" Lucia screamed.

"You sure?" The thing's voice was as cold and dry as the grave. The zombie holding Lucia relaxed its grip and stood back up, removing its lips from her neck. Lucia shuddered. Had it bit her? Would she turn? She pictured herself as a sad pregnant zombie roaming the woods and felt like crying. No, that didn't matter now. Nothing did.

Oddly, Lucia felt an innate sense that she needed to buy

some time. Woman's intuition. But for what? One last miracle that the cruel world somehow owed her? She felt like laughing at that absurdity. To what point? Everyone was dead except her brother and perhaps Michael. Where was he? He should have been back by now. Was he dead? Had he abandoned them? If so, then she hoped his death would be prolonged and painful.

"Wait! I thought you said I was safe as long as I answered your questions."

"Yes, and I am all out of questions."

"I don't know where he is. I swear to—"

The wolf threw up its hand. "Enough." Again, he made no motion or said anything, but the zombie holding Lucia painfully tightened its grip and leaned down, jaws wide. It seemed like slow motion to Lucia. The kiss of death. She knew there was no stopping it this time. She closed her eyes as it drew close.

"Wait! Stop." Roman said, sounding hurt and desperate. "I killed him. He's dead."

Lucia looked at Roman in shock. "What do you mean?"

Roman ignored her, never taking her eyes from the wolf. Lucia realized the zombie had also stopped, though its grip was still painfully tight on her wrist.

That was when she heard footsteps approaching on the snowy gravel. Oddly, a metallic clank came with every other step.

The wolf grinned like its namesake and turned, arm extended like a circus ringmaster. The sea of zombies parted to show a single zombie standing at the far side of the circle, its face a mask of blood.

The mask obscured details, but Lucia could see a white flap of torn skin hanging from the zombie's forehead. There was a dent in its exposed skull. It started forward, an odd metallic clank coming from every other step. The sound drew Lucia's eyes to its ankle where a bear trap pointed jaws sawed back and forth with each step revealing bloody bone.

Then Lucia noticed the vintage hunting outfit, the sun glinting off the bent rifle the zombie held in one hand. Silver wolves. Lucia screamed in recognition and shock. Michael. The zombie was Michael!

"What did you do to him?" Lucia gasped, looking at the wolf.

"We?" The wolf said slowly as if tasting the word. "We did nothing." It turned to Roman. "Tell her. Your sin is fresh and delicious."

Lucia also turned to look at her twin. "Roman?"

Roman looked at Michael, then at her, and then hung his head.

Then it all came crashing down on Lucia. "You did this? All of this? You killed Michael?

Roman slowly shook his head. "No, I..."

"You're going to lie to me now, really?"

Roman slowly shook his head as if trying to escape a bad dream.

Rage filled Lucia, burning through the pain, through the numbness. Abruptly, as if anticipating her next move, the zombie let her go. Lucia lunged forward and slapped Roman as hard as she could. She slapped him again. Then she switched to punches.

Roman grabbed her hands, a hurt and angry look on his face. "Stop. Stop it! I had to. He would have killed us."

Wait," She said as a malignant thought occurred to her.

"You drugged me?"

"I, uh." He mumbled, refusing to meet her eyes.

"You killed my baby."

"What?" Roman looked up, stunned.

Lucia poked him hard in the chest. "You killed us! You killed my baby!" Lucia screamed at him. She fell back, sobbing.

Roman's eyes widened as he looked down at her belly in shock. His face drained of color, and his eyes began to tear up. "No! I never meant..." The damning words confirmed his treachery.

The wolf laughed then, sounding like gravel falling on a cold grave. A second later, a zombie lunged forward and bit Roman on the neck, and he cried out in pain and horror.

Lucia was too shocked, too numb to respond. Her whole world had crashed in on itself. She felt weirdly disassociated, like a spectator to her own execution.

Michael's zombie stopped as he reached the edge of the circle.

The wolf grinned its namesake grin. "Finally, the shepherd."

"Do... I know you?" Michael asked. The words were thick and slurred with pain.

Lucia gasped in shock. Michael was still alive! How? How was he even standing?

# CHAPTER TWENTY-EIGHT

**M**ichael watched the wolf through a nearly overwhelming haze of agony. He could endure it as it was nothing to the pain he had felt when he had lost Steph. He could feel his body dying, and knew there were only a few minutes left. He had one final task to complete. Then he'd be back with Steph. Forever.

He looked at the twins. Lucia sat on the ground, staring at him in horror and shock. He imagined he looked like a complete mess. Unfortunately, Lucia didn't look much better and Roman sat in a stupor beside her, the bite on his neck sealing his fate.

"You should know us," the wolf said, drawing his attention back to it. "You interfered in our hunt."

This sparked confusion in Michael. He didn't recognize the wolf. It didn't matter, he reminded himself. Lucia and her baby needed to get to safety. He couldn't fail them like Rachel. Then he remembered Steph's voice from the dream telling him that Rachel had always been walking that path. Sudden insight struck Michael, "The girl on the cliff's edge. Wait, you were the hunter?"

"Yes."

"But that is impossible. I killed you."

The wolf laughed, and the hair stood up on Michael's neck at the sound. The wolf said, "You can't kill us. We are legion."

"I saw you die." Michael went on stubbornly. I kicked your stinking corpse over the cliff."

The wolf smacked its lips, and then its body undulated violently once as if it had reigned in volatile anger. "That was just a meat suit. Its loss was merely an inconvenience until I found this one. Hiding in a hole in the ground. But his sins and intent made him mine." The wolf's eyes flickered to Roman momentarily, then returned to Michael. "You can't kill us. There is always another."

That meant the wolves could move from body to body, from sinner to sinner. That made horrific sense to him now, not that there was anything he could do with that knowledge. He turned to look at Lucia. She needed to get safely away. That was the only thing that was important. Would the wolf keep chasing her, hunting her? He could not let that happen.

But what could he do? How could he kill something apparently immortal as long as sin was in the world, especially this world? He didn't know, but at the same time, there was an odd feeling in his mind, almost like a forgotten word on the tip of a tongue that hinted that there was a way. Michael just needed to figure it out, and fast. He only had a scant few minutes remaining.

He turned to the wolf and said, "You've been following us for a while?" That was a little too close to the way the wolf spoke for his comfort. "You've been following me?" That question felt right to him for some reason.

"Yes."

"Bethsdale? The town?"

"No."

"The farmhouse."

"We saw the smoke, yes. Followed but could not see you." The thing cocked its head to the side like a cat. "Where did you go?"

The church, but that wasn't important. His gut was telling him that the farmhouse was the key. Something significant had happened there, but what could it be? Was there something in the interaction with the ghosts that was key? If so, he didn't know what it could be. "Please, Steph," Michael whispered, "give me insight."

The wolf growled, "We grow weary of the obvious, human." Two zombies grabbed Michael by the arms and dragged him toward the wolf. A sharp pain shot up from his mangled ankle as it dragged on the snowy ground, and he nearly dropped the rifle before clutching it securely to his chest. The gun's barrel was bent and unsound, but he might be able to pull off one last trick with it.

"Wait, what about the zombies we ran into with the bikers?" Michael asked as the two zombies stopped in front of the wolf. He noticed Lucia looking at him askance as if she, too, was wondering if there was a point to these questions. Michael noticed that his vision was beginning to narrow and dim like a vignette. Not much time left. Roman suddenly twitched violently. The boy didn't have much time either. None of them did unless Michael figured out the riddle.

The wolf waved his hand in a circular motion. "Yes. We

saw you, then lost you in the feast." It said with a depraved grin, then held up an impatient hand as if anticipating his next question. "Yes, we made the zombies wait for you in the mist." Its head tilted as if listening to inner voices. "We grow weary of your questions."

"So, you control them?" Michael winced at the obvious question, but it felt right to him for some reason. He was so close to figuring it out. And so close to death, too. He needed to figure it out now.

The wolf stepped up to him, grinning. "Yes." It purred, gesturing to the zombies frozen around them.

"They are like you then?"

The grin on the wolf froze. It looked at Michael and cocked its head to the side like a cat again, watching its prey curiously.

Michael knew he had hit upon something there, but what? The thing was like the zombies, but how? A weakness, perhaps? Fire! Its weakness was fire! It would permanently kill the wolf. Michael *knew* it, could feel it in his gut. He remembered the last road flare in his pocket. He was in striking range but needed to get the twins free of the zombies first to be safe.

Michael looked at Lucia, then at Roman. The boy looked in rough shape. His skin was a splotchy pale and red, and his eyes were bloodshot. Nothing could be done for Roman. He would turn within minutes. Michael felt he had the same amount of time. One last roll of the dice. If they could work together to save Lucia, then it was worth it. First, he needed to get Roman's attention. "Roman."

The boy did not react. He stared off at nothing in a haze. Michael prayed that the boy wasn't too far gone. "Roman, I'm sorry."

Roman's head shot up in surprise. He blinked at Michael as if trying to focus his vision. Lucia looked up too, and her eyes narrowed as if trying to figure out why he had said that. The wolf's lips pulled back in a rictus snarl as it realized something was up.

"Sorry, I couldn't take you and Lucia out fishing on the boat like I promised. I'm sorry about everything."

"Enough of this human." The wolf hissed. What are you up to?" It grabbed him by the throat, but Michael focused only on Roman.

Roman's eyes cleared up, but all Michael could see was confusion. Lucia was also giving him a confused look. "The boat." Michael mouthed at them, then made a subtle motion with his head.

Roman looked at the dock and back at Michael. After a very long second, he nodded and drew his feet up underneath him.

"Enough!" The wolf snarled and raised his hand to strike. No more time left. Michael gathered his remaining strength and tore his arms free from the zombies holding him. Yelling, he slammed the bent rifle into the wolf's face and pulled the trigger. The gun backfired, the small explosion rocking both of them. Michael felt hot, searing agony in his right hand and knew he had lost several fingers. The wolf screamed in dual-toned pain and rage, and the zombies writhed and howled in tandem.

"Run!" Michael yelled at the twins.

Roman lurched to his feet, his movements off balance. He looked at the mayhem around him in wonder, then suddenly snapped out of it and ran to his sister's side. Lucia was still sitting, staring blankly at the chaos. Roman said something to his sister and then heaved her to her feet. They started a slow limping run towards the dock.

Michael turned to face the still writhing wolf. Now for the next trick. He quickly thrust his hand into his pocket, pulled out the flare, and promptly dropped it. Michael looked down in surprise, and remembered that he was missing several fingers when he saw his mangled hand. All the zombies abruptly stopped writhing, turned en masse to glare at Michael, and screamed in unison.

The wolf slammed hard into him, knocking him back. Michael rolled away from the flare and ended up facing Lucia and Roman to find them halfway through the twisting and contorting zombies. They weren't far enough. He looked back to see the wolf and saw that its formerly well-groomed face was a bloody, ruined mess. One eye was missing and the other was glaring balefully at Michael. It lunged at him, and Michael quickly rolled underneath it and ended up on top of the flare. He barely had time to pick it up before the wolf was on him, hitting and tearing

"Run!" Michael screamed as the zombies swarmed him and the wolf. He again screamed as he felt the first bite, the second. In a few seconds, it wouldn't matter. Battered by the storm, he kept his hand clamped on the road flare. He then jumped at the wolf and slammed the flare into its chest and heard the sizzle as the flare ignited. Just as he was about to pass out, he saw the world ignite around him. Then everything went white.

# CHAPTER TWENTY-NINE

"**M**ichael!" Lucia screamed as she watched the zombies swarm her protector. "No!" Roman grabbed her arm and began to insistently drag her to the dock. She wanted to tell him to stop, that saving her was for nothing. "Stop!" She screamed. All she wanted was to join her son and Dom in heaven. Several zombies turned towards them.

"Wait here," Roman said, his voice full of pain. He had only moments left. Both of them did, the way things were going. Why fight and prolong it? There was nothing left for her to live for. They were all dead anyway.

Roman growled as he engaged the first zombie. He hit it hard with a fist, and the undead thing rocked back. Lucia was shocked to see it ignore her twin and instead make a beeline towards her. Roman lowered his fist, looking stunned. He watched as two other zombies walked past him, and as he watched them, a sadness showed on his pale face. He lowered his head with an agonized grimace and began breathing hard.

"Roman!" Lucia cried out as the first zombie reached her. It clutched at her with both hands. For a brief second, she thought again of surrendering. No! She was a fighter, and she would go out fighting. Lucia tried to run away but her battered body was too slow. The zombie grabbed her arm, refusing to let go.

Lucia spun away, momentarily breaking its grip. It quickly latched back on, and Lucia threw her arms up, hands pressing on its chest. She tried to push it away, tried to break the grip again, but she was too weak. The zombie snapped at her with rotten teeth, its insistent movement slow in the bright sun. That was her only saving grace, a momentary respite as the two other zombies reached her struggle. Behind them, she could see Roman, head still down, his chest heaving. He twitched as if fighting a battle inside him. Several other zombies walked past, ignoring him. Only moments left now.

"Roman!" Lucia screamed again as she fought to keep the zombie from biting her. "Snap out of it!" The two other zombies arrived and pushed in at her, throwing her and the zombie she was fighting off balance. The momentum spun Lucia away, and she could no longer see her brother. Seconds left now.

This was it. One bite and death would follow. Would her zombie endlessly walk the land, forever pregnant? With a zombie baby in its womb? The thought horrified and sickened her. She had only wanted to die someplace nice for her baby, but this ugly world did not care what she wanted. Still, Lucia fought on. She'd fight bitterly to the very end. She didn't know any other way.

There was a loud crack, and one zombie careened off her and dropped to the ground. Two more cracks followed, and the other zombies fell beside it. Stunned, Lucia looked down and saw that the zombie's heads were caved in. She glanced up and saw Roman standing near her. His head was down, chest still heaving. He was holding tightly onto a small log, his knuckles white with effort. Several zombies were down in his wake.

"Roman?" Lucia asked nervously.

"Run!" He screamed at her in an almost inhuman voice. Lucia was too shocked, too overwhelmed to move. Roman snarled and lunged at her. Lucia tried to throw up her hands to block him, to stop him somehow from biting her, but Roman instead took her arm with one hand and started to drag her towards the pier again. He still held the small log tightly in his other hand, using it to eliminate any zombies that went after them. No, not Roman. Only her, Lucia realized with a distant horror. The things practically ignored Roman, making it easy for him to dispatch them with his newfound, albeit double-edged immunity.

Abruptly, all of the zombies were running in their direction. Lucia looked back, trying to see what was going on. Was it Michael? Was he somehow still alive? No, she thought when she saw a tall pillar of green fire growing behind them, consuming the zombies that weren't moving fast enough. Michael was dead, and they were next.

She didn't need Roman's prodding to run. She ran as fast as she could, faster than she thought her exhausted and battered body could run. Roman still held her wrist in an iron grip, pulling her straight towards the boat dock without looking back.

Lucia screamed as several of the zombies caught up to them. She watched in shock as they ignored her and continued running beside her. Roman ignored everything, single minded in heading towards the dock. Lucia almost tripped and would have fallen if it weren't for Roman holding her hand. Falling would be a death sentence; the stampeding horde behind would trample them.

Lucia looked back and saw a fast-approaching wall of green flames sweeping through the zombies. "Run!" This time, she was the one who was screaming it. She could feel the sparks stinging her skin as she ran.

She felt her feet hit the wooden boards of the pier, and her exhausted legs buckled under her. Roman held her arm, dragging her without slowing as he ran towards the rowboat. She looked back again and saw the bright, iridescent fire greedily consuming the zombies as they attempted to run down the pier or as they attempted to jump into the water. The flame continued to roll forward as if a powerful force was pushing them.

The conflagration caught up to them just as they reached the docked rowboat. Lucia cried out as they were enveloped, and then Roman jumped. She was airborne for a second and then landed hard in the rowboat, next to Roman, nearly capsizing it. His clothes were smoking, and his exposed skin had second-degree burns and pockmarks.

Lucia quickly looked at the exposed skin on her hands and felt her face. The skin was red and tender, like a mild sunburn. She had only been a second behind Roman. Why was he burned worse? Then she saw the bite on his neck and knew. Roman was close to turning and more susceptible to fire. Roman gave a feral growl as he tamped out the smoke on his clothes. He bared his teeth for a moment, and Lucia braced herself, unsure if it was from the pain or if he wanted to attack her.

Then he resolutely turned around and sat down. He

grabbed the oars and started rowing.

Lucia watched as the flames consumed the remaining zombies, the hunter's lodge, everything. It was as if all of the evil was purified. Michael was gone. No one could survive that inferno. Hopefully, now his spirit could rest. Hopefully, they all could rest soon.

Roman stopped rowing and stayed still, twitching as he fought the evil within. The evil that Lucia now realized had always been a part of him. Now, it was physically manifest.

They drifted in the water for a few moments. Lucia watched with growing concern as Roman's twitching became worse. Battered and wrecked, emotionally and physically, she did not have it in her to fight a zombie, let alone one that had been her brother, on a boat in the middle of a lake.

Then, the trembling movements stopped.

"Roman?" She asked tentatively, reaching a hand out to touch his shoulder.

"Don't touch me!" He snapped over his shoulder, voice guttural and corrupt. She let out a breath of relief even as she pulled her hand back. No, he had not turned yet, but it wouldn't be long. She had caught a glimpse of his right eye and saw it was completely bloodshot. Like a zombie.

There was a loud bang and explosion as the side of the lodge blew out. Roman looked up briefly, then lowered his head and started rowing again. She heard a soft gasp and saw that he was twitching again. No, she quickly realized, her twin was sobbing. Lucia stared impassively at his back, having difficulty feeling any compassion for him. This was all Roman's fault. All of it.

No, she realized with a sigh. Not all of it. The wolf showing up was not her brother's fault, but they may have been better prepared for when he showed up if Roman had not been so stupid. No doubt in his twisted mind, he had only been thinking of protecting her. That was his only intent, she realized and softened a little, only for the second it took for her to remember that her baby was dead because of him.

So, she watched him cry, with tears in her own eyes, conflicted as she wanted to both console and condemn him at the same time. He was her brother, after all, and only family could make you feel this way.

Then Roman's rowing slowed down, his head still down. Just the two of them. Soon, it would be one. And then...

Roman began trembling violently again, and the battle began anew. He started rowing harder, the movements growing more erratic, to where they began spinning in a slow circle. Lucia realized with a sudden insight that Roman was running away, as he always did. Finally, he threw the oars down in their oarlocks with an anguished cry.

They spun lazily in the middle of the lake. Lucia saw that the hunter's lodge, what was left of it after the explosion, was engulfed in flames. Many of the cabins were as well. Grey ash swirled in the air, covering the snow where it had not melted away from the heat.

"I'm sorry," Roman said finally. His voice was agonized and strained. "I made such a mess of things. I'm an idiot. I'm such an idiot!" He picked the oars up and started rowing again, then stopped. "Never meant to harm you or your baby. I was only trying to protect you. Both of you. I... just didn't do good enough. Didn't protect you from me." He stood up, still shaking and jerking, and put a foot on the edge of the boat. "There's one last thing I can do. I promise I won't screw it up."

"No!" Lucia shouted despite herself.

Roman looked at her then with sad, bloodshot eyes, and she felt that unmistakable jolt of pain in her soul. His skin had a gray pallor, and the bitemark was red and swollen with infection. "I don't have long before… Just know that I am sorry." His head turns slightly back as if referencing the mess behind them. "Sorry for everything. I'm a screwup. We both know that. Please forgive me. Please remember me like I was when we were younger. and not the monster I am now." He looked at her then with eyes from when they were kids. Lucia saw pure, raw remorse in them.

"I will," she said, beginning to cry. She meant it. One last grace to give. Forgiveness was easy when time was finite.

Roman nodded and jumped from the boat without another word, slipping into the water. Lucia braced herself as the boat rocked violently. She watched the water, expecting Roman or his zombie to surface. After a minute, she let out a screaming wail of anguish. All gone, everything. Everyone. Lost.

Lucia sobbed as she took up the oars and rowed once, then threw them back against their oarlocks. What's the point of going on? All was lost. Everything. She began to cry harder and then stopped with a gasp, a look of shock on her face. Then she felt it again, a subtle kick in her stomach womb. Another kick, stronger this time! Her baby was alive! He had just been sleeping!

Crying tears of joy now, Lucia grabbed the oars and started rowing again, jaw set with determination. She would have her baby, and they both will survive. Somehow. She would make sure of it. The world be damned.

# ACKNOWLEDGEMENTS

First and foremost, I want to thank my mom for instilling in me a deep love of reading. As a librarian, she kept me surrounded by a nearly endless supply of books, which fed my ever-growing appetite to read anything I could get my hands on. From that foundation, a love of writing grew naturally. My wild imagination soon found new paths to explore and worlds to build.

A huge thank you to my editor, Abigail. Not only for lending her expertise to a genre far outside her comfort zone (too gory!) but also for being a true friend to both me and my wife, Kami. Your support means the world.

Tom, thank you for the encouragement, the friendship, and for helping me not stress about the gunplay in this book. Your reassurance and perspective made a bigger difference than you know.

Next, Jared. He not only went above and beyond in designing the stunning cover art for this book but also generously mentored me through the process and became a great friend along the way. Your creative insight was invaluable.

To my beta readers, thank you all, but especially Ashley and Jackson. Ashley, your detailed, moment-by-moment feedback was incredible. And Jackson, thank you for creating my first piece of fan art, it was both inspiring and unforgettable.

And finally, above all, my wife, Kami. This book would not exist without you. Some of the characters were born from your strength, your heart, and your unshakable authenticity. I wrote this book for you, first and foremost, to keep a promise, and to give you the best birthday gift ever.

# ABOUT THE AUTHOR

## Cj Wheeler

The author lives with his wife in Florida. His lifelong fascination with dreams led him to a degree in polysomnography, the study of sleep. Now, he dreams up entire worlds, transforming vivid imagination into words on a page.

www.ingramcontent.com/pod-product-compliance
Lightning Source LLC
Chambersburg PA
CBHW070306260626
47160CB00003B/742